THE SHADOW WING

CROW INVESTIGATIONS BOOK SIX

SARAH PAINTER

Text Copyright © 2021 by Sarah Painter

Published by Siskin Press Limited

Cover Design by Stuart Bache

ALSO BY SARAH PAINTER

The Language of Spells

The Secrets of Ghosts

The Garden of Magic

In The Light of What We See

Beneath The Water

The Lost Girls

The Crow Investigations Series:

The Night Raven

The Silver Mark

The Fox's Curse

The Pearl King

The Copper Heart

CHAPTER ONE

Maddie looked different. Partly because she was wearing a red bobbed wig over her brown hair and heavy-framed glasses with, Lydia assumed, clear lenses, but also because there was a calm stillness that she didn't associate with her cousin. After another second, Lydia realised another reason she felt so alien; there was barely a wisp of Crow. She reached out her senses, giving Maddie a virtual pat-down, but came back empty. There was the smallest taste of feathers and, with concentration, she could feel the warm lift of a thermal current as she lifted and flew...

'Stop it,' Maddie said sharply.

Lydia stopped. She shifted her balance, wondering what sort of weapon Maddie would be carrying and whether she was going to chat before she killed her. She felt strangely calm. In some ways, it would be comforting to die at the hands of somebody familiar, rather than a stranger. Keeping it in the family.

'What's funny?' Maddie said.

Lydia realised she was smiling. 'It's nice to see you. I mean,' she tried again, 'not nice, exactly. It would be. If we weren't on this roof and if you hadn't been sent by Mr Smith to kill me, but still. You look well. I like your glasses.'

Maddie didn't move.

The sky was clear and, behind Maddie, the Houses of Parliament were bathed in morning light. There was warmth from the spring sunshine, which helped to counteract the coolness of the breeze. Up high, the traffic was quiet and, if it hadn't been for the assassin opposite, Lydia would be grateful for the view.

'I didn't know it was you,' Maddie said after a moment of silence.

'You threatened my best friend,' Lydia said, feeling a surge of pure anger.

'It was in the packet.' Maddie waved a hand. 'I was told the target would come running if I sent that message.'

'And here I am,' Lydia said, spreading her hands. 'I thought you weren't taking orders anymore?' At that moment she felt her legs begin to move. She took one step toward Maddie, her body lurching and off balance, and then another. She hadn't told her body to move, it was simply doing so. Which was terrifying. She tried to push back, to regain control of her muscles, but it made no difference. It was as if the connection between her mind and her body had been completely severed.

When she was inches away from Maddie, close enough to wrap her hands around her throat or throw a punch, Maddie said: 'That's better. Now we don't have to shout.'

'How did you do that?' Lydia's mouth flooded with saliva and she thought she might be sick.

'You like my party trick?' Maddie's tone was playful, but her eyes were flat and lifeless. They reminded Lydia of Charlie's shark eyes, but only if the shark had been dead for hundreds of years. And hated other sharks.

'It's incredible,' Lydia forced herself to say. The fear was pounding through her now, and her traitorous legs were liquid. It was one thing to be killed, quickly and neatly by a professional, but to have her body taken over, forced to do things while she was fully awake, that opened a whole chasm of terrible possibility. 'Is this why you're so good at your job?'

Maddie tilted her head. 'You're being very agreeable. Do you think if you flatter me, I'll let you go?'

'I'm just surprised, that's all. You didn't seem the professional type. You were always so...'

'What?'

'Scatty. Undisciplined. Childish.'

Lydia's lungs squeezed and the air whooshed out. She couldn't move her muscles in order to refill them and the panic was instant.

'You're trying to annoy me into finishing this quickly,' Maddie said, her voice even. 'Dangerous tactic.'

Lydia's head was pounding with the lack of oxygen and her panic was beating its wings wildly against the inside of her chest. Just when dark speckles appeared in her vision and she knew she was close to passing out, Maddie released her diaphragm and allowed her to drag in a breath. If she had been in control of her body, she would have slumped down, but she wasn't so she stood, back straight, and pulled in air until her head cleared. After a few breaths, she managed to speak. 'Just making conversation.' Lydia's lungs felt like they were on fire and Maddie was still keeping her spine unnaturally rigid, but she struggled on. 'Do your parents know you're back in town? Do they know you're contracting for the government? I bet they'd be very proud.' In the middle of her last sentence, when she thought Maddie was as distracted as she was going to be, Lydia threw as much of her power as she was able. Maddie took a stumbling step back as it hit, and Lydia felt Maddie's control over her body loosen. She had been ready and threw a punch into the side of Maddie's head, knocking her out.

At least, that was the idea.

Maddie ducked and the blow glanced off her temple. Lydia felt the syrupy sensation of her limbs being taken over, and she fought against it, trying to grapple with Maddie. With a twisting motion, Lydia found herself grasped in front of Maddie, a knife at her throat. Maddie seemed utterly unaffected. 'That was fun,' she said, her breath tickling Lydia's ear. 'Hardly anybody dances with me anymore.'

'We've got all day,' Lydia said, trying to match Maddie's tone.

'Sadly, you do not.' Maddie walked Lydia toward the edge of the roof.

'Why are you working for Mr Smith?' Lydia kept talking to try to mask her fear. If she pretended she wasn't terrified, maybe she could make it so. The breeze seemed stronger here, at the edge of the building, and the traffic noise louder. Lydia could glimpse the street below. Far below.

'I don't know who that is,' Maddie said.

'Government spook. Nice suits. Why are you taking orders at all? You're a Crow.'

Maddie stopped moving.

'How much do you know about the department that gives you orders? I know Mr Smith has been rogue himself or, at least, head of a very hush-hush department. The kind that gives the government full deniability.' Lydia was speaking quickly, trying to find a way in now that Maddie seemed to be listening. 'And I'm the head of the Family, now. You know that, right? Have you asked yourself why they want me dead? I've been working on forming alliances, keeping the old truce from breaking. If I'm murdered, all hell will break loose.' Lydia had no idea if this was accurate. It was entirely possible that Aiden, or even Maddie, would step neatly into her place and Maria Silver would do a dance on her grave.

'The thing is,' Maddie said, after a moment. 'I know I warned you about this. I told you to fly.' And with that, she pushed Lydia so that she was hanging over the edge of the roof. Her body was under the control of Maddie, both physically and magically. Her tiptoes scrabbled for purchase on the stone edge and her mind slowed with the mortal fear. Every single impression, the feel of the wind on her skin, the sounds of the city, the harsh call of a crow. Many crows, in fact, as a group flew into view. A murder of crows, Lydia thought. How appropriate. It was possible that she was being hysterical. Losing her mind. She heard laughing a moment before she realised that it was hers.

'What's funny?' Maddie's voice was almost interested and Lydia could detect a neediness beneath her words. The neediness of a girl who had felt left out. Maybe not the coolest in her gang of friends, maybe marginalised, overlooked. Or maybe Lydia was still grasping at straws.

'I knew they'd played me, but I thought you'd got away. But here we are.'

'I did get away,' Maddie said. 'I make my own choices.'

'Not how it looks,' Lydia said. Then, taking a gamble, 'Charlie's still using you.'

Lydia felt a jerk of movement and closed her eyes. This was it. She was going to plummet to the concrete. She thought of Fleet and felt a deep throb of sadness.

Instead, she landed on her backside on the roof. The jolt sent a spike of pain up from her tailbone through her spine and into her neck, but she wasn't free-falling toward a pavement, so it was a definite win.

'What has Charlie got to do with this?' Maddie was standing over her and she hadn't even broken a sweat. The controlled power of the woman was breath-taking. And terrifying.

Lydia had no idea what Mr Smith had told Maddie, or even if he was her official handler. She tried to weigh up what would most offend Maddie. 'Charlie is working with the government. The spook who has been trying to recruit me teamed up with him last year.'

'Your Mr Smith?'

'Yeah. I named him.'

'Imaginative,' Maddie said. She was poised on the balls of her feet, but was clearly thinking.

For a moment, Lydia allowed herself to imagine a scenario in which she walked away. 'I didn't take Charlie's place just to start taking orders from somebody else.' She tried to keep her voice steady, to match Maddie's strength. It wasn't easy as her whole body hurt and her mind was still a tangle of fear.

Abruptly, the tension in Maddie's body shifted. Lydia tensed. This was it.

'You look tired,' Maddie said. 'You should check your vitamin D level.' And then she turned away.

Lydia twisted to watch her leave. She walked, casual and unhurried, back to the entrance to the stairwell. At the door, Maddie glanced back, and Lydia tried to read her expression. Was she going to change her mind? Come back and finish what she had started? She found herself raising a hand, half goodbye wave and half salute. Maddie smiled and then left. Lydia lowered her hand, unsure whether she had been in control of it.

WALKING FROM THE HOSPITAL TO WESTMINSTER Bridge, Lydia was in a daze. The colours of the day were too saturated, and the morning air felt like tiny needles on her skin. Her legs were wobbly, but she could still feel the adrenaline in her system, the urge to run or fight. Anything, in short, other than walk sedately past the South Bank lion. There was a Nando's next to the statue, and Lydia felt suddenly ravenously hungry. She pictured chicken in a pitta bread with a pile of chips on the side and saliva flooded her mouth. It was before nine in the morning and she didn't even like Nando's very much. It was a reaction, Lydia told herself. Near-death experiences made her hungry, apparently.

She ducked into a chain coffee shop just before Parliament Square and bought a cheese and ham toastie and a pain au chocolat. She was gripped with the realisation that she had never tried an iced coffee. She had always meant to, but hadn't got around to seeing what all the fuss was about. She could have died and then she would never have known. Iced latte in one hand and a fragrant paper bag in the other, Lydia headed for a seat in the square. She passed the statue of Winston Churchill looking, as ever, like a grumpy egg in an overcoat, and perched next to Millicent Fawcett instead.

She ate the toastie without really tasting it. After licking the grease from her fingers, she pulled out her phone and stared at the screen. She wanted to call Fleet. Not just for the comfort of hearing his voice, but because he was the person she wanted to tell. Things seemed both more real and more manageable when shared with him, which was probably what all the love songs and poetry had been bleating on about.

But he was still a copper. If she told Fleet about Maddie, he would call in the cavalry. He would have to. It was probably a public health issue or something. There would be protocol. Guidelines. A handbook of some kind. And if the police started marching around the place, making a fuss, Maddie might take it poorly. And take it out on Lydia. Or Emma. Hell Hawk.

Lydia lifted her drink, surprised by the coldness of the cup. She had forgotten that she had bought an iced coffee in a moment of madness. If she couldn't tell Fleet, what could she do? How could she protect Emma? It was terrible timing. Emma was probably rushing to get the kids ready for school, but she pressed dial anyway.

'Hey hey!' Emma's voice sounded happier than Lydia expected. Lin Manuel Miranda was singing in the background, Archie joining in enthusiastically, if not accurately.

'Shush a minute,' Emma said, and the music dipped in volume. 'Mummy can't hear Lydia. Sorry. You all right?'

'Fine,' Lydia said. 'Is this a bad time?'

'We're in the car,' Emma said. Her voice took on a theatrical tone. 'We're going on an adventure.'

Emma's next words were drowned out by excited cheering.

Lydia felt tears in her eyes as she heard Maisie and Archie and Tom whooping and squealing, Emma dissolving into delighted laughter. 'Sorry, sorry. Tom and I are delirious, we've been up since three so that we could pack in secret. We didn't want to tip them off early.'

'Where are we going?' A chanting had started and Emma shushed them again, without much success.

'We're back on Sunday. Shall I call you then? We can catch up properly.'

'Great,' Lydia said. 'Have a good time.'

After hanging up, a WhatsApp pinged from Emma.

Sorry about the chaos. We're taking the kids to Center Parcs. V excited.

They were heading out of London. That could only be a good thing, even if it was a temporary reprieve. Lydia tapped out a quick reply and then took a slurp of her coffee. It was like milkshake. Not unpleasant, but not coffee. She ate the pain au chocolat and felt a little better. She still wanted to phone Fleet, but the urge was manageable. And now that the fear had subsided a little, clear thoughts were breaking through.

The ten-shilling note that Mr Smith had slipped into her coat was tucked into the inside pocket of her leather jacket. She unfolded it carefully, feeling the softness of the old paper. This was a method used by Charlie, something he had used to show people they were marked. Mind games and menaces. Typical Charlie, in other words. Still, it was Crow business, twisted and used against her. Now she saw that it was a symbol of the greater betrayal to come. Mr Smith had ordered a Crow to kill her. Her own cousin.

Lydia drained the cup and stood to put her rubbish into the bin. Millicent Fawcett was carrying a banner. It said: Courage calls to courage everywhere. She stared at it for a moment. Was Millicent telling her to call for help? Or to make a stand and inspire others? Or just to remember her courage? That was good. She had courage. And in that moment Lydia realised that she had something else... Fury.

CHAPTER TWO

Lydia wanted to do something. Take immediate and decisive action. Ideally something destructive. Unfortunately, there was nothing physical she could burn down. She had linked Mr Smith to JRB, a corporate entity that had been trying to stir trouble between the Families, and it was entirely possible that he was the man at the top of that particular tree. But the only physical location for JRB was a deserted rented office which was used as a postal address and nothing more. And she knew as much about the organisation and its key players as when she had first heard of them, which was, practically speaking, nothing.

What she did know didn't make her predicament easier or more comfortable. Mr Smith was on the payroll of the British government, running a super-secret shadow department which sat somewhere between MI6 and MI5. She couldn't exactly storm the hulking fortress of MI6 to demand a reckoning. And if his activities went beyond his official capabilities, the service might not even be aware of what he was doing. Worse still, this might be the way the secret service routinely operated. It was secret, after all, and Lydia imagined there were plenty of black-ops-style shenanigans that the powers that be couldn't officially sanction, but for which they, nonetheless, gave tacit approval. Her head hurt with the sheer weight of things she didn't know.

Until she discovered more about Mr Smith's role at JRB and the size of that organisation, and figured out the scope of his department and influence within the secret service, Lydia had to assume that danger could come from any angle. Knowing that she had handed her uncle to a man who was now trying to have her killed spiked her fury. But fury wasn't going to help her, now. She had to *think*.

Lydia wasn't naïve enough to believe that Mr Smith would be working entirely alone. And there was no way she could find out how far his influence within the service went and whether he was taking orders from high up. For now, she had to act as if MI6 were her enemy, too. Which meant no blabbing to Fleet.

If she was being smart, Lydia would run. There was a chance that Maddie would tell Mr Smith that the job had been done and her body had hit the pavement, making a bit of modern art all over the road outside St Thomas's. That would buy her time. And even if Maddie did go running to him to talk about how she'd been thrown by his choice of target and hadn't, on this occasion, fulfilled her brief, he still had no idea of her location at this exact moment. She glanced up as she walked past a bus stop, seeing the camera mounted on the streetlight nearby. He would have quick access to the city's CCTV and she would need to use an ATM to get cash, which would also be traceable, but if she went right now, she could be in Glasgow by the afternoon, and hiking away from a remote station in the highlands by nightfall. Or she could jump on the Eurostar to Paris. Then nick a car and drive to Italy. If it had been an official operation, then he could put an all-ports warning on all transport hubs out of the UK, but if it had been unofficial... Well, Lydia didn't know exactly what he would do, then. Just send Maddie back after her, she supposed. Or somebody like Maddie. How many killers-for-hire did Mr Smith have in his back pocket?

She hesitated, her mind quickly tracking through the steps to running. The nearest place to buy a rucksack and a pack of underwear, the fact that she needed to destroy her phone, buy a couple of burners. Her passport was back at the flat. Would she be able to go and collect it, or was that too risky? Once she crossed the channel, she could keep driving. Go all the way to Russia. Russia was big. A person could definitely lose themselves there.

Underneath all this, another track was playing. Lydia finding Mr Smith and putting him in a choke hold. Her mum and dad's faces when they were told she had disappeared. Fleet moving on with his life with another, less insane, girlfriend. Maddie, frustrated at her failure, paying a visit to Emma. Her stomach flipped and she turned blindly, going to cross the road and start moving if just for the relief of motion.

A man wearing bulbous headphones and staring at

his phone walked right into Lydia, and she almost fell off the kerb and into a black cab. It was a quintessential London moment. The traffic. The idiot pedestrian. The brush with death. She smiled.

She pulled her phone from her jacket and, instead of dropping it and stamping it into oblivion with her DMs, she made a call. She wasn't running. She was Lydia Crow, and London was her home.

LYDIA HADN'T SEEN PAUL FOX SINCE HE CRASHED A dinner date with Fleet, intent on stirring trouble. Truth be told, she was nervous. There had been an awkward possible-marriage-proposal a few weeks back, and she wasn't sure where things stood between them. She was pretty sure it had been a business proposition more than a romantic declaration, but still. They had a history.

She had texted her request and he had told her to meet him at a pub in Whitechapel. She was asking a favour, so it was reasonable for him to summon her to his manor, but still, she was on edge as she made her way to the side street off Brick Lane.

It was a traditional boozer, complete with a slightly sticky floor and button-leather and wood furnishings, plus the obligatory old geezers on bar stools engrossed in their pints and the racing paper. Paul was sitting with his back against the wall, watching the door. Thankfully, he was alone. Lydia didn't think she could handle his siblings, too. She was annoyed to find that she still felt off balance and she channelled that, straightening her spine as she approached Paul's table.

'This makes a nice change, Little Bird,' Paul said. 'You coming to me.'

'Don't get used to it,' Lydia countered. She was trying very hard to ignore the animal pull of Paul Fox. No matter how much she prepared herself it still hit her afresh each time she saw him. 'I'll buy you a drink, though. What do you want?'

He tilted his head. 'You want to buy me a drink?'

'Not if you're going to be weird about it.'

He looked at her for a beat. 'You're worrying me. Sit.'

Lydia didn't want to make a habit of obeying Paul Fox, but she was trying to be conciliatory, so she dragged the chair that was opposite Paul to the side of the table and sat. She wasn't going to snuggle up to him on the bench, but this way she didn't have her back to the door.

Moments later, the bar man appeared with two coffees, which he placed on the table with great deference.

'I didn't think this place did table service,' Lydia said.

'They make an exception,' Paul said. 'Coffee all right? I can get us something stronger if you want to kick off a party.'

'Coffee's fine,' she said. It was disgusting, actually, but she pretended to take a sip. It was an excuse to take a beat to collect her thoughts. Now that she was here, Paul watching her with a bright light in his eyes, her plan didn't seem quite as clever. She had to force the images of red fur, dark earth, and the crunch of tiny bones from her mind. She clenched her right hand, feeling her coin appear in her palm. The shape of it was comforting.

'What's different?' He asked finally. 'With you?'

'I don't know what you mean.'

'Suit yourself, Little Bird.' Paul sipped his coffee and pulled a face.

'You remember my cousin? Maddie?'

'I do,' he said cautiously.

'She's back.'

He went still. 'In London?'

Lydia nodded. 'She's working.'

The look of caution increased.

'You know.' The realisation hit. 'You already know. What she does these days.'

Paul touched the edge of his cup with a thumb and forefinger, rotating it once. And then again. Finally, he nodded. 'I have an idea, yeah.'

'And you didn't tell me?'

Paul smiled thinly. 'You rejected my very generous proposal. I don't think I need to apologise for not giving you full access.'

'That's not how this works,' Lydia said. 'This is business, not personal. You are the head of the Foxes, I am the head of the Crows.'

'We don't really have a leader-'

Lydia held up a hand. 'Don't give me that bollocks. You're the head of your family. Whatever you want to call it, they're not listening to anybody else.'

'Nevertheless,' Paul began.

'No, not nevertheless. And who calls a marriage proposal "generous"? That's some shady shit. No wonder I said no.'

Paul smiled like he had won the lottery. 'I knew you cared.'

She felt a flush creep up her neck. 'I don't care. I just want a bit of respect.'

His smile vanished. 'Don't we all.'

Lydia squeezed her coin and took a deep breath. 'She threatened my friend. Emma.'

'The one with the kids?'

'My friend from school.' Back when she had been a rebellious teen there had a been a short, intense fling with Paul. She squashed the memory of pressing up against him, body on fire, mind delirious with hormones and lust. She was older and wiser now. Well, definitely older.

'What are you doing to do about Maddie?'

'Find her. Kill her.' The words were out before Lydia could think. But they made sense. How else could she ensure Emma's safety? She had to stop Maddie for good.

'That's fair. And you want a hand?'

'I was hoping you could keep an eye out for Maddie. Let me know if you hear anything. And something else...' She swallowed. 'Can you spare anybody to watch Emma? She's out of the city for the weekend but will be back on Sunday. I can do some shifts, but I can't cover the whole time. I can pay.'

'Protection?'

Lydia nodded. She waited for Paul to ask her why she wasn't asking Fleet, to take the opportunity to stick the boot in about her copper boyfriend and make some snide comment about him not being able to help her. Instead, he reached for her hand, the one holding her coin, and wrapped both of his around it. Looking straight into her eyes with a sincerity that was unnerving, he promised that his family would keep a personal eye on Emma and her children day and night.

She felt a mix of relief and apprehension. 'You're going to send your brothers?' There was nothing like being given a good kicking to make you wary. But at least she knew they were capable. 'If they hurt her, I will-'

'They're strong,' Paul broke in. 'And fast. Trust me, you want them watching out for your friend. They have good instincts. And they will-'

He broke off, eyes shifting toward the entrance. Lydia hadn't heard the door open, but there was a man walking toward their table. He had a weather-beaten face and a red beard shot through with grey and was carrying a walking stick that looked like a twisted tree branch, worn smooth and shiny with use. He was wearing a tunic and trousers which appeared to be made of pieces of leather and fur. Lydia would have said that he had wandered from a cosplaying event, except that the clothes were extremely well-worn and were giving off a distinctive, authentic aroma. Nobody looked askance, which made Lydia think the man was a regular and perhaps made sense of why Paul had asked to meet her here and not in his hidden den.

He nodded to Paul and changed his trajectory from the bar to their table. She desperately wanted to put a hand over her nose and mouth against the smell, but she sensed this would not be polite.

'Long time,' Paul said. 'Did you do as I asked?'

The man nodded and reached out an open palm. His nails were caked in dirt.

18

Paul leaned beneath the table and produced a plastic carrier bag. He held it out of reach, his own hand outstretched. There was a curious moment, both men eyeballing each other and neither one speaking or moving. Then the man dressed like an extra in an extremely low-budget Lord of the Rings, put a folded piece of paper on the table and slid it toward Paul.

After unfolding and reading, his face betraying nothing, Paul handed over the carrier bag.

The man moved away with surprising speed and was out of the door before Lydia had time to gather her thoughts.

'What was that about?' She had thought about not asking, not wanting to give up power by showing her interest, but then had decided that she couldn't be bothered to play games. Besides, if Paul felt a little bit superior, he would be more likely to drop his guard.

Paul pocketed the paper and smiled tightly. 'Just business.'

Lydia nodded. She tried an understanding expression.

'What are you doing?' Paul said, unnerved.

'Empathising,' Lydia said. 'There's always something, isn't there? It's exhausting. Sometimes it almost makes me miss Charlie.'

'It's not the same. I'm not...'

'I know, I know.' Lydia waved a hand. 'No formal hierarchy. Free spirits. I'm not trying to insult your family.'

His mouth twisted. 'Makes a change.'

Lydia pressed a hand to her chest. 'You wound me.'

He smiled then, properly, and Lydia felt it in her gut. And a bit lower down. Bloody Fox magic.

'I had better go,' Lydia said, not moving.

His teeth were white, and she imagined them grazing her skin. His eyes held hers and she couldn't help but notice how black and large the pupils were and, was that her imagination, or were there rings of gold around the light brown irises? They were mesmerising. Alight with a knowing desire. A desire which promised good times in a safe, warm den. She swallowed hard and forced herself upright.

'I'm looking into that firm, JRB.' Paul said, seemingly oblivious of the effect he was having. 'The place that sent the Russian to mess with my Family. What?' He raised his eyebrows. 'You're not the only one worried about it. If there's a war we'll go to ground, but that doesn't mean we won't suffer. Besides,' Paul smiled a different sort of smile. The sort that promised pain, not pleasure. 'I wish to settle the score.'

CHAPTER THREE

When Lydia walked into The Fork, the scent of fried bacon and toast almost made her cry. She hadn't cried when an assassin had summoned her to die, but the sight of Angel scowling from behind the counter and the familiarity of the cafe with its breakfast-scented air and steamed-up windows almost broke her. That was what she got for drinking a milkshake instead of a proper coffee.

'Feed me,' Lydia said. 'The works.'

Angel raised an eyebrow. 'Rough morning?'

'And tell Aiden I'm waiting for him.'

Angel, sensibly enough, didn't say 'tell him yourself' or 'I'm not your secretary' or any of the other phrases Lydia could see piling up behind her lips. Instead, she caught sight of something in Lydia's face and tone and simply nodded.

Once she was at her favourite table, her back to the wall and with a full English in front of her with both coffee and orange juice on the go, Lydia felt her strength returning. Aiden appeared, pulling his beanie off his head and sitting opposite. Lydia was using a piece of fried bread to mop up the remaining egg yolk. The weight of the food in her stomach was comforting, but she had the feeling she would be ready to eat again in a matter of minutes.

'All right, Boss?' Aiden said, eying her plate enviously.

'How is everything going? Anything on fire?'

Aiden shook his head. 'All cushty.'

Lydia took a sip of her orange juice to cut the grease from the bread. 'I need to tell you something because you've a right to know. And I need you to be on the alert. But it must not go any further.'

Aiden straightened up. He looked so young to Lydia, but she knew she didn't have a choice. He had proved to be reliable and trustworthy so far and he was a Crow. One of her own. Trust didn't come easy, but that didn't mean she shouldn't keep trying. She had already checked that there was nobody sitting near their table, but she glanced around once more before continuing. 'MI5 or MI6 or a department that flits between them has its sights on us. They've been interested for a while and been looking to use us as assets. Or to burn us to the ground, cut out any threat we might pose to national security.'

'That's fucking ridiculous-'Aiden broke in, affronted. 'What have we done to the country? We're not bloody terrorists.'

A man eating a bacon roll on his own a couple of

tables over lifted his head and Aiden lowered his voice. 'And how the feathers did we get on their radar?'

Lydia wiped her fingers on a paper napkin and scrunched it up. 'I was in contact with that department. I had hoped it would be mutually beneficial. More for us, than them, obviously,' she smiled and Aiden nodded his understanding. 'But that's off the table. My contact seems to want to end our relationship in a permanent manner.'

'That's okay,' Aiden said, visibly adjusting to the news. 'We don't want anything to do with them, anyway, do we? I mean, we're all right on our own. Always have been.'

'Hopefully,' Lydia said. 'They do seem keen to make a statement, though.' She wasn't sure whether she should tell Aiden the full truth. Hadn't, in fact, been planning to, but the words tumbled out. 'The department took out a hit on me.'

'They what?' Aiden's eyes were wide.

'You heard,' Lydia said, pushing her plate away. She wasn't saying the ridiculous phrase out loud again, once had been enough.

'But you're still here,' Aiden said, admiringly. 'Good job, Boss.'

Once upon a time, Lydia had found Aiden's boyish enthusiasm annoying. Now, she had the awful urge to give him a hug. What was wrong with her? She drained the rest of her coffee. 'I need you to ask around. Discreetly. See if anybody important has made any shady new friends recently. I'm not arrogant enough to think I'm special and

23

if Mr-,' she broke off, stopping the name she had given her spook falling from her lips. A breath. She continued. 'If the secret service were looking to recruit me as an informant, they may have tried their luck with other Crows, too. I'm particularly interested in John and Daisy. I need you to watch them. Covertly. Can you handle that?'

'I mean, I go round there quite a bit. And there's that Easter thing on the weekend.'

Lydia had completely forgotten about the family party. The invite had come via email and she had assumed it was a duty invitation, rather than a sincere one, which had given her the very happy excuse to bow out. She didn't have the closest relationship with Uncle John and Aunt Daisy, John having made it perfectly clear that he didn't think she ought to be Charlie's replacement.

'I won't be there,' Lydia said, 'you can make my apologies.'

'Right,' Aiden said, looking like he wanted to say something else.

Before he could, Lydia barrelled on. 'And I want you to look around for anything out of the ordinary, but don't worry too much. It'll be too busy. I need you to keep an eye on them both. See if there is anyone new in their lives. Any suspicious activity.'

'How will I watch them both? Can I ask my brother to help?'

Lydia shook her head. 'Just do your best. I want this to stay between us for the moment.'

'Why do you think they might be targeted?' There was an element of insult in his voice.

'I don't, really. But an outsider could assume John is senior. And I thought they might be vulnerable to a spot of bribery.'

That slur on John and Daisy mollified Aiden. He nodded sagely. 'Especially since they lost Maddie.'

'Exactly,' Lydia said. 'Just keep your eyes open. And, while you're at it, let me know if anybody in the Family is flashing cash.'

'I just got the new PlayStation,' Aiden said lightly. 'Full disclosure.'

'That's all right,' Lydia said. 'I know you're not stupid enough to cross me.'

UPSTAIRS, LYDIA HAD JUST SAT DOWN BEHIND HER desk and was contemplating the drifts of paper and line of dirty mugs, when her phone rang. It was Maria's assistant, and the spurt of annoyance at Maria Silver and everything she stood for felt like a welcome breath of fresh air. The assistant was doing his very best to make an appointment for Lydia at the Silver offices. 'No, thanks,' Lydia said cheerfully, in exactly the same way she had done the last three times he had called. It was nice to have a bit of normality in a very strange day.

'Ms Silver would very much appreciate a meeting at your earliest convenience. If tomorrow isn't suitable, how about Wednesday? Or Thursday? She is in court during the day, but you could come in for eight. A breakfast meeting. Or five-thirty.' There was a note of desperation in his voice.

'You can tell Maria that if she wants to see me, she

can make an appointment at my office. I'm not running over to Holborn just because she has clicked her fingers.'

'You don't understand,' the assistant said, sounding utterly miserable. 'That's not how she works.'

'But it's how I work,' Lydia said, enjoying herself far too much. 'You take care, now.'

'Who was that?' Jason spoke near her ear, making her jolt in her chair, her hands coming up in fists.

'Feathers!'

'Sorry,' Jason said, not looking sorry at all. 'You're jumpy.'

'It's been that kind of day.' And, before she could stop herself, the whole story tumbled out.

Jason hovered next to her desk, listening intently. 'So you've got Aiden keeping an eye on John and Daisy?'

'I didn't tell him the real reason, of course,' Lydia said. 'But, yeah. He'll be watching them.'

'I don't understand why you went to the roof in the first place. What the hell were you thinking? Why didn't you call the police? Fleet?'

Speaking to Jason was the closest thing to talking to herself. She trusted him, of course, but since nobody else could see or hear him, it really added a layer of security which helped her to open up. Still, she had to force herself to include the part where Maddie had threatened Emma. It had been bad enough telling Paul. Saying it out loud again made it even more real and she felt her fear spike.

'You could have taken me, at least. I could have helped. Maybe the two of us would have had a chance...'

JASON DIDN'T FEEL PHYSICAL THINGS LIKE A normal person, but he still had lots of mannerisms from when he had been alive. Conversely, when he was very upset, he forgot to use them. Now, instead of slumping in shock or sitting down, he went stock still for a full minute, as if someone had pressed 'pause'. Then his outline began to vibrate. His physical form flickered in and out of existence and Lydia had to put her hand on his arm until he settled.

Oddly enough, his reaction made her feel better. He was horrified, and that eased the shock of the situation a little. Lydia supposed that this was what people must be babbling about when they said 'a problem shared was a problem halved'. It was nowhere near that effective, but it was something, and Lydia felt a surge of gratitude.

'What do you think she will do next?'

He meant 'will she change her mind and finish the job?' a thought which had been pinging in and out of Lydia's mind all day. 'I don't know. Mr Smith said that an assassin had gone rogue. Assuming he meant Maddie, that gives us hope that she might decide to ignore this order and disappear again.'

'Unless Smith is rogue,' Jason said. 'And that we can trust anything he told you.'

'Yes,' Lydia agreed, suddenly feeling exhausted. 'Assuming that.'

. . . .

27

RELIEVED THAT SHE DIDN'T HAVE PLANS WITH FLEET and would have a little bit of time to recover her game face, Lydia had fallen into her bed and slept a deep and profound sleep. She had expected nightmares and insomnia but instead she dreamed of flying. It was so immersive that it took her a while to get properly conscious the next morning. She had dragged herself into the shower and taken her coffee out onto the small roof terrace, letting the morning drizzle and mild spring air rinse away the last dregs of sleep.

The pressure sensor under the carpet in the hallway set off a beeping alarm so that Lydia had prior warning whenever anybody approached her door. Seconds after it sounded, Lydia tasted the clean bright tang of Silver, so she wasn't at all surprised when she opened the door to find Maria Silver glaring at her.

'So this is where you work,' she said, sweeping into the flat.

'Come in,' Lydia said drily, following her into the main room which served as both her living room and office. There had been murmurings in the Family that she ought to move into Charlie's house or, at least, rent an office more befitting of the head of the Crow Family but she had resisted. The main reason for that resistance had, at that very moment, materialised behind Maria Silver's back and was making little bunny ears above her head.

'Tea? Coffee? Valium?'

Maria's frown intensified in confusion.

'Have a seat,' Lydia said, indicating the chair in front of the desk that she used for clients.

Maria was walking around the room, looking at it with an attention that Lydia found unsettling. She was wearing a tight black pencil skirt and a fitted jacket with a red silk blouse peeking from underneath. She looked like money and danger and sex and Lydia pitied the defence lawyers that found themselves opposite her in court.

Jason had moved with Lydia to her side of the desk and was making eye contact, waggling his eyebrows in a questioning manner. Lydia raised hers in reply with the tiniest of shrugs. She had no idea why the head of the Silver Family had decided to grace her office with her presence. They hadn't spoken since Maria had agreed to visit The Fork in a show of solidarity against Mr Smith and his shadowy government department. That had been a week ago and, given that Maria had spent the previous year vowing to kill Lydia, it was a very new, very tenuous truce. Lydia kept her balance light, ready to dive for the floor if Maria produced a weapon.

Jason circled around and got closer to Maria which made Lydia feel a bit better. Jason was a ghost, but he was surprisingly handy in a fight.

'You live here?' Maria inspected the sofa before sinking gracefully to sit. She crossed one exquisite leg over the other and laid her arms across the back of the seat, forming a compelling image. It was calculated, of course, as with everything Maria did. The woman was a master of performance.

Lydia sat in her office chair. She leaned back and put her DMs up onto the desk, crossing one leg over the other in a less elegant motion. 'What can I do for you, Maria?'

'You owe me,' Maria said.

Jason sat next to Maria on the sofa and leaned close. He blew lightly on her neck and Lydia was interested to see Maria shiver.

'We're allies,' Lydia said. 'You want a favour, all you have to do is ask.'

'You did ask,' Maria replied. 'And I delivered. I stood with your family, provided the necessary optics.'

Lydia had wanted to demonstrate to Mr Smith that she had a successful alliance with the Silvers and that further attempts to turn the Families against each other would be futile.

'Not just optics, I hope,' Lydia pushed a little Crow into her words. 'This alliance is only going to work if it's genuine. No more scheming behind my back. The Silvers and the Crows are allied. That means if our fortunes rise, so do those of the Silvers, and vice versa.'

Maria's expression didn't change, although there was the slightest twitch of her left eye. 'Naturally.'

She was lying, but so was Lydia. Alliance meant cooperation while it was mutually beneficial. When stars fell, all bets would be off. 'Good, then. I repeat, what can I do for you?'

'The cup,' Maria said simply.

'What about it?'

'You told me it was fake. Were you lying?'

'I was not.'

'So you will find the real one for me.' It wasn't a request.

Jason pulled a face at Lydia and mimed throttling Maria, both of which she did her best to ignore. 'Why me? You looking to save some cash?'

'Because you know the significance of the piece and because you are properly motivated to carry out a task of this importance. You have incentive that money cannot buy.'

'And what's that?'

Maria smiled. 'My continuing kind wishes.'

CHAPTER FOUR

'You're not going to do it, are you?' Jason was frowning as he filled the kettle and hit the switch to turn it on. She was glad to see that he had regained one hundred per cent solidity and was back to looking almost alive. 'Isn't it a good thing Maria doesn't have it?'

'I have to,' Lydia said. 'Gotta keep the alliance in good order.' Lydia knew that her position as the head of the Crows was only as secure as the peace she managed to keep between the Families. She had lost points for winding up the more criminal parts of the Crow empire and knew there were plenty of whispers about her being too weak. She couldn't afford to have anything else slip.

'You don't trust her, though? I mean, do you really think she's on our side?'

'Feathers, no,' Lydia said, smiling at Jason. 'But I have to act as if I do. Believe her, that is.' Lydia had told Maria that the Silver cup, a Silver Family relic which lived in their crypt beneath Temple Church, had been swapped with a fake. She had been in the process of telling her that her supposedly dead father, Alejandro, was not in the crypt either, which had, understandably, been the headline. Lydia hadn't even been sure that Maria had taken in the news about the cup at all as she hadn't reacted and they had soon been back to their usual fare of mortal threats. Lydia ought to have known better. Whatever else she could say about Maria Silver, the woman was sharp. Nothing got past her.

Jason dropped a tea bag into a mug.

'No hot chocolate today?'

He shook his head. 'It doesn't feel like hot chocolate weather anymore.'

'Fair enough,' Lydia said. The sun was streaming through the living room windows, and would be drying the terrace from the night's rain. 'Is it beer weather?'

'Too early,' Jason said. 'And you're working.'

If someone had told Lydia that she would be living with the ghost of a man who had died in the 1980s and that he would treat her with a kind of motherly concern, she wasn't sure which fact would have seemed less likely.

She took her tea and sat behind her desk, feet up. The Silver Family cup had been donated to the British Museum at the time of the truce as a show of goodwill, but had been stolen forty years ago. Lydia had seen the cup in Alejandro's office and knew it was the real deal by her reaction to it. Namely, she had hurled her lunch all over Alejandro's nice carpet. The next time she had seen the cup it had been in the Silver Family crypt and that had most definitely been a replica and not the real thing. Which begged several questions. Did Alejandro place the replica cup in the vault and, if so, did he know it was a fake? If he had been knowingly handling a replica in order to keep the real cup hidden elsewhere, why hadn't he told Maria about it? And, for the grand prize, where the feathers was the real cup?

Lydia sipped her tea and closed her eyes, chasing the threads of her thoughts. Whether Alejandro knew or not, the replica was clearly good enough to fool the rest of the Silvers, which meant exquisite workmanship.

When she had been on the trail of an enchanted statue, Lydia had visited a shop in the silver vaults. Perhaps they could provide details of likely silversmiths.

As for the real cup, the most likely possibility was one which made Lydia shiver. If Alejandro had kept hold of the real cup, placing a replica in the crypt to hide that fact, there was a chance it hadn't disappeared along with him. The government department paying for his relocation package would have bled Alejandro dry and that, logically, would include confiscating any valuable Family relics. They would have argued that it would have endangered his new identity, and explained that it was for his own protection, but the result of that argument made Lydia taste blood and fury. A Family relic sat in a secure room of some shady government department. Worse still, Mr Smith handling the cup, maybe working out some way to harness the power contained within it.

Her tea was cold, and she was gripping the mug so tightly it was in danger of shattering. Lydia pulled herself upright, her DMs thudding onto the floor, and put the mug onto the cluttered surface of her desk. She slid her phone over and tapped a quick message to Emma. She had called to check in on her twice already and knew that if she did so again, she was really going to freak out her friend. After a moment's thought, she constructed a bright and breezy message about avoiding her tax paperwork and then waited, breath held, until the little checkmark indicated that Emma had read the message. Seconds later and a reply appeared. It was heavy on the emojis which meant that Emma was as busy as ever. Alive. Happy. Safe.

SINCE OPERATION BERGAMOT HAD BEEN OFFICIALLY wound up and his bosses seemed to have accepted that Fleet's private life had not affected his loyalty to the force, Fleet was no longer out in the cold at work. At least, that was what he said. Lydia didn't know how much he was playing up the positives in an effort to make her feel less guilty. Lydia knew that Fleet's decision to go public with their relationship had caused him no small measure of professional pain.

He texted to ask about dinner plans and Lydia hesitated before replying. She had been spending more and more time at Fleet's comfortable flat. Partly because she was determined to match his commitment to the relationship but mostly, if she was honest, because she didn't feel as comfortable in her own flat since Ash had died in it. The cleaning crew had done an exemplary job, but they hadn't been able to expunge her memory. Not only was a troubled soul snuffed out before his time, in a truly unpleasant manner, but he had been under Lydia's protection. She had failed him. And what was to stop her failing the remaining people in her life?

Jason breezed through the room as she hesitated over the screen. She knew that he preferred her to stay in the flat overnight, and the added responsibility for his well-being pulled at her.

'What are you scowling about?' Jason asked, suddenly on high alert.

Lydia shook her head. 'It's nothing. Just thinking.'

'I'll make you some toast,' Jason said. 'Carbs cure everything.'

Lydia didn't bother to argue. Now that he could touch things, Jason found making food and drinks extremely therapeutic. Who was she to disrupt his equilibrium?

The smell of toasting bread floated through the open door to the small kitchen and Jason was singing a Bowie song quietly.

Lydia had never been very good at sitting still. She paced the room until Jason floated through with her food and then wolfed it down. He had been right. Buttery toast made everything better. Not solved. Not okay. But better. 'Thank you,' she said, dabbing her finger in the crumbs.

'I miss eating,' Jason said suddenly.

'Do you?' Lydia was surprised. He had never said as much before.

'It's new,' he said. 'It's been creeping up ever since you came along. Feelings of all kinds.'

Lydia opened her mouth to speak, but Jason rushed on.

'It's good. It's all good. I mean, I like feeling more real. I like being able to touch things and think clearly and care about... Things. It's like being alive.'

It hit Lydia. It was like being alive, but he wasn't alive. It was close but no cigar.

'But there's a cost to wanting things,' Jason continued, sounding forlorn. 'Feeling things. I am aware of what I'm missing. What I can't have. I'm aware that I'm dead and that there are so many things I will never have again.'

Lydia didn't know what to say. It put a lot of things into perspective. She probably ought to have an epiphany about living life to the full while she was breathing, but she just felt an aching sadness for Jason. He didn't deserve to have been cut down prematurely. He didn't deserve this half-life existence.

'But this is better than before,' he said quickly. 'Before you came was way worse.' He was getting upset, Lydia could see his edges vibrating and a sliver of space opened up beneath his feet where he seemed to have forgotten about gravity.

'How so?'

'I was barely here. But I had no control. No peace. I spent a lot of time in that other place, I think.'

Sometimes, without wanting to, Jason disappeared. It could be for five minutes or five days, but when he came back he was always shaken. He said he couldn't remember where he went or whether it was just like passing out, a blank space, but Lydia didn't know if he was lying. All she knew for sure was that it terrified him. She put a hand on his arm, now, letting the cold seep into her arm until he stopped vibrating and looked solid again. 'What can I do?'

Jason smiled crookedly, looking like himself again. 'Don't leave me.'

'Never,' Lydia said.

Jason still looked as if he wanted to cry, so she added: 'Who would bring me toast?'

DCI FLEET ARRIVED ELEVEN MINUTES AFTER HE had texted to say he was on his way and would be about ten minutes. There were many things Lydia appreciated about her kind, smart, handsome boyfriend, and his reliability was definitely high up the list. Which came as a surprise. As a younger woman, she had never imagined that would be an attribute to set her heart racing. Turned out, she had more than enough unpredictability in the rest of her life.

She kissed him hello in a thorough manner and was pleased to see him looking faintly dazed. Having a steady adult relationship was one thing, but it was good to see that she could still make Fleet temporarily forget his own name.

'I brought food, but it can wait.'

'No it can't,' Lydia said, plucking the paper bag from Fleet's hand. 'It smells amazing and I'm starving.'

'You forgot to eat again?'

That did happen when Lydia was engrossed in work, but today she had still been ravenously hungry.

She didn't know if everybody reacted to near-death experiences with hunger, but it appeared that she definitely did. She also really wanted to jump Fleet. All of her appetites had kicked into high gear, which made a kind of sense when viewed as an evolutionary survival instinct. Or she was just twisted.

Once they were ensconced on the sofa with glasses of red wine and forks, Fleet turned serious. 'Any sign today?'

He meant, had she seen Mr Smith covertly or not-so-covertly following her or seen anything out of the ordinary that could indicate his attention. Fleet knew that it wouldn't be anything more than that as Lydia had promised him faithfully that she would call him immediately if Mr Smith approached her.

'Nothing.' Lydia speared a piece of red pepper from the sweet and sour chicken, trying to hide her guilt. 'I think he's moved on.'

'No you don't,' Fleet said shortly.

'Well,' she waved her fork, 'who knows what's going on with him?'

'That's the problem,' Fleet said. 'We know that he was removed from Operation Bergamot, but we don't know what to expect from his department next. He doesn't seem like the type to just stop.'

'I agree,' Lydia said. 'And his pet project has been destabilising the Families. I don't see him dropping that out of the goodness of his heart. I just wish I could be sure he was working alone. If we knew he was the sole operator behind JRB and considered a lone nutter at the service, we would only have one problem to solve.'

'You know I reached out to MI6 to ask for information on his department, but there's still nothing coming back. I'm just a copper and not a very important one. Unless I offer a trade, I don't think we'll get anything.'

'No trade,' Lydia said. The last thing she wanted was more attention from the government.

'I know,' Fleet stuck his fork into the chow mein and reached for his wine. 'And I agree. Mr Smith is clearly personally obsessed with the Families, but we can't be sure there aren't others. Especially with Charlie in custody.'

That was one word for it. Lydia's Uncle Charlie was most likely in a facility deep underground being experimented on to see if Mr Smith could work out the hows and whys of his Crow power. While most of modern London had decided that the legends of the four magical Families were exactly that, just myths and folk tales, fed by exaggeration and repetition, Mr Smith was more clear-eyed. He knew the powers existed and he seemed hell bent on harnessing them. Or, and this seemed increasingly likely now that he had ordered Maddie to kill her, eradicating them. 'Charlie might be dead,' Lydia said.

'I know,' Fleet said quietly and Lydia loved him for not ducking the hard truth and for the steady way he held her gaze.

'Do you think I would feel it?'

Fleet put his wine down and reached for her.

There was a place that made Lydia feel cherished and safe. A place where there was no professional killer stalking the streets with Lydia's name written in her

41

workbook, a place where she hadn't been forced to betray her flesh and blood to save her father's sanity, a place where she wasn't normal but that her difference made her special and strong, a place where she was loved. Settled against Fleet, his arms around her and her cheek resting in the space between his collar bone and chin, the scent of his skin and that sensuous glow which was part delicious warm male and part the intriguing signature of Fleet, Lydia felt like she could breathe.

THE NEXT DAY, LYDIA HAD BEEN AWAKE FOR OVER an hour when Fleet turned over in bed and opened his eyes. 'Hey,' she said as she watched him wake up.

Fleet smiled with his soft morning face and Lydia felt the warmth spread through her chest. This unguarded version of Fleet was private and all hers. He threw a warm arm over her body and hauled her close. She closed her eyes, feeling her racing thoughts slow for a few precious seconds.

'Bad night?' Fleet asked.

'Been worse,' Lydia said. He knew that she hadn't been sleeping well, but not the exact reasons why. Every time he brought up Ash or Mr Smith or her family, she deflected him. She couldn't talk to him about those things or how she felt about them, and she definitely couldn't talk to him about the real reason she couldn't sleep. She had no wish to remind the man she loved that he was sleeping with a monster. A murderer.

Over and over, Lydia ran the moment she had panicked and thrown her power through the lift doors.

She hadn't even known she could do that. It had been like throwing a ball, if that ball was indescribable and full of pain and fury and dragged out of her own atoms. The man she had killed, Felix, was a professional killer. He murdered people for money. Lydia reminded herself of this fact multiple times a day, but it didn't help. She hadn't meant to kill anybody. She had lost control and a man died. If that had happened once, it could happen again. What if she hurt somebody else? What if she killed an innocent person?

Once they were both up and mainlining coffee, Lydia felt Fleet looking at her. 'What?'

'Nothing. Busy day today?'

'Tracking down a magical item for my sworn enemy,' she said. 'The usual.'

She took another sip of coffee and tried to remember where she had left her keys. Jason often tidied up behind her, so she looked in the top drawer of her desk. Nope.

Fleet ought to have left to make it to work on time, but he was still by the doorway, coat over one arm. 'You're not looking for the Pearls, are you?'

Lydia closed the drawer and looked at him. 'Why would I do that?'

'Revenge. For Ash.'

Lydia felt stung. The thought hadn't occurred to her. The Pearls were extremely powerful, but they appeared to be trapped in their underground court. While they weren't snatching kids or following Lydia, she was going to leave them well alone. Besides, she had enough on her plate with Maddie. Why go poking the hornets' nest when you're already on fire?

Fleet's eyes were gentle. 'I would understand. If you were.'

Lydia shook her head, unable to speak.

'But you barely got out of there alive. The house was torn up. I've never seen anything like it.'

Lydia was transported back to the court, the Pearl King's unflinching inhuman gaze. She shuddered. 'As long as they stay put, I'm not going to bother them. My job is to prevent a war between the Families, not start one.'

'Good,' Fleet said after a beat. He looked surprised and it hurt.

Was she losing her humanity? Shouldn't she want to avenge Ash? She prodded the thought like it was a sore tooth. 'And I'm more concerned with Mr Smith and JRB.'

'You still think they are one and the same?'

'He's working his own little department at MI6 and we know not everything was official, but we don't know where the lines are drawn. I'm pretty sure he has been trying to destabilise the Families, though, keeping us off balance and apart. He was masquerading as a courier for JRB and said he was undercover, but I think he is JRB. Or, at least, I hope he is as I have no other leads.'

'They certainly seem to have an aligned purpose. How can we prove it?'

'To what end? He's using the company as a shell to funnel money and provide cover, but I'm guessing he has several set up. If we get too close to JRB, what's to stop him winding it up and using the ones we don't know about?'

'You want to go after Mr Smith personally?'

Lydia hadn't told Fleet that Maddie had summoned her to the rooftop by threatening Emma or that she had been contracted by Mr Smith. She knew that she had a bad old habit of keeping things close to her chest, but this instance was different. Fleet would take the information to the police. He *was* the police. And that risked Maddie going after Emma in retribution. Lydia would not risk her friend's life. Police protection would be too little and for too short a time. Maddie had proved that she could kill difficult targets, crime bosses and political leaders and heads of private armies. One mother in Beckenham with the local cops dozing outside in an unmarked vehicle wouldn't even provide a challenge. 'If I can,' Lydia said. 'But not if it's going to come back on the Families. I've got a lot of work to rebuild the trust between the leaders. I need to calm things down or we're going to have another problem. Maria Silver doesn't want her Family cup just for sentimental sake. I've got to assume she's aware of its power and is looking to use it.'

'Do you think she can?'

'No idea,' Lydia said. 'My training didn't cover anything like it and it's not like there is a big book of magic that can give me the answers.'

'Have you spoken to your dad? Henry might know more than he's told you.'

'Undoubtedly,' Lydia said. 'Speaking of fathers. Have you ever thought about finding yours? He might be able to tell you about your heritage.'

Fleet's eyebrows drew down. 'Fine. I take your point.'

45

'I wasn't making one.' Lydia was bewildered at his sudden hostility. 'It was an honest question.'

'No,' Fleet said shortly. 'I have never been tempted to track him down. He left. And I'm not interested in forcing a relationship with a stranger.'

CHAPTER FIVE

Confronted with questions she couldn't answer and truths she would prefer to forget, Lydia turned to practical matters. She might not be the biggest fan of her current client, but she had a job to do. And it would provide a welcome distraction from her dark thoughts and the dreaded feelings.

The thing about the Silver cup was that it contained power. Whoever had obtained the cup most likely knew that, but it didn't follow that they had the necessary skill to use that power. If they did, that was going to be a bigger problem. What Lydia had, however, was the ability to sense that power. Of course, London was a big city and the cup relatively small. There were a million hiding places and Lydia could hardly go wandering around every part, hoping to pick up its scent.

In the absence of other ideas, Lydia decided to trace its history. She had assumed that it had been stolen back from the British Museum by the Silvers, but perhaps a third party had been involved. If so, had they swooped in and taken it for a second time? Alternatively, maybe the people who had been involved in making the replica of the cup which had been placed by Alejandro below Temple Church had fallen for the real thing? People didn't have to be aware of the Family powers to be affected by them. What if someone had become obsessed and decided to take it for their own personal collection? These thoughts weren't anything close to solid leads or even solid ideas, but Lydia had started with less. That was the thing with investigative work. You just had to start digging, however unpromising the ground.

Roisin Quin had agreed to meet Lydia later that day, on her lunch break from her job in the medieval European and Anglo Saxon department of the British Museum. The sunlight pouring through the arching glass ceiling of the central atrium and bouncing from the white marble was almost blinding and Lydia was relieved when Roisin led her through a wide passage, past the public toilets, and down a spiral flight of stairs to a hallway lined with doors.

The education suite had a number of classrooms and small libraries with study desks and round tables for small groups. One room was filled with excitable primary-age kids, with a pile of brightly coloured backpacks and lunch bags against one wall and a slightly harassed teacher calling for attention. The kids reminded Lydia of Archie and Maisie and she dug her fingernails into her palm to stop herself from pulling out her phone and calling Emma. Maddie had only threatened them as a way to get Lydia to meet her on the roof. She had no reason to hurt them. Apart from anything else, they were valuable leverage for the future. Lydia's guts twisted, and her thoughts ran the now-familiar little maze, like a rat in an experiment looking for the exit, to the inevitable conclusion. There was nothing else she could do to protect them at this moment. She either had to get strong enough to take Maddie out, or she had to do exactly as she asked. Even if she could convince Emma to move her husband and children out of London, Lydia had no idea where would be safe. Maddie had killed highly guarded targets around the globe. And the act of her running might draw her interest, like a tiny mammal scurrying in the earth catching a hawk's eye. Still. Perhaps the Silver cup would offer a well of power that she could somehow harness. Or, she could use it to bargain with Maria for some professional protection. The woman had an impressive security detail and Lydia could hire the same kind of thing for Emma. And her parents. And Fleet. The weight was back on her chest.

Lydia had been distracted by her thoughts and she realised, when Roisin opened the door to a room with a conference table in the middle and an interactive white board on the wall, that she hadn't caught the woman's last few sentences.

Roisin was standing in the doorway, a questioning look on her face. At Lydia's blank expression, she repeated herself. 'We have a study room and a library attached to the department which are accessible to members of the public. If there is a particular item you are interested in, you fill out a study request form and add the objects requested. If possible, they will be collected for your appointment. There are strict handling rules, of course, but all guidance and equipment such as gloves are provided.

'We have over four million items which aren't on display, but there is a database with photographs and so on. Just make sure you fill out all the details correctly for the object request. It's not a simple undertaking to collect the items and nobody will just nip off to swap it for you.' She smiled as if having made a joke and the phrase had the delivery of a well-worn line.

'I understand,' Lydia said. 'I wanted to speak to you about an item that went missing from the collection in the late seventies.'

Roisin frowned. 'Missing? I wouldn't know anything about-'

'According to my research you're the expert on early Modern Europe. I want to find out about a piece which was made at the beginning of the early seventeenth century. It went missing from the museum in the seventies, but I know that a replica was made at some point. I'm not saying it was anything to do with the museum or that it was used to hide the disappearance, just that I have seen a very convincing replica of the item.'

'I do know what you're referring to,' Roisin said reluctantly. 'It's not exactly something we like to shout about. This is a very secure place, even more so these days. The items we care for are in the very best of hands.'

'Doubtless,' Lydia said. 'But this item, an ornate silver cup, was stolen from the collection and, to my knowledge, hasn't been recovered. Made in the early seventeen hundreds by the Silver Family and gifted to the museum as part of a truce in the nineteen forties. I have a personal interest in the truce.' Lydia produced her business card. 'Note the name.'

Roisin glanced at the card but didn't take it. She put her hands on her hips, instead. 'I thought you said you were doing a piece for The Guardian?'

Lydia had forgotten the cover story she had used on the phone to Roisin. Her mind seemed to be jumping from task to task, unable to keep continuity as she spent almost every waking second expecting Maddie, or a new hired assassin, to pop up and kill her. She tried a different tack. 'Look, forget about the cup. I'm not here to make accusations or get anybody into trouble. I assume replicas of very old items are made sometimes? For security. Or educational purposes?'

Roisin frowned. 'The provenance of our collection is well documented, all items are tested for validity before being catalogued. In the rare cases we display replicas, they are clearly marked as such.'

'That's not what I'm... Let me start again.' Lydia's hand itched to produce her coin. It would be so much easier to nudge Roisin with a little burst of Crow. She would go spacey and cooperative and would automatically and truthfully answer every question Lydia put to her. But Roisin wasn't a criminal. As far as Lydia knew. She was a citizen and, as such, Lydia felt she ought to go lightly on the mind control. She was descended from a long line of Crows who had used their abilities to build a criminal empire, but that didn't mean she had to follow in their footsteps. There had to be rules. She hadn't ousted her Uncle Charlie just to morph into him. She tried a smile and saw Roisin get even more discomforted. 'I am not suggesting anything untoward about your collection. But I imagine that occasionally there is need for reconstruction work. Would you be able to point me in the direction of the craftspeople capable of such work?'

Roisin's shoulders went down a notch. 'It's highly specialist.'

Lydia felt her coin appear in her palm and she folded her fingers around it, willing it to retract, to disappear to wherever it went when not in the physical realm.

Roisin stared into the middle distance for a moment, as if captured by a passing vision. Then she blinked. 'The Silver Family cup?'

Roisin looked properly out of it. Lydia had deliberately placed her coin into her jacket pocket and left it there, willing it out of existence at the same time, but some Crow whammy had clearly leaked out regardless. She was definitely stronger. A thought which thrilled and horrified her in equal measure.

Roisin sat down behind the nearest computer, seemingly on autopilot.

'It's not in the online collection,' Lydia said. 'I already checked.'

'Right,' Roisin said. 'I just...'

'You just wanted to make a show of looking in the hope that I would sod off.'

She started. 'No. No, not that. Not at all.'

'If you say something three times, it doesn't make it true,' Lydia said sweetly. 'I think you know exactly what

I'm talking about and I want you to show me everything you've got on the Families. Now.'

The photographs showed the cup exactly as she remembered it. Tall and ornate with two handles. Like a trophy. It would be just like the Silvers to award themselves one. In the image, Lydia could see the same aged silver that had been so cleverly replicated in the fake cup currently residing in the Silver Family tomb. What she couldn't see, from the photograph, was the blindingly shiny silver overlay that she had seen from the real thing. The unmistakable sheen of Silver power which had made her throw up in Alejandro's office, just from being near to it. Looking around the busy reading room, the lack of nausea was a blessing, but it would have been handy to confirm for certain that the cup given to the museum had been the real deal.

Whoever had catalogued the cup had been thorough. There were photographs from different angles and one of the base. Four smudges in a row caught Lydia's eye. She magnified the image until the smudges revealed themselves to be stamped markings. One was recognisably the shape of a lion, one a letter L, and one was round and indistinct. The first mark was the most complex and the image too pixelated when magnified for Lydia to make it out.

'The lion is a quality mark, to show it's sterling silver. This is a leopard's head,' Roisin pointed at the round-ish shape. 'It tells you which Assay office tested and hallmarked the cup. Leopard is the symbol for the London office.'

Lydia squinted at the blob. 'I'll take your word for it. What about this one?'

'That's the maker's mark. It was registered with the Assay office and we got the details from them.'

'Their records go back that far?'

Roisin's face was alight with the fervour of a true fan. 'The Assay office began assessing the quality of metal goods in 1300, and the hallmarking office set up in 1478. The records aren't perfect back to that date, of course, but by the sixteen hundreds, they were writing things down. And this piece was important. It was made for the king, after all. See the crown, there. That's to commemorate that it was made for James I. We know the stamp from other royal items. I know it looks like any other crown, but they really are distinctive when you get into it.'

Lydia was studying the maker's mark. 'Is that a G?'

Roisin nodded. 'And that's a "C" on the other side of the hand. Hands have been a common symbol to indicate fine workmanship over the years, but this symbol with the palm facing out can be traced to a French maker.'

'You traced the maker?'

'I found this,' Roisin said, clicking to open a file. It was a photograph of a book page packed with black ink. The script was impossible to read as far as Lydia could see, but Roisin pointed to a line. 'This lists the date and the initials GC. The surname is here, see? It says "Chartes" which certainly ties in with the probable French origin.'

• • •

BACK AT THE FORK, LYDIA FOUND HER OLD notebook and confirmed what she had thought. She had recognised the name 'Chartes' from an old case. Lydia had been on the trail of a statue of a knight and she had ended up in the silver vaults. A man named Guillame Chartes had sold the statue to Yas Bishop in her capacity as JRB employee from a shop he ran down in the vaults. A shop which had mysteriously disappeared when she had looked for it a second time.

Yas Bishop was the only other person, apart from Mr Smith, that Lydia had found connected with JRB. And Maria Silver had killed her. The Silvers represented JRB. Mr Smith was high up in JRB. Possibly the sole owner. In fact, Lydia's working hypothesis was that JRB was just a shell corporation, a cover for Mr Smith's pet projects. The ones that didn't fit into his official capacity in his shady department with the British government's secret service. It was all so murky and Lydia had the familiar urge to shine a bright light on the whole lot. Preferably using a flame thrower.

Jason was sitting on the sofa with his feet up, laptop glued in place. He had been ignoring her pacing but finally sighed and looked up from the screen.

'Sorry,' Lydia said, and stopped.

'It's not you,' he said. 'Just someone in the crew is arguing for the sake of it.'

Jason had made a bunch of hacker friends online. If 'friends' was the right term. Colleagues? Cohort? Gang members? 'That's the internet for you.'

'I suppose.' Jason shook his head, clearing the distraction. 'What's on your mind?'

Lydia went over her thoughts, marvelling at how much better it felt to talk the whole thing out. By the end she still didn't have a clue how to find out more about JRB, how to confirm that Mr Smith was a one-man-band, or how to find the cup, or whether she should, but she felt a little better.

'That's a weird coincidence,' Jason mused. 'The name being the same as the guy you met in the vaults. You reckon it's his ancestor? Family firm?'

'Could be. Some families do hold to the same line of work for centuries,' she said, smiling at Jason. 'But it doesn't really help. I'm not sure what I was expecting to find. Looking at the original is a nice history lesson, but it doesn't help me find it now.'

'You're going to find out who made the replica, though, right?'

She nodded. 'That's next. It gives me something to do. Something to tell Maria when she demands an update. And who knows? Maybe it will give me a lead.'

Jason was staring at the wall, thinking. 'That silver statue sent people crazy, didn't it? Could the cup have the same effect? You said it was imbued with Silver power... Maybe that's why it was down in the tomb? To protect people from it?'

Lydia stopped pacing. 'Is that something you could search for? People admitted to hospital with psychosis?'

'I can try,' Jason said. 'Everything is recorded digitally now, but it depends on whether there is a centralised system. If medical records are kept by each individual hospital and institution, it will be harder. What about arrest reports?'

He made a good point. And Fleet would look if she asked.

That evening, Lydia called into her local deli before heading over to Fleet's flat. She wanted a good bottle of wine and his favourite crisps. She figured she should bring gifts before she hit him with a request. The sign had been flipped to 'closed' but Ciro opened the door when he saw it was her.

'Evening, Ms Lydia,' he ducked his head.

At first it had been strange when men and women old enough to be her grandparents bowed and scraped, their anxiety around her now that she was the head of the Crows palpable, but she had adjusted quickly. That was something she would have to watch, she thought, as she picked up two sharing bags of crisps and waited for Ciro to fill a plastic pot with fat green olives. If she wasn't careful, she would get used to it. Or even start to think she deserved their deference. She had to act the part left by Charlie Crow but she had to be careful she didn't start believing her own hype.

She asked after Ciro's children and grandbabies while he packed two bottles of red into a canvas shopping bag along with the olives and crisps. 'Anything else today?'

'No, that's perfect,' Lydia said. 'You're a lifesaver, thank you for opening for me.'

'Of course, of course.' Ciro ducked from behind the deli counter to open the front door for Lydia.

She didn't try to pay, knowing from experience that

this would send Ciro into paroxysms of panicky genu-flections and she didn't have time to reassure him. Instead she pushed a little extra warmth into her smile. It wasn't much, but she told herself it was better than nothing.

Fleet hadn't been home long when Lydia arrived. He was still in his suit with his tie loosened and hadn't even got himself a beer.

'Have you eaten?' He asked after kissing her hello.

'No. I brought olives,' Lydia hefted the bag onto the kitchen counter and began unpacking.

Fleet slipped off his jacket and hung it over the back of a chair before getting wine glasses and a bowl for the crisps. 'I've got some Greek salad and flat bread.'

Lydia wasn't big on salad, but she was too tired to think about takeaway, let alone cooking, so she gratefully agreed. She wandered through the flat, telling Fleet about her educational trip to the museum and hearing about his caseload, while music played through the speakers.

Fleet was just about to bring plates over to the sofa when he stood still. 'Can you smell that?'

'What?'

'Something's burning.' He turned to check the stove. 'I've not used the oven. I don't-'

'I can't smell anything.'

'Could be from another flat.' Fleet crossed the room at speed. A moment later, he had the front door open and was in the stairwell.

Lydia trailed after him.

He was turning slowly, frowning in confusion. 'You really can't smell it? It's definitely smoke. Really strong.'

Dutifully, she took a couple of deep snorts. Traces of urine and refuse. Somebody in the building cooking curry. A hint of Fleet. 'No.'

He shook his head and they went back inside.

Lydia retrieved the plates, and they sat on the sofa. She forked up some cucumber and feta cheese and washed it down with a generous gulp of wine.

'It's gone,' Fleet said after getting stuck into his own meal. 'That was weird.'

There was a possibility that Fleet's olfactory hallucination was a result of a head or nose injury, maybe something which hadn't been picked up in A&E after their car crash, as the doctor had been distracted by his gunshot wound. Or, and Lydia decided not to voice this opinion, it was his precognition gleam playing merry havoc with his senses. She glanced at the ceiling. 'Have you tested those recently?'

'The smoke alarms? Yeah. And they have that little light which shows the battery is good.' He looked at her seriously. 'You think it was a sign?'

'I don't know.' She wasn't going to lie to him. 'How have you been? Had any premonitions today?'

Fleet looked down at his salad and speared a piece of tomato. 'Hard to tell.'

Lydia waited.

'I mean... I have thoughts about what might happen all the time. Often I'm right, but that's experience of being an adult in the world. Doesn't make it precognition.'

Lydia put her plate onto the coffee table and drained the rest of her wine. 'Keep an eye on it. Maybe you could start tracking when something comes true? If you have a strong feeling or vision, maybe?'

'Perhaps,' Fleet put his empty plate on top of Lydia's and sat back, rubbing his face. 'I don't want to think about this.'

Lydia climbed onto his lap. 'Lucky for you, I have an excellent alternative.'

He smiled up at her and she felt the kick low in her stomach. 'Is that a fact?'

'It's a promise,' she said, and kissed him.

CHAPTER SIX

Since talking to Fleet about fathers and answers, Lydia had been wishing she could speak to hers. She was still trying to keep away from Henry Crow, in case her presence made him ill again, but she had another idea. The next day was bright and warm and it seemed like as good a time as any to visit the cemetery. With a ghost for a flatmate, the idea of asking her dead relatives for information didn't seem completely pointless. And who knew? Maybe they would answer. If you didn't ask, you didn't get.

The Family tomb was surrounded by bluebells and wild daffodils, ivy ramping across its surface and the old yew tree alive with small birds chattering. As Lydia crested the hill, three crows swooped down and perched on the stone tomb. The small birds took off in fright and the corvids regarded Lydia in an expectant manner. She greeted them politely, as she had been taught to do from an early age, and was rewarded with what might have been an acknowledgement. A slow tilt of their heads, six

bright eyes fixed upon her, waiting. Feeling faintly fool-
ish, Lydia faced the tomb and asked the question she had
been mulling over on her walk. 'Where did my abilities
come from?'

Nothing.

'I mean, I know that I'm a main bloodline Crow and
that's why I have Crow power. Like my father and
grandfather. But how did we get it in the first place?'

Lydia hadn't expected an answer, but when the crow
simply cawed and flew up into the tree, she couldn't help
but feel a little snubbed. Then she remembered that she
was carrying an offering, and that she was in entirely the
wrong place to get answers.

The yew tree had a couple of sturdy limbs which
were invitingly low to the ground. Lydia caught one and
swung her legs up, trying to imagine her father doing the
same when he had been her age. She got herself into a
crouch and shuffled along, holding a branch above for
balance until she could reach the trunk. She rose slowly,
gripping the trunk. Her first thought had been to climb
higher but now that she was standing, she felt like she
had plenty of height. Her view of the cityscape was
obscured by branches and a thick canopy of pale green
leaves.

Henry had told her that this was the best way to
pay her respects. That her Family had never cared
much for churches or carved stones on the ground, that
they preferred a perch up high. Somewhere with a
view, where you could hear the wind through the
leaves and feel the sun on your feathers. Now that she
was in the tree, Lydia could see the remains of previous

offerings. Small scraps of frayed material, worn to threads by the weather, were tied from upper branches. She had never noticed them from the ground, partly because they were high up and partly because they were black and didn't exactly stand out. Lydia produced her coin and made it stick to the trunk while she tied the piece of black silk around the nearest branch.

'What are you doing?'

The voice startled her and the world tilted sideways for a sickening second. She gripped the trunk and took a couple of breaths.

Peering down through the foliage, she saw the man she expected. Not just from his familiar voice, but from the strong scent of Fox which had wafted upward, carried on the breeze.

Lydia didn't bother replying to Paul, just saved her concentration for getting back down out of the tree in one piece. Her father might have happily shimmied up and down it in his youth, but Lydia's activities had always been more urbanite. Having never been keen on heights or plants, she wasn't a natural tree climber. Above her, her offering flapped in the breeze, looking uncannily like a wing.

Once she had reached solid ground, she put her hands on her hips and faced the Fox. 'What are you doing here?'

'Charming,' Paul said. 'Thought you would like a status report on the surveillance of your friend.'

Yes. The huge favour Paul and his family were doing. Lydia closed her eyes briefly and called for strength. She forced a pleasant expression onto her face. 'Thank you.'

Paul's lips quirked into an amused smile. 'That must have hurt, Little Bird. Don't strain yourself.'

'Shut up.'

'That's more like it. She's fine. No sign of anyone hanging around. And I've put a tracker on her car so if it goes AWOL we'll be able to find her.'

Lydia ignored the clutch of her chest as she imagined Emma being forced to drive somewhere with Maddie. She could see it so clearly, Maddie in the passenger or rear seat, knife held to Emma or, more likely, just using the threat of violence to Archie and Maisie to gain Emma's compliance. It was unbearable.

'Hey, she's going to be okay.' Paul took an uncertain step forward. 'I swear.'

'You can't know that,' Lydia said, noting that his words seemed sincere. 'But I appreciate you saying it. I do.'

He looked away, embarrassed.

'Now. How did you know to find me here?' She gestured at the tomb.

Paul smiled, the moment of uncertainty erased and swagger firmly back in place. 'I'm keeping an eye on you. We all are. For your own protection, of course.'

Well, that was creepy. But also, weirdly comforting. Next to JRB and Maddie, attention from the Fox Family seemed almost quaint.

'So, what were you doing up there?' Paul lifted his chin, his usual teasing tone and sardonic expression back in place. 'I didn't have you down as a tree hugger.'

'I'm not, as a rule.' She turned and looked back at the yew, the branches stretching over the family tomb. 'I brought something for the grave, but my dad said the Crows didn't care much for the ground. He said it was more respectful to leave offerings in a decent perch.'

'Well it makes a kind of sense. If you believe they're here.'

Lydia rubbed at the tree debris which she had acquired, knocking curls of bark and sap from her jacket and jeans. 'Honestly, I don't. But I'm desperate.'

'Desperate?'

As always, Paul Fox made her instantly wish she had kept her mouth shut. 'Don't get excited,' she said in her most withering tone.

He grinned at her, flashing white teeth.

She was too tired to spar with Paul. The way things stood, their old animosity felt like school playtime. Whether it was sensible or not, he felt like something safe and comforting. Familiar. Lydia had a new bench-mark to divide her friends and enemies. Had they attempted to kill her?

She sat cross-legged next to the tomb, resting her back against the cool stone and looked at the vista of London laid out beyond the roll of the hill and the nearby rooftops. Paul sat next to her. Close, but not touching.

They didn't speak for a while and Lydia felt her heart rate calm and her breathing slow down.

'I'm sorry,' Paul said, after a while.

She glanced at his profile. 'What for?'

'About your cousin. It must be hard.'

She watched his face for a beat longer, but there was no malice in his words. No laughter. 'It doesn't feel real. Any of it. I mean, Maddie. I remember her running around and stealing desserts at Uncle John's birthday and making herself sick. She could be a pain, but a contract killer? An assassin? It makes no sense.' Another memory surfaced as Lydia spoke. She and Maddie at another family gathering. Bored of the grownups talking, they had escaped to the garden and were playing underneath the fuchsia bush in the far corner. They had found a dead sparrow and given it a burial. Maddie had cried for half an hour after until Lydia had distracted her with a bag of Skittles. How could that child have grown into a murderer?

Paul shrugged. 'What else does a restless young woman with a flexible moral attitude, an uncanny ability to influence people, move objects with her mind and stop hearts do? If they're not heir to the Crow Family business,' he said, waving a hand at Lydia.

'I am nothing like Maddie,' Lydia said, although she could taste the lie on her tongue.

Paul turned his head to look into her eyes. He smiled gently. 'I can tell you what they're really well suited to, and it's not secretarial work.'

'Charlie wanted to use her as a weapon,' Lydia said. 'He wanted to do the same with me, but we both refused. In our own ways.'

'You can say a lot of things about your Uncle Charlie, but he wasn't a fool.'

Lydia noted Paul's use of the past tense. He believed Charlie to be dead, then. 'But why would Maddie let the

66

government do the exact same thing? She left the Crow Family because Charlie tried to use her.'

'And she hated him for it. I remember,' Paul said.

'So, why let them do it?'

'Maybe they made her a better offer?'

An expression crossed Paul's face that Lydia didn't recognise. 'What?'

'Just... I just thought of what they might have offered Maddie. And it's not good.'

Lydia opened her mouth to ask, but Paul was already speaking.

'Retribution.'

CHAPTER SEVEN

Paul had planted the seed of a very unpleasant idea in Lydia's mind. That Maddie wasn't back in London by accident or even because Smith had contracted her for a job, but instead for her own personal reasons. The assumption was that the rogue assassin Smith had mentioned and Maddie were one and the same, and that certainly seemed to fit. And if the service had lost control of Maddie, that might mean they would be willing to help Lydia to take her out of the picture. A rogue assassin couldn't be a good thing for them, either.

She found Jason in his bedroom, sitting on the floor with his legs stretched out and the laptop open. Knowing him, he hadn't moved all night.

'Can you look for unexplained deaths from the last two years?'

'Where?'

'Worldwide.'

Jason's eyes widened. 'Um... That's...'

'Too many,' Lydia said. 'Feathers. You're right.'

'What are you looking for?' Jason asked.

'A pattern in Maddie's work. Or evidence against her for the jobs she's already done.'

'To take to the police?'

Lydia ran her hands through her hair. It needed a wash, but it was hard to focus on mundane things when she was walking around with a target on her back. 'I'm guessing assassins are considered disposable once they're compromised. Their value lies in the way they move through the population unseen. And Mr Smith, or whoever else has been giving her work, won't want her in custody alive in case she makes a deal in return for information.'

'So, they'll send another assassin to shut her up?'

'Maybe,' Lydia said. 'I really have no idea. But it's what I would do.'

Jason pulled a face. 'No you wouldn't.'

'Okay. Probably not. But it's what I would think I ought to do. If I was being smart.'

'What if I narrowed the search down to unsolved murders?'

'They're likely to not all be marked as murder, though. Like that hit and run in Greece. That was recorded as an accident.' Lydia balled her fists in frustration. She had to do something. Couldn't just wander around waiting for Maddie to decide to fulfil her contract or for Smith to get tired of waiting and send a new assassin. She had to *do* something. 'What about narrowing down by country? Start with the UK or Greece? Her known locations?'

'It would be a start. I can create a program that will

comb for certain parameters easily enough, but the problem will be the data generated. There will be a lot.'

'Yeah, I'm sorry.' Lydia knew she was being unreasonable. Demanding the impossible. 'Don't worry...'

Jason had an unfocused look in his eye and he muttered something that sounded like 'script'. Lydia decided to shut up and let him think. She went and put some bread in the toaster and poured an orange juice. A few minutes later, Jason wafted into the kitchen. 'I could ask some of my friends to help. I don't think they're likely to tell anybody, but it's all just screen names. I don't know who they are.'

'Could you give them small parts to do? Not give them the big picture, kind of thing?'

Jason hesitated before nodding. 'That should be safe enough.'

LEAVING JASON TO COMMUNE WITH HIS LAPTOP, Lydia headed to the silver vaults in search of silver-smiths. A chatty young man with a passion for the subject, pointed her toward a jewellery company in Mayfair. They had an in-house studio for silver and goldsmithing and they supplied the Gold Cup and the Hunt Cup for Ascot every year, he told her. 'They've got a royal charter and have been around since the seventeenth century.'

'Early seventeenth, do you know?' Lydia was thinking about the cup the Silver Family had made when the king gave the lawyers use of the Temple Church.

The man paused. 'Yes, sixteen ten, I believe.' His mouth twisted into a smile. 'Don't quote me.'

Mayfair was not Lydia's natural environment. The expensive stores went beyond the flashy gilt promise of lesser brands, and spoke of establishment and permanence. Tiffany and Givenchy and Burberry, all housed in buildings which looked like banks. Or temples, which, Lydia realised, were much the same thing.

White columns carved with intricate patterns led to a recessed portico and the entrance to the shop. A shop so swanky it was called a 'house'. The silver vaults contained a glittering array of silver, of course, a cascade of fine items with stories of wealth and privilege, as well as desperation and cunning. This place was something different.

Once admitted, Lydia was surrounded by the hush of true wealth. Recessed lighting provided subtle inducement to look here, or there. To admire this exquisite piece or that. The ambience was a cross between a museum and a high-class brothel. Lydia quashed a snort of laughter. That probably wasn't the vibe they were aiming for, but now that she had thought it she could see it everywhere. The desirables laid out wantonly, batting their expensive gems in the punters' direction. The way they wouldn't glitter quite as much when removed from the expert lighting and velvet display case, moulded to show the necklace or whatever to its finest advantage.

Lydia realised she was light-headed. She wasn't tasting Silver. This was just a vast building filled with ordinary silver and gold. Nothing to trouble her senses.

She hadn't drunk any alcohol the day before, so it wasn't a hangover, and Jason had made her a bowl of cereal before she had left home, so it wasn't hunger. She put a hand out to steady herself and felt smooth glass. A subtle gasp to her left indicated that laying fingers on the polished case was a social faux pas. Lydia ignored it and concentrated on sucking in oxygen until the speckles at the edges of her vision receded.

Once she was reasonably sure she wasn't about to keel over, Lydia was able to focus on the man standing close by. He was extremely well groomed and had the glowing skin of a good dermatologist and a comfortable life. As a result, Lydia would have guessed his age at somewhere between thirty and fifty. She also wasn't surprised that he was taking in her general appearance with something close to horror. 'Are you unwell, madam?'

Madam. Lydia would lay money that she was younger than the man, which meant he was being deliberately insulting. Or, perhaps, it was part of his training. Some weird custom among the British upper class. Well, she was a Camberwell girl and wouldn't have the first idea about any of that. She smiled widely and deliberately relaxed her stance. She wasn't going to be subservient in the face of snobbery, but she didn't want to appear threatening, either. This place would be wired up directly to the police and it would be embarrassing for Fleet if she was the cause of an emergency call out. 'I wanted to ask about a job that was done here.'

His face closed. 'We don't give out details about our clients to the press.'

'I'm not a journalist,' Lydia said. 'I work at the British Museum. Research. Roisin Quin,' she held out her hand.

He shook it automatically. 'I don't understand...'

'We're talking ancient history,' Lydia said, smiling again. 'Sometime in the period from the nineteen forties to around nineteen eighty.'

'That's a large stretch of time to check records. Even if we were able to do so. As I say, client confidentiality... It's simply not information we give out.'

'I don't need the client information,' Lydia said. 'I need the name of the person who made the item. You have a studio here, I believe? You must keep staff records.'

Now the man looked thoroughly confused. 'You want the name of the person who made the item? It might be more than one, you know. Pieces are rarely made in isolation. And we don't keep records of individuals.'

'You don't keep staff records? I find that hard to believe.'

The man shifted. 'I mean to say, we might not be able to pinpoint who worked on a particular piece. Besides, we're not about to open up private records to just anybody.'

'Not even for the greater good?' Lydia had her coin in her hand and she squeezed it lightly. 'The historical record of our beloved city.' Well, that was laying it on a bit thick. Lydia was doing her best impression of how an academic historian associated with the museum would speak, trying to emulate Roisin's verbiage. Surprisingly, it seemed to be working. The man was visibly more at ease.

'There's no harm in me taking a peek at your studio, at least?'

The man brightened. Perhaps at the opportunity to offload Lydia onto somebody else. 'No harm at all,' he said.

'Lead the way.'

The studio was in a half basement with a low ceiling, a row of barred windows high up the walls, and wooden desks strewn with chisels, pliers, and other tools. There were tall chests with shallow drawers, spools of wire, tool chests, and a forest of angle-poise lamps.

The air was tinged with the scent of heated metal and something acidic but, Lydia was grateful to note, no Silver tang. The metal she could smell was entirely natural. A woman wearing a heavy work apron and carrying a long metal file looked at Lydia curiously as she took her place back at a desk, but otherwise nobody stopped what they were doing.

'There's a research library next door,' her guide said. 'But you want to speak to Barbara. Barb. She's worked here forever.'

Barb turned out to be a sprightly pixie of a woman, and Lydia would guess her age at around three hundred. If her senses hadn't been telling her otherwise, she would have assumed the woman had Pearl blood. She had some of that ethereal vitality, with eyes that were bright blue and as sharp as a child's and the complexion of a Mediterranean matriarch. Or a woman who had spent the best part of her life under a tanning bed.

While her face was entirely creased by wrinkles, like a shrivelled apple, Lydia had the inescapable feeling that Barb would be able to beat her in a fair fight.

'Healthiest substance to work with,' Barb said after the guide had introduced them and told her that Lydia was interested in the silversmithing side. 'Antibacterial.'

'Right,' Lydia said. She had never thought of silver has anything except potentially lethal.

'I've been here since the sixties. Started at fourteen.'

Hell Hawk. That was commitment. 'Gosh.'

Barb's eyes narrowed. 'You're not interested in silver-smithing history, girl. And I've not got time to waste.'

'It's about a replica.'

'This way,' Barb led the way out of the studio and in through the next doorway. The library. Which was a smaller room than the word suggested, but lined with shelves and with a small table in the middle and a couple of chairs. Barb sat down and indicated that Lydia should do the same.

'You're with the police?'

'No, I'm with the British Museum.'

'No you're not,' Barb said, her eyes narrowed. 'But no matter. No skin off my teeth.'

Lydia was finding it difficult to keep her place in the conversation. She decided to take control. She produced her coin and spun it in the air.

Barb's eyes were drawn to it, as Lydia had known they would be. She felt guilty, using her power when she ought to use normal persuasion, but that was like carrying a sharp axe and trying to cut down a tree with a spoon. 'A silver cup went missing from the British

Museum in the seventies and at least one replica has been made of it. Probably since it went missing, but I can't discount the possibility that the replica was made before, after the war sometime.'

'What cup?' Barb's voice had the dreamy quality of the hypnotised.

'The Silver Family cup.'

Barb nodded slowly. 'Three.'

'Sorry?'

'We made three here. Expensive job. Especially for that sort of client.'

'What sort of client?' Lydia asked, expecting her to say something disparaging about magic folk or the rumours surrounding the Families.

Barb gave her an imperious look. 'Not royalty.'

'Right.'

'Did you work on the cup yourself?'

'I did,' Barb said. 'Well. I saw it. I was sweeping up shavings from the floor and not much else back then. I was an apprentice, but it was a slow start. I was a girl, after all.'

'But you remember this being made?' Lydia couldn't believe her luck. 'Do you remember if they worked from the original or from photographs?'

'Photographs and drawings, I believe,' Barb said. 'But better than that, we had the original moulds for the body and the handles. There was detail work to be added, of course, but the moulds were key.'

'How was that possible? The original was made over three hundred years earlier. And the British Museum have no records of any such item.'

77

'There was a man. He didn't work here, but he came in for that job. That's one of the reasons I remember it so well. That has never happened since. Not once. The boss here is very particular about who is allowed in the workshop and especially not to touch anything. It's to do with our reputation. And he doesn't want anybody stealing design ideas, either.'

Lydia felt a tingling. 'And the man brought the mould for the cup?'

'That's right,' Barb said. 'And he supervised.'

'Can you remember his name?'

Barb shook her head. 'Sorry. No.'

Lydia could see she was telling the truth, even without the Crow whammy. She pocketed her coin and made to leave. Finding out where the replica cup had been made wasn't exactly helpful to its current where-abouts, but at least she now knew there were three replicas floating about.

'He had a funny name,' Barb said.

'Sorry?' Lydia turned back to the small woman.

'Foreign, like. French, I think it was.' She smiled dreamily. 'Ooh la la.'

CHAPTER EIGHT

Lydia knew she was dreaming, but the fear was real. She was on the roof and Maddie was smiling like it was Christmas and her birthday rolled into one. She could see her bright lipstick and the hectic light in her eyes, but she couldn't hear anything except the wind rushing in her ears. Lydia knew it was bad. She knew that something awful was about to happen, but her fear was tinged with excitement. The wind was whipping Maddie's hair around her face, giving it a life of its own. Then they were high in a clear blue sky, flying together and she could feel her wings beating and her muscles working in exactly the way they were made to work and there was nothing but pure exhilaration. Freedom.

'It's time,' Maddie said in her ear and they were back on the roof.

Fleet was kneeling in front of her. She couldn't see his face but knew the back of his head, his shoulders, his suit.

'Do it,' Maddie said.

Lydia had a knife and she stepped forward, reaching to draw it across Fleet's neck. His body tumbled forward and she woke up, heart racing and drenched in sweat.

ONCE SHE WAS UP AND CAFFEINATED, LYDIA knocked on Jason's door. 'Sorry if I disturbed you last night.'

Jason was sitting on the bed with his laptop open. He looked at her over the screen. 'You were shouting in your sleep. Bad dreams?'

Lydia nodded. 'Nothing I can't handle. I'm heading out.'

'Okay,' Jason frowned. Lydia didn't usually inform him of her movements.

She hesitated. 'If I'm not back in a couple of hours, could you... I don't know. Call Fleet? Or message him?'

'What are you doing?'

Lydia gave in. 'Looking for Maddie. I can't just sit around waiting to see what she decides to do.'

'Is there any point in me pointing out this is a bad idea?'

'None at all,' Lydia said, smiling as cheerfully as she could manage. She headed for the door before Jason could talk her out of it. She had to act.

When Maddie had disappeared from her parents' home and Lydia had been charged by Uncle Charlie to bring her back, she had found her hiding out on a canal boat in Little Venice. That had been courtesy of Paul

Fox, but when he said he hadn't seen her, she believed him. At least, she thought she did. Lydia couldn't tell if she was just tired of second-guessing everybody or whether it was some Crow-level gut feeling.

Without expecting to find Maddie in such an obvious place, Lydia checked the canal first. The boat Maddie had used before was occupied by a middle-aged couple who seemed as normal as it was possible to be. Lydia had printed some information sheets from the council website on canal bylaws and handed one over as her cover, introducing herself as a council worker on a thankless, box-ticking task. They were perfectly pleasant, and she got zero Family reading from either one of them.

Next was Uncle John and Aunt Daisy, Maddie's parents. Aiden hadn't noticed any unusual behaviour or heard any useful gossip. Certainly nothing about Maddie being seen around her family home. Still, Lydia felt that she needed to check for herself. It wasn't that she didn't trust Aiden to do a good job, it was just that... She was a control freak who didn't trust anybody.

Uncle John wasn't Lydia's biggest fan. He thought she was too young, too inexperienced and too female to be head of the Family, and he hid it poorly. He let her into his Camberwell house with a palpable reluctance. 'To what do we owe the honour?'

Lydia fixed John with her best shark-stare. She had learned it from Uncle Charlie and, she liked to think, had learned it well.

John dropped his gaze and led the way to the

kitchen. 'Daisy's not here. She's at the gym. Or out with the girls. I forget which. It could be shopping.' He shrugged in a faux-apologetic manner. 'I wasn't really listening, I'm afraid.'

'I'll take a coffee, thanks,' Lydia said, taking a seat the large table. 'Do you have any biscuits?'

After a brief session of small talk, which neither of them enjoyed, Lydia cut to the chase. In short order, she ascertained that John hadn't seen or heard from Maddie and, to the best of his knowledge, neither had his wife.

Lydia had never been keen on John and his attitude toward her hadn't warmed her feelings, but she didn't wish him actual bodily harm. Which was why, when he asked why she was asking about Maddie, Lydia didn't lie. At least, not completely. 'Can you keep something between us?'

He nodded.

'Maddie has been seen in central London. I don't know if she is hanging around for a long visit or whether she has already flown away, or if the person who reported seeing her was mistaken, but...'

'When?'

'Last week.'

'I had a feeling,' he said, abruptly. 'When I was in the garden on Friday. You know when you feel like someone is watching you?'

It was Lydia's turn to nod.

'But I couldn't see anyone. And it could have been one of the neighbours looking out of their windows, nothing to worry about. But I felt it on the back of my neck.'

'It might not have been her,' Lydia said, realising that she was suddenly in the strange position of reassuring him. John was clearly unhappy.

'You're right,' he said. 'Why wouldn't she have come in to say "hello" if it had been her. If she had been so close to us. She would have visited.'

Lydia made a non-committal noise.

John walked her to the front door. He probably meant to seem polite, but it felt like she was being seen off the premises.

'Tell me if she gets in touch or if you see her,' Lydia said, not bothering to hide the command in her tone.

At that moment, Daisy opened the front door. She was visibly shocked and alarmed at the sight of Lydia, which set her wondering whether Maddie had, in fact, been around. Or perhaps they were hiding something else. Or they just hated her guts.

'We missed you on Sunday,' Daisy said stiffly, hanging her beige coat on a peg and giving Lydia the lightest of air kisses.

The Easter Sunday garden party. Egg rolling for the little ones and a booze-laden BBQ for everyone else. 'I was working,' Lydia said.

'Of course you were,' Daisy said. 'We all know how stretched you are. With your little business as well as your Family role. We did wonder if it would be too much for you on your own, didn't we, John?'

He nodded stiffly, eyes wary. John was no fool, and he knew that Daisy was sailing very close to the wind.

Lydia smiled thinly and produced her coin, lazily

flipping it over the back of her knuckles. Daisy stopped speaking.

'I appreciate your support,' Lydia said. 'And I know where to come when I need help. It's important to know that family is on side.'

John swallowed and Daisy's eyes widened.

'She meant no disrespect,' John blustered.

Lydia stared him down.

'We meant no disrespect. I mean, neither of us... We respect you.' John seemed unable to stop speaking, while Daisy just stared at Lydia with her mouth open. Frozen.

Lydia let the silence play out for a few seconds longer than was comfortable before flipping her coin into the air and catching it. 'I'll be in touch.'

Now that John and Daisy had joined the growing number of people who knew that Maddie was back in London, the guilt at not telling Fleet was gnawing at Lydia's insides. She was distracted by a fresh source when he called her mobile to ask why she wasn't at his flat. She had forgotten that she had promised to meet Fleet's family, and that they had agreed to go together from his place. 'Sorry, sorry. I'm leaving right now.'

'I'll pick you up,' Fleet said.

Lydia knew her hair was in need of a wash so she pulled it back into a pony tail. She considered getting changed into smarter clothes but then figured that it wasn't likely to make enough of a difference and that she needed all the comfort she could get. A quick look in the mirror revealed an unhealthy complexion, so she added some red lipstick to brighten and distract from the dark circles under her eyes. The face looking back at her was the one she had seen in her nightmare and she hastily rubbed the lipstick off again, erasing Maddie's ghost.

By the time she was outside the cafe, looking out for Fleet's car, she was thoroughly rattled.

After apologising for forgetting and for not having anything to bring his aunt, Lydia slumped back in the passenger seat and tried to calm herself down.

'It's all fine,' Fleet said, not for the first time, as he pulled into a parking space.

The engine ticked as it cooled and Lydia made no move to leave the car. 'Will she like me?'

'Of course,' Fleet said easily. 'She has excellent taste.'

'Will she mind that I'm not...'

Fleet raised an eyebrow. 'What?'

'That I'm a bit paler than you. A lot paler than you.'

Fleet ducked his head to look into her eyes. 'She knows.'

Lydia wanted to tell him that that wasn't a complete answer, but she also knew that she might not want to push him for the whole one. She might not like it.

Fleet's aunt lived in a high rise with open balconies. The buzzer was extremely loud and set off a cacophony of barking from inside the flat. 'I didn't know she had dogs.'

'She doesn't,' Fleet said. 'Too much mess. But my cousin-'

He was cut off by the door opening and a small round woman pulling him into an immediate embrace.

She was wearing a red floral-patterned dress which brushed the floor. 'Don't let the dogs out,' she said, her words muffled by Fleet's body.

Two tiny Yorkies were attempting to wriggle through the gaps between her body and the door frame. Lydia stepped up closer and prepared to duck and grab.

Fleet disentangled himself and pulled Lydia by the hand to follow the woman who was retreating into the flat, shooing the dogs as she went. He closed the door and Lydia stooped to unlace her DMs. Fleet had warned her that his aunt had a no shoes rule.

The living room wasn't large and it was filled with bodies. Fleet's aunt was in an aggressively paisley armchair, three young women were squashed onto the too-small sofa, and several small children were on the floor. They leaped up and onto Fleet, shrieking with what Lydia could only assume was delight. Fleet hugged them and twirled them and swung one very small girl high up into the air until she laughed so hard a stream of snot came out of her nose.

The Yorkies were sniffing Lydia's feet. 'Let them sit down,' the aunt said and the three young women jumped up.

'I don't see why...' One of them began and then stopped with a single searing look from Fleet's aunt.

'It's very nice to meet you,' Lydia said, stepping forward, narrowly avoiding standing on a tiny dog. It made a startled little 'yip' sound even though she didn't touch it. Traitor.

'Call me Auntie,' Fleet's aunt said, with a wave of

her hand. Lydia caught the three young women making wide eyes at each other.

'Go on and fetch the tea,' Auntie said. 'A body could shrivel up waiting.'

ONCE LYDIA WAS WEDGED ON THE SOFA NEXT TO Fleet, had drunk two dainty china cups of tea and eaten a slice of lime cake which was sticky with syrup, she was beginning to think she might just survive this exposure to Fleet's family.

'Your daddy is Henry Crow.'

It was a statement, not a question, but Lydia nodded anyway. 'Yes, Auntie.'

'He ought to be with your family. Leading.'

Well that was a slap in the face.

'Not that you're not capable, child,' she waved a hand. 'But he shouldn't have left his responsibility.'

'Auntie...' Fleet cut in and received a blistering look from Auntie in return.

'You stay out of it, child,' Auntie said, heaving herself upright. 'And you. Come along with me.'

Lydia followed Auntie down the narrow hallway. Behind one of the flimsy doors was a small room. It was the kind of size which got called 'a lovely space for a baby' because you couldn't fit anything larger than a cot into it. There was a chest of drawers, the surface crowded with framed pictures, melted wax and the stubs of half-burned candles. It had the look of an altar.

'That's my sister,' Auntie said, pointing at a picture

of a smartly dressed woman with a gangly looking boy. 'And Ignatius.'

Lydia scanned the other pictures. She saw one of Auntie when she was younger, shoulder to shoulder with Fleet's mother. Two pretty unsmiling women in flowery dresses. There were a couple of men flanking them. 'Is that...'

Her lips pursed. 'His daddy? No. No pictures.'

Auntie clearly wanted to say something else and Lydia waited.

'I saw something,' she said eventually. She patted her chest. 'In here.'

Lydia nodded to show she understood, but didn't speak.

'That boy in there.' Auntie jerked her head in the direction of the living room. 'He's very precious.'

Lydia was embarrassed to find her eyes welling with tears. 'I know that.'

'Then you should do the right thing.'

There was a prickling sensation along Lydia's skin and she consciously unclenched her fists. 'And what's that?'

Auntie gave her a long, assessing stare. 'Do you know what you're doing to him?'

Lydia wasn't sure if Auntie could somehow sense her Crow power and the way she powered up those around her, or whether Fleet had confided in her about his increasing clairvoyance and she was putting the blame on Lydia regardless. Or, and this was very possible, that she was talking about something else entirely. The fact that Lydia was as white as her Scandinavian ancestors, perhaps? Or the fact that she was a private investigator and not good wife material. Or, maybe Auntie simply disliked the thought of Fleet attaching to anybody. She was clearly protective of her nephew. 'I won't hurt him,' Lydia said. She wanted to add that she loved Fleet, but her throat had closed up and she didn't trust herself to get the words out without seeming unhinged. Once upon a time, she had prided herself on her toughness. These days, she seemed to have lost the barrier she had kept between herself and other people. It was exhausting.

Auntie's expression didn't soften. 'I'm not saying you'll mean to hurt him, but he'll be hurt just the same.'

The door swung inward and Fleet appeared, looking deeply unhappy. He shot Auntie a look which could have stripped paint from a car. 'We've got to get going. Are you ready, Lyds?'

'Sure am,' Lydia said and escaped in front of Fleet.

OUT IN THE CAR, FLEET TURNED IN THE SEAT. 'I'm sorry about that.'

'How much did you hear?'

'Nothing. But it's not a good sign when Auntie takes a guest away on their own. I can guess enough to know that you are probably really freaked out. I'm sorry.'

'It's fine,' Lydia said, cupping his cheek. She was surprised to find she was telling the truth. There was something to be said for having a professional hit hovering over her head, it really put 'scary' into perspective. 'Bring it on.'

89

He kissed her before starting the engine. 'Are you sure you're okay?'

'Your aunt is protective of you. It's nice. And I'm not keen to start comparing family drama.'

Pulling into the traffic, Fleet nodded. 'Fair enough.'

BACK AT HER FLAT, ONCE SHE HAD EATEN A restorative plate of pasta and they had shared a bottle of wine, Lydia checked in on Emma. She had to be careful not to alarm Emma with her increased contact, but the only alternative was to ask Paul and that held its own set of problems. After a moment, she did it anyway and got a fast text message back telling her that there was no cause for alarm. Well, as Paul put it, 'her dull life is singularly unenlivened'. He added a suggestion that they meet for a drink to 'discuss all the boring details' which Lydia ignored.

Curled up and preparing to sleep, Fleet breathing evenly beside her, Lydia pushed thoughts of her nightmare out of her mind. She had no intention of having a bad dream again and she told her subconscious so in firm tones. In the safety of the dark, she could admit to herself that the visit with Fleet's family had been a little unsettling. But, she reasoned, the fact that she had dreamed about hurting Fleet before Auntie had said she would do so, was comforting. Perhaps Fleet's aunt had a bit of the gleam that she sensed in Fleet. If she had heightened perception, then perhaps she had sensed the psychic imprint left by Lydia's nightmare. Perhaps Lydia's deep fears that she would cause harm to Fleet had leaked out in the presence of a highly sensitive individual. It made sense. And, as it was based on dreams and fears, it didn't mean anything. She was in control of her actions and she would never hurt Fleet. So she could go to sleep.

CHAPTER NINE

The next morning, Lydia was woken by her landline ringing in the next room. She ignored it and was successfully staying asleep when her mobile rang. A shot of adrenaline and one clear thought – Emma – brought her to sudden consciousness and she grabbed the device from its place on the floor. It was a terse message from Maria's assistant, requesting a progress report. The entire purpose was to remind Lydia that she was working for Maria and to rub it in as much as possible.

Fleet was awake by this point and she updated him on her progress on finding the silver cup. It didn't take long.

'What are you going to do if you find it? Give it to Maria?' Fleet asked once she had finished.

'I don't know,' Lydia said, sitting up against the pillows. 'I told her I would find it, I was very careful not to say what I would do with it after.'

'Sneaky,' Fleet said.

'It's her fault for not pinning down the wording of our agreement. It's not like she didn't know who she was dealing with.'

'And she's got legal training. She knows about contracts.'

'Exactly,' Lydia said, refusing to feel bad. She might have called a truce with Maria and the Silver Family, but that didn't mean she liked or trusted them. And it didn't erase the past.

Fleet was silent for a moment. 'You know there's a good chance Alejandro took the cup with him when he left?'

Lydia shifted to a more comfortable position. 'Or he gave it to the government as part of his immunity deal. I know.'

'And if that isn't the case, it might be better if you don't find it.'

'What do you mean?'

'Wouldn't it better for it to stay lost? Collecting dust in someone's trophy cabinet rather than... Well, whatever Maria wants it for. What does she want it for?'

'Pride, I think,' Lydia said. She could imagine Maria displaying it in her office to remind people of her heritage. The ultimate status symbol. 'Although it is chockful of Silver power. Maybe she could use that somehow. I honestly don't know enough about their potential.' The Family lore said that the Silvers used to be able to convince a person to do anything they wanted, just with the power of speech. They could make a person stroll off a building, thinking they could fly. They could suggest someone didn't need their property, car or cash, and they would just hand it all over with a smile. If Maria was brought up on those bedtime stories, maybe she thinks the cup is the key back to glory.

'Have you got any leads?'

'Not yet. I've spoken to the expert at the British Museum and seen the pictures and description from before it went missing. Not surprising, she was pretty cagey about how it got nicked. Doesn't look very good for the museum security.'

'I can look up the report, if you like?'

'I don't want to waste your time. I know where it ended up, after all. I need to know who has it now, not who took it back in the day.' Lydia sat up and began pulling on her clothes. All this chat had just reminded her of how little progress she had made. She had to get going. 'There is something I hoped you could look into for me.'

Fleet had sat up behind her and he dropped a kiss onto her bare shoulder. 'What's it worth?'

She shot him a look. He held up his hands. 'Joking. What do you need?'

'You remember the effect that the silver statue had on Robert Sharp and Yas Bishop? I was wondering whether whoever picked up the Silver cup might have suffered the same problems.'

'You want me to search arrest reports for mention of a cup?'

'If someone is cognitively compromised, they might be babbling about it. That would get recorded in the report, wouldn't it?'

'Should be. I could look for reports that had

contacting mental health services listed as an action. There will be quite a few.'

'I saw the cup with Alejandro last year in the summer. That gives us a time frame, at least.'

'It's still going to throw up a lot of results,' Fleet said. 'Just to warn you.'

'That's okay. And thank you.' She turned back to kiss him and he cupped her cheek with one hand.

She could be a little late.

AFTER FLEET HAD GONE TO WORK, LYDIA FORCED herself up and into a hot shower. Padding through the flat with still-damp hair, clean skin and a hoodie for comfort, she felt ready to face the rest of her day. Strong enough to make coffee, at any rate.

Lydia was sipping from a novelty cupcake-shaped mug, the only clean one left, and contemplating the prospect of returning Maria Silver's phone call, when Jason mercifully appeared from his room to distract her.

'You know you asked me to look for Maddie's handi-work? I've got something,' Jason was carrying his laptop. He didn't need to sleep so didn't look any different to usual, even though Lydia knew he had been working non-stop since she asked him to trace Maddie's movements.

'In Albania. Just over the Greek border.'

'What makes you think it's Maddie?'

'Location, partly, this was just two weeks after the hit and run in Greece. But also because of this,' Jason spun the laptop around so that Lydia could see the screen.

An image was open and, for a moment, Lydia thought it showed a gigantic black bird. She blinked and the picture became clear. It was a man hanging from a tree, arms spread wide. He was wearing a long black coat which was open, the material mimicking wings. Lydia squinted at the scenery. The tree had a thick trunk with peeling white bark and the sky was blue.

'It's an oriental plane,' Jason said. 'I looked it up. And in the next image you can see some olive trees. And a bit of old blockwork. The man was found in the Butrint national park, there's an amphitheatre and all sorts. Looks very nice.'

'Apart from the man in the tree,' Lydia said.

'Yeah. Apart from him.'

Lydia flicked her attention back to the figure and forced herself to focus on every aspect. She used the technique her old boss had taught her of breaking the image into a grid of one centimetre squares and examining them in order. You had to look at the image overall, too, but breaking it up was important for the detail. And for not allowing emotion to cloud your vision. She realised that the long coat wasn't just opened, the material had been cut up the back and the two long flaps folded up and attached at the wrists. The man's arms were straight out, unnaturally so, with something cylindrical poking out of the cuff of the coat. Maybe the handle of a broom, threaded through the coat sleeves.

The material looked dry. The man was somewhere in his forties or, at a push, fifties. Slim and in good shape.

He was wearing black trousers which had an expensive cut and seemed to fit well and black socks. His shirt was also black, buttoned right up to the neck, but it looked loose on his frame.

'Are there more?'

'A couple,' Jason flicked through the images. One was taken from closer to the body and at a high angle. It showed a slice of ground beneath the figure and there was something brown at the edge of the shot.

'What's that?'

'The report of the scene described a pair of shoes near the trunk of the tree. Could be those?'

'Makes sense,' Lydia said, looking at the flash of brown.

'What about this makes sense?'

'Brown shoes. That's why she took them off. They didn't match the aesthetic.'

'You're sure it's Maddie, then?'

Lydia nodded. 'I mean, look. She's dressed him up as a crow.'

'He might have just liked wearing black.'

'Not with brown shoes. And I don't think he was wearing the shirt or the coat when he turned up to meet Maddie. The shirt doesn't fit him properly. She guessed on the size.'

'It's not bad,' Jason said, squinting at the picture. 'Could have been something he bought himself.'

'She guessed well,' Lydia said.

'So who is he?'

'Sergio Bastos. The report doesn't give much detail and he's got a severely minimal online presence. Jobs listed as a stint in the SAS and "analyst" for GCHQ and then he drops off the net. And there's a note on the report which indicates the file was closed almost as soon as it was opened.'

'What does that mean?'

'I think it means he was Maddie's handler.'

Lydia leaned back in her chair. 'You are amazing. How hard was it to break into the Albanian police database?'

Jason looked embarrassed. If he was alive, he probably would have blushed, but instead he began hovering slightly above the ground. 'I only hacked the staff database to get some contact details. Then I bribed an officer for the report.'

'All via email?'

Jason smiled paternally, like she was a toddler. 'It's a little bit more complicated than that.'

'Right. Well. Well done.' How likely was she to go to prison in the event of Jason being prosecuted for bribing an officer of the law? I mean, she could hardly say that a ghost did it. Then another thought struck her. 'Where did you get the cash?'

'I invested in bitcoin last year. Been doing a bit of trading in crypto ever since.'

LYDIA HAD BEEN CHECKING IN ON EMMA EVERY DAY via WhatsApp, keeping it light and breezy. Still, Emma had picked up on the increased contact and invited Lydia round to the house.

Maisie and Archie were in the living room watching

CBeebies. Emma had put the kettle on and was making tea. 'I've got wine if you want, but I can't join you.' She pulled a face. 'Spring fair at the school tonight.'

'I would have thought that meant alcohol was even more necessary.'

'Tom is working and I have to drive. I'm in charge of the tombola and I'm not lugging all those tins on foot.'

Lydia rummaged in her bag and brought out two large bags of chocolate. 'I bought these for the kids but I wanted to check with you first. I didn't know if they are allowed it or...'

'Oh, yes,' Emma said. 'All my sugar-free ideas went out the window as soon as they started school. Sometimes I pay Archie to do his homework with Dairy Milk.'

Lydia laughed to show she got the joke, although she wasn't sure how serious Emma was being. She was trying to be normal, but her face felt like she was wearing a mask and she was sure Emma would notice. She was her oldest friend. Her only friend, in fact, until she had met Jason, and nobody knew her better. At least, nobody had known her better. But she tried very hard to keep her Crow Family weirdness away from Emma and her safe, normal life. Maddie's text flashed across her mind and she felt the roil of fury and fear in her stomach. Her own cousin, threatening Emma.

Emma put her elbows on the table and cradled her mug with both hands, regarding Lydia over the rim. 'What's up?'

'Nothing,' Lydia said, looking at her tea. There were little bubbles on the surface and the milk hadn't quite dissipated, yet. Her stomach turned over again.

'You're very pale,' Emma said, reaching out a hand to her forehead.

It made Lydia feel about five years old, but she was alarmed to discover she didn't mind. 'I'm fine.'

'That's what you always say.' Emma took a sip of tea. 'And you're usually lying. Let's face it, you're here. That means something is definitely wrong.'

Lydia opened her mouth to say that wasn't fair, but then she closed it. Emma had a point. And, besides, the words hadn't been said sharply or with a single drop of malice. Emma gazed at her steadily. Accepting. Knowing. And somehow still her friend.

'I love you,' Lydia said, her eyes prickling with unexpected tears.

'Oh Jesus,' Emma said in alarm. 'What's wrong?'

Lydia smiled and shook her head. 'I'm fine, honestly.'

'Don't say that when it's clearly not true,' Emma said. 'Are you ill? Just tell me.'

'Nothing like that.' Lydia couldn't tell Emma about Maddie. She couldn't run away or hide successfully and would only live in fear. 'I've just been feeling a bit off recently.' As she spoke, she realised it was the truth.

'Are you pregnant?'

'No!'

Emma gave her a long look. 'Are you sure?'

'Stop it, yes.'

At that moment an unearthly howling started up. 'I'll just...' Emma headed to the living room to deal with whatever crisis had befallen her children, and Lydia sipped her tea and catalogued her symptoms. She had been feeling tired. And there had been a couple of almost-fainting episodes. On the other hand, her Crow abilities seemed more powerful than ever. Just that one thought and she could feel her coin in her hand. She slipped it into her pocket and tried to clear her mind, but there was a humming at the edges. A vibration in her body and mind which felt like a prelude. A tuning up. A warning.

'They're tired,' Emma said when she returned. 'Don't know how they're going to cope with the excitement of the fair.'

Lydia wasn't sure if she was being sarcastic or not. Perhaps a school fair was exciting when you were a small child. Lydia couldn't remember.

'So, are you working too hard? I know you've got a lot on your plate. I mean, you're the big boss, now, right? That's got to be stressful.'

When Lydia had first taken over from Charlie it had been extremely stressful. Now she had settled into a good routine. She had impressed upon the Family that there was a new order and that certain old practices were no longer acceptable. Now that had filtered through, Aiden took care of the day-to-day. She still had to speak to him regularly, though. And, worst of all, be 'seen' in Camberwell. Once every fortnight she sat in The Fork and people came and aired their grievances, begged favours, and offered deals. Plus, she was still trying to keep her investigation firm going, not to mention be a half-decent partner to Fleet. She shrugged. 'It's not so bad.'

'Do you miss him?'

For a second Ash's face flashed in front of Lydia and her guts twisted. 'Who?'

'Your uncle,' Emma said.

'No.' And she really didn't. Things were tangled and tricky and Mr Smith had turned out to be very bad news indeed, but at least that was a clear kind of hatred. It was easier. Her guts twisted, again, as if to call her a liar. And then they cramped and she rose hastily.

'Tummy bug?' Emma's face was the picture of concern.

'Or something,' Lydia said as she rushed from the room.

CHAPTER TEN

Lydia was in the training room at Charlie's house. It had a wall of mirrors which gave her a perfect view of the coins she was spinning all around the room. She made them spin and then stop, swoop together like a flock of starlings and then disappear, leaving only her true coin. When she felt warmed up, the vibrations humming through her mind and body and the sound of wings filling her ears, she threw a bundle of energy at Charlie's punchbag. She had hoped to knock its stand over, maybe even cause some damage to the bag itself. What she hadn't expected was for the metal stand and weighty bag to fly back into the mirrored wall with such impact that a large starburst crack appeared.

She bent over, breathing heavily, but she didn't feel light-headed. For a few moments, she felt clear headed and strong, like an unexpected pause in a hangover, but then the fog and sickness crept back. She sat on the floor cross-legged and looked at her fractured reflection in the broken mirror. Her power definitely seemed to refill. It wasn't something that got used up and that was good. The problem was, she hadn't meant to hit the punchbag with that amount of force. It was like the burst of energy she had thrown through the lift doors killing the hitman, Felix. And if the punchbag had been a person, they would also be dead. The point of training was to stop that from happening, not to repeat it.

'What do I do?' She asked out loud, but none of the multiple Lydias in the mirror answered.

LYDIA HAD INTENDED TO DO ANOTHER HOUR OF training, but the cracked mirror was mocking her so she trailed downstairs to make some coffee instead. She switched on the machine and downed a glass of water while it warmed up. What she really wanted was a proper drink. The last few months of laying off the whisky hadn't left her feeling any healthier. If anything, she felt worse. Although her power seemed much stronger. Either she was an alcoholic in withdrawal or the whisky had been dampening her power to a manageable level and now she was suffering as it grew. The unanswered questions made her head hurt, so she helped herself to a swig of Charlie's single malt. The burn in her stomach and the smoky aftertaste was soothing, so she took another swig. And another.

'Day drinking,' a voice said from behind her, making her jump. 'Not a good sign.'

Maddie was lounging in the entrance to the hall. She wasn't wearing a wig this time, but she still looked different to the girl Lydia remembered. Her brown hair was expertly highlighted and fell in shiny curls below her shoulders and there was a hardness in her face.

Lydia gripped the bottle tightly. 'It's nice that you care.' She was making a quick inventory of her chances. She had no gun, the knives were held on a magnetic strip next to the cooker, too far away for comfort, and she was still feeling exhausted and odd after her training session. She was facing an experienced killer with nothing but a glass bottle. She relaxed her hold on the neck, letting her arm fall to her side, as if this might make Maddie forget she was holding it.

'So,' Maddie moved into the room and looked around. 'You really have taken over.'

'Aiden's on his way,' Lydia said, 'we have meetings here.'

Maddie shook her head. 'Gotta hope that isn't true. For Aiden's sake.'

There was a block of ice in Lydia's stomach, the cold radiating along her limbs and creeping into her chest. It was dread. She instinctively knew that dread would paralyse her. Root her feet to the floor and leave her helpless. She reached instead for bright hot fear. That she could work with.

'Don't look so tense,' Maddie said. 'I'm not here to kill you.'

'Change of orders?'

Anger flashed across her face and Lydia mentally kicked herself. This wasn't the time to annoy the woman. Old habits died hard, though.

'I told you,' Maddie had opened the fridge and was gazing inside. 'I don't follow orders.'

'You've been working for the government, though. Their top international assassin by all accounts.' Maybe flattery would get her off guard.

She closed the fridge door and prowled to the large glass doors overlooking the garden. 'I hated it here.'

'Me, too,' Lydia said. 'I still do.'

Maddie was turned away, gazing out into the garden, and Lydia took an experimental step back toward the hall. An image of Sergio Bastos's dead eyes flashed into her mind and she pushed it away.

'Why do you come here?'

'Duty.' Another step back. 'And the training room is handy.'

'I only did the jobs because they coincided with my own plans. It suited me. When it didn't suit me anymore I stopped.'

The entrance to the hall was close. Then it was a short run past the stairs and the living room. She couldn't remember if she had locked the front door. 'They're not too happy about that,' Lydia said. 'You make them nervous.'

Maddie shrugged, still looking out to the garden. 'They know what I can do.'

Lydia was calculating whether she could get out of the front door and down the street ahead of Maddie. How much of a head start she would need to get somewhere busy and safe. Or safer. Perhaps Maddie would happily shoot her in a crowd.

'I can see you in the glass,' Maddie's voice was conversational. 'It's rude to leave the party early. Especially without saying goodbye.'

Lydia stopped moving. She wondered whether Sergio had known Maddie was going to kill him before she did, or whether it was a surprise. That split second when he saw the clothes she had brought, perhaps. 'What do you want?'

'Answers.'

Maddie turned away from the window and Lydia was struck by how much older she looked. There was nothing physical, no fine lines on her skin, but there was a new knowledge in her eyes. Perhaps it was because Lydia knew what she had been doing for the last year or so, and that coloured her view, but she didn't think so. Looking into Maddie's eyes was like staring into the entrance to a long dark tunnel.

'Why are you on a hit list?' Maddie tilted her head very slightly. There was a cleaver in her right hand and Lydia had no idea when it had appeared. Or from where.

'I told you,' Lydia said, swallowing. There was no point in lying. 'I wouldn't join Mr Smith so he opted to take me out, instead. I refused to be his weapon, and he obviously decided he didn't want me to be a threat.'

'That's it?' Maddie held the cleaver up and carved strokes through the air. 'This is a well-balanced blade. Charlie splashed out.'

Lydia licked her lips. They were as dry as her mouth. 'I've been looking into a company called JRB. They seemed to be behind a number of attacks on the Families. I assumed they were trying to destabilise us, disrupt alliances and maybe start a war. I found out that

Smith is part of that company. High up. Maybe he even is the company. I'm still looking.'

'Why?'

'Why am I looking into it?'

'No. Why is this company interested in messing with the Families?'

Lydia shrugged. She told herself that this was just a normal conversation. That Maddie wasn't, at this moment, admiring her reflection in the surface of the Sabatier meat cleaver. 'I don't know. There's probably money to be made. Or it might be fear. Of what we could do as a combined force.'

Maddie snorted. 'Yeah, I don't see that happening.'

Lydia thought of the Pearls and the Foxes and the Silvers and the Crows all standing shoulder to shoulder on the field of war, a common purpose, and felt herself smile. Which was wrong, of course. She shouldn't be smiling. Was it part of Maddie's power that she had used some sort of mind control? It occurred to her that she could be like an animal walking into the slaughterhouse, being calmed with a soothing word from her handler. She squeezed her coin in her hand and tried to focus. 'Agreed. But I guess not everyone knows that. From the outside, it must feel threatening.'

'Good,' Maddie said and smiled.

For a second, Lydia saw her cousin as she had been. In that moment they could have been back at a family party, sneaking away together to eat cake and avoid the grownups.

'I know you've been looking for me,' Maddie said, and the illusion disappeared.

'I'm scared of you,' Lydia said. 'When I'm scared of something I like to know where it is.'

'I'm not an it.'

Lydia wanted to say 'prove it' but she didn't want to goad Maddie.

'You need to stop,' Maddie said.

'Okay.'

Maddie shook her head. 'I mean it. You're going to get yourself hurt.'

Lydia had a wild urge to laugh. Safety tips from the knife-wielding assassin. She still couldn't get a read on Maddie, couldn't feel Crow from her at all. It was creepy. Her mind expected it and the absence made her feel off balance. She wondered if Maddie knew. Before she could phrase the question, Maddie had turned back to the glass doors and was sliding them open. 'I'm taking this,' she raised the cleaver.

Lydia didn't know what to say to that, so she kept her mouth shut.

Maddie slipped through the gap in the doors and didn't look back.

FLEET HAD BEEN AT THE GYM AND WAS SHOWER-fresh and relaxed when he arrived at the flat. The bullet wound in his shoulder was healing well and his work seemed to be at least fifty per cent less annoying than it had been, which made Lydia happy for him. There was a very small part of her that wished he was still being driven mad by management bullshit so that he would stop being a copper entirely, but it was a very selfish part

111

and she liked to pretend it didn't exist. Besides, there were times when Fleet's badge came in handy. This, however, was not one of them.

'So, there's this thing,' Lydia began.

'Okay,' Fleet said, looking guarded. 'Why do I feel as if I should be worried?'

'You know Mr Smith said that he was trying to find an assassin?'

'The one who shot me?'

Lydia appreciated that he didn't say 'the one you killed'.

'No, not Felix. He's a local contractor. Was a local contractor.' Lydia found small glasses in the kitchen and brought them through. She poured a couple of generous measures of whisky and handed one to Fleet. 'Mr Smith was talking about someone who had been working for the service. Someone who had gone rogue. They thought she had something to do with the death of the MP in Greece. The one who paved the way for Alejandro's political rise.'

'She?'

He was quick. Lydia took a slug of her drink and willed Fleet to do the same. He didn't. Just looked at her steadily.

'How do you know it's a woman?'

'I've met her,' Lydia said in a rush. 'It's Maddie.'

For a second or two, Fleet didn't move. Then he nodded. 'Okay. Tell me.'

Lydia finished her glass of whisky and told him about Maddie summoning her to the roof of the hospital. About how strong she was. How she had an order to kill her and had been going to make it look like Lydia had taken a swan dive. How she had changed her mind.

'When was this?'

'Couple of weeks ago,' Lydia said.

The tension in Fleet's face went up a notch. His warm brown eyes had gone flat and unreadable. Lydia wasn't sure if it was concern or fury. Probably both.

'And you're telling me now,' Fleet said in an extremely careful way. 'Interesting.'

Lydia fetched the whisky and poured another shot into her glass. She held up the bottle but Fleet put his hand over his glass.

'She threatened Emma. If she got the idea that the police knew, she might have... I don't know.' Lydia wasn't going to say the words out loud.

'Is Emma all right?' He asked immediately and Lydia felt a rush of love and gratitude.

Lydia nodded. 'Paul put his brothers onto her.' She wished she could grab the words out of the air.

Fleet had definitely flipped to anger, now. 'You told Fox?'

Lydia skipped over that tricky detail to the main event. 'Tonight, I was at Charlie's, training, and she turned up.'

'Wait... What? You saw her today?' He took a step closer, raking her body with his eyes. 'Are you hurt?'

'No fighting,' Lydia said. 'She didn't even threaten to chuck me off a roof.'

Fleet did not seem ready to joke about it. His hands were bunched into fists and there was a muscle jumping

113

in his jaw. Lydia watched him take a deep breath and let it out slowly. 'What did she want?'

'I don't know. Maybe just to chat?'

'Jesus Christ, Lyds. I can't... You can't keep being so... Flippant. This is serious. You could have been hurt. You could have been killed. She could have...'

'I am aware,' Lydia said, draining her glass.

'You should have told me,' Fleet said.

'I'm telling you now.' She should be being conciliatory. Apologetic. Part of Lydia knew this, but it wasn't a large enough or loud enough part to override the idiotic rest of her brain. 'Did you want to order takeaway? Or we could raid the cafe kitchen.'

'I'm not hungry,' Fleet said. 'I'm going to head home.'

'Don't be like that. Let's talk about it.'

'So now you want to talk?' Fleet shook his head. 'Ignore me. I'm just... I need to process.'

'Okay,' Lydia said. She understood that impulse. He wanted to go and sort his head out. Then he would come back and they would talk it through properly and everything would be fine. Everything had to be fine.

An hour later, the pressure sensor outside the flat told Lydia she had a visitor. She recognised Fleet's shape through the obscured glass and got a hit of his particular signature, a bonfire on a beach, a warm salt-tinged breeze ruffling through palm leaves.

'I'm sorry,' he said as soon as she opened the door.

Lydia stepped into his arms. 'Me too.'

After a moment, Fleet pulled back slightly. 'I'm ready to talk.'

'We should make up properly first,' Lydia said. Mostly out of the need to be naked with Fleet but also, partly, to put off the talking part.

Jason was on the sofa, the laptop sitting innocently next to him, waiting for them to pass through before picking it up again.

Lydia was towing Fleet by the hand, but he stopped and stared at Jason and, for a moment, Lydia thought he could see him. He had glimpsed him once but hadn't mentioned seeing him again.

'New laptop?'

'That's my old one,' Lydia said.

He stood for a few seconds longer, frowning in Jason's direction.

Lydia watched Fleet staring and then she squeezed his hand. 'You see him, don't you? Jason.'

'Jason?' Fleet glanced at her quickly and then back at the ghost.

'Hi,' Jason said, waving in an exaggerated way.

'Did he...' Fleet swallowed, grey showing under his skin. 'Did he just wave at me?'

'Yep,' Lydia said. 'If you're going to pass out, please get on the floor. I don't want you to knock yourself out.'

'I'm not going to faint,' Fleet said, but he didn't sound sure.

At that moment Jason flickered and disappeared.

'So,' Lydia said. 'That's my flatmate. His name is Jason. He makes a mean hot chocolate. And he died in the nineteen eighties.' Murdered on his wedding day. By

Charlie. But Lydia decided not to say that bit out loud. She didn't know where Jason went when he disappeared or whether he became invisible and could still hear her. She had decided long ago that was a hornets' nest she would prefer not to kick. It was easier to live with a ghost if she decided that he couldn't become invisible and hang about without her knowledge.

'You know its name.'

'Not it. He. Jason. He's my friend.' Lydia was going to explain that Jason was also her partner and that he was extremely handy when it came to internet research requiring hacking, but she thought that might be a revelation too far. Fleet still looked a bit queasy.

He looked at her for a moment. 'I thought it was more a... I don't know, casual haunting thing. One of your... Side effects. Of being...'

'A Crow? Seeing Jason is a side effect, I guess. And I have made him stronger. He wasn't able to touch things before, and he disappeared a lot, but now he can make me coffee.'

'That's...' Fleet ran out of words and the pause stretched on.

'Weird? Handy? Amazing?'

He nodded, a trademark sunshine smile appearing. 'All of the above.'

LYDIA POURED THEM BOTH A STIFF DRINK AND waited for Fleet to take the conversational lead. She was still wary of how much he was able to process in one lump. She was a lot. She had always been a lot and her life just kept getting stranger.

Finally, Fleet drained the last of his whisky and spoke. 'So. We need to leave London.'

'She's been working as an international assassin, I don't think it would make a difference.'

'Witness protection. New identity. You know the drill.'

'I'm not leaving,' Lydia said.

'This is serious, Lyds. You've got no choice. I would come with you,' Fleet said. A beat. 'If you want me, that is.'

'I'm not leaving,' she repeated. She was not having this conversation.

'She is going to kill you,' Fleet said starkly. His expression bleak. 'I can't stop her. You can't stop her. You need to hide.'

Lydia met his gaze. 'She was there to do a job. When she discovered it was me, she chose not to do it. I don't think we should be so quick to assume she is going to top me.'

'What if Mr Smith ups her fee? Offers her something she really wants? And that's assuming she's in her right mind. She's not normal, Lyds, we have no idea what she's going to do.'

'I'm not normal, either. Does that make me an unpredictable psycho?'

He frowned. 'That's not...' He stopped. 'We're not talking about you.'

'I'm not hiding,' Lydia said. 'So we need a new plan.'

. . .

OUT ON THE TERRACE, WHISKY BOTTLE AND GLASSES on the table and the fairy lights on, it could have been a normal social occasion. The three crows which were perched on the railing watching them were a little unusual perhaps, as were the house sparrows which were sat along the roof line. A magpie flew down and stood on the table, eyeballing Lydia like it was trying to tell her something. 'I know,' Lydia said to it. 'I'm an idiot. Warning received.'

The magpie tilted its head and half-flew half-hopped over to the railing to join the crows.

'At least the birds agree with me,' Fleet said easily, pouring them generous measures.

'Hey,' Lydia complained without conviction. She was just glad he was here. No amount of crazy seemed to be too much for Fleet and the small part of her that had been waiting for the other shoe to drop, for Fleet to realise that Lydia wasn't alluringly mysterious, that she was just strange, broke free.

'Here's the thing,' Fleet said. 'I know you don't want to trade with MI6, but I don't think we have a choice. We need to find out what is going on with Mr Smith's department. We need to know if there is an official kill order out on you or whether that was off the books.'

'Are there official kill orders? I thought all of that was clandestine.'

'There are books and then there are *books*,' Fleet said. 'Someone will know something.'

'How will it help, though? To know if it's just Mr Smith or goes further?'

'So that we know who to trade with to get it

rescinded. The only way to stop Mr Smith going after you is to make you more valuable alive.'

Lydia put her glass down so quickly she was surprised it didn't smash. 'I'm not working for him. That's the whole point...'

'Not for him, but what about for MI6?'

'No,' Lydia said flatly.

'Okay, not working for, but what about working with? Helping with enquiries? Being a useful contractor from time to time? Isn't that worth your life?'

Lydia was about to say 'no'. She was nobody's weapon. Nobody's tool to be taken out of the box and used, but Fleet wasn't finished.

'Isn't that worth Emma's safety? Her life?'

Lydia glared at Fleet but it didn't make him any less right. *Hell Hawk.*

CHAPTER ELEVEN

The sun was out and the sky was blue, and Lydia felt a darkness in her heart which made her want to set fire to things.

'You've got nothing to worry about,' Fleet was saying as they approached the columned exterior of the Tate Britain. 'You don't have to agree to anything. Let's just see what we can get without promising anything. She wants to cultivate a source as much as we do.'

Lydia clenched her teeth and squeezed her coin in her fist. She didn't want to be a source. She didn't want to be anywhere near another bloody spook. When she thought of Mr Smith the rage rolled over in a hot wave of fire. She knew this was unhelpful, but she couldn't help it. It wasn't that he had proved to be untrustworthy, it was the extent and breadth of that untrustworthiness which burned. She had misread the situation, the relationship, the man, and that had shaken her more than she would ever admit.

Inside the gallery, there was the usual hushed air of

people appreciating art. The walls were pastel tones and the ornate white cornice was a foot deep. Two women stood in front of a bronze sculpture of a man grappling with a python. The figure had extremely impressive musculature and Lydia didn't blame them for their intense interest.

Fleet was walking slowly, looking at the art as if he were any other visitor. Lydia emulated him as best she could, but her mind wouldn't stop racing. She was in partial fight-or-flight mode and had been since meeting Maddie on the hospital roof. She knew it wasn't sustainable, this level of hypervigilance. She would crash and burn.

'See the brushwork, here,' Fleet said, pausing in front of another dark and dreary oil painting. He took her hand and squeezed it and she felt the message. Be calm. Unclench your jaw. At least standing still meant she could stop counting her strides. Her footsteps were audible on the parquet flooring, despite the sturdy soles of her DMs and it had become an obsession since they had walked into the large room. Lydia forced herself to look at the painting.

Her heart stuttered. The painting showed a terrified horse, brought to the ground with its head twisted back to stare, wide-eyed and panting at the lion biting its back. The lion looked faintly comical, but the horse's fear was palpable.

'George Stubbs.' A woman with salt-and-pepper hair and red-rimmed glasses had stopped next to Lydia, her gaze focused on the canvas. 'He was obsessed with the subject for over thirty years. Created at least seventeen works which depicted horses being frightened or attacked by lions.'

Fleet nodded. 'Ms Sinclair. I know you wanted to meet Lydia.'

Lydia had now met two members of the secret service to her sure and certain knowledge. Mr Smith had first appeared at her gym and later as a courier, looking completely at home in both guises. It was only once she knew his role that she saw him in a suit. Ms Sinclair, on the other hand, was wearing a complicated amount of grey-toned, layered separates and she looked like an art critic or a professor of something vaguely trendy. Scandinavian studies, perhaps. Or film.

'Very pleased to make your acquaintance,' Sinclair said, glancing at Lydia before resuming her study of the art. 'Apologies for not bringing you into the office. It's easier this way.'

'I wouldn't have come,' Lydia said, and Fleet squeezed her hand. Warning her to play nice, no doubt.

'I always wonder what started it,' Sinclair mused, her eyes roving over the painting. 'After all, lions aren't exactly common in England.'

'Maybe that's what attracted him,' Fleet said. 'The lure of the exotic.'

Sinclair looked at Fleet approvingly. 'Exactly so. People fear what they don't understand, but they adore the novel.'

'Is that what I am?' Lydia was already fed up with this covert shit. Why wouldn't spooks just get to the point? 'A novelty?'

123

'Hardly,' Sinclair said. 'Crows have been of interest since the service was first created.'

'What is it you want?' Lydia said. 'In return for the information I require.'

She looked at Lydia properly, then. 'You grossly misunderstand the nature of this meeting. I am merely considering an exchange, we are a long way from discussing terms. Didn't your uncle teach you the art of negotiation? First the introductions, then you give me something to create good faith, then you sweeten the pot and then, maybe then, I will consent to a mutually beneficial deal.'

Lydia produced her coin and flipped it into the air where it hung, motionless just in front of Sinclair's face. 'Didn't your boss teach you not to piss off a Crow?'

'Lyds,' Fleet said. 'There's no need...'

'There's every need,' Lydia said. 'I'm not in the habit of wasting time. Especially when dealing with death threats.'

'I told you,' Sinclair was addressing Fleet, now. 'I don't know anything about that.'

'Well, what is the point of this, then?' Lydia cut in. 'If you have nothing for me, I'll be heading off. I hear there's a van over the road which does insane falafel wraps. Hard to believe, I know, but I'm willing to give it a try.' She made as if to leave.

'You're making a mistake,' Sinclair said. 'DCI Fleet, you need to make her understand.'

Fleet shrugged. 'I can't make Lydia do anything. I don't believe anybody can.'

· · ·

OUTSIDE THE GALLERY, LYDIA CROSSED TO THE river and stared at the moving water until she was fairly sure she wasn't going to punch anything. She knew it wasn't smart to piss off a valuable contact, and that Fleet had no doubt put his professional reputation on the line in order to set up the meeting in which she had just acted like a furious child, but she couldn't stop the swirl of panic and mistrust. Her whole life, she had trusted herself and had felt that she had pretty decent instincts. She had made mistakes, of course, like dating Paul Fox, but she had known full well they were mistakes at the time. She just hadn't cared. When she began training as an investigator with her old boss and mentor, it had been like coming home. This job had been perfect for her with the weird hours, the working alone and the need to assess people accurately. Immediately, she had excelled and Karen had said it was like she was born for it. Now, she was second-guessing her every impression and inter-action. It was exhausting and disabling.

Fleet arrived, quietly standing next to her for a few minutes before speaking. 'Well, that could have gone better.'

'I don't trust her.'

'You don't have to. You just have to use her.'

'That's what I thought about Mr Smith,' Lydia said. 'Look where that got me. You were shot. You could have been killed.'

'Just a graze,' Fleet said, trying for levity.

'I don't know what to do. Everything I've tried with JRB and Mr Smith has made things worse.'

'That's not true.'

'Tell that to Ash,' Lydia said and then wished she could take the words back.

Fleet put his arm around her shoulder and pulled her close. 'I know. I'm sorry.'

Lydia let herself lean against him and she closed her eyes. With the sounds of her city and the river flowing past and Fleet's signature glowing around them, she felt a moment of calm. Broken by her mobile buzzing.

It wasn't a number Lydia recognised, but she answered. 'This is Miles Bunyan,' the caller said, mercifully preventing Lydia from having to admit that she didn't recognise his voice. 'You found my daughter.'

Lucy Bunyan. Taken by the Pearls and retrieved by Lydia. Much to the annoyance of the Pearl Court. Best not to think about that.

'Yes, Mr Bunyan, of course. How are you?'

'Lucy set fire to her bed last night. Luckily nobody was hurt. I keep an extinguisher in the kitchen and I managed to put it out, but I'm worried. Of course. That's not normal. And it could have been so much worse. I've told her, if she does anything like it again we'll have to call the fire brigade. The police will have to be involved. She could be convicted.'

'Slow down, Miles,' Lydia said. 'Is everybody all right? Was Lucy hurt at all?'

'No. Smoke inhalation and an overnight in the hospital but I'm allowed to pick her up this afternoon. That's why I wanted to speak to you first. What do I do to help her?'

Lydia thought of Ash, unable to function in the real world after decades in the Pearl Court. Lucy had been with them for a relatively short time and had seemed unscathed. She had talked of being at a fun party. Apparently, she wasn't as unaffected as she had appeared.

After promising that she could call round that evening, she finished the call and filled Fleet in.

'Poor kid,' Fleet said. 'There's a chance it's unrelated. I mean, she's the age for acting out.'

Lydia appreciated his attempt to ease her guilt, but she wasn't buying it. Lucy was another casualty of the magical Families of London. It wasn't enough to be the head of the Crows or to keep the peace or to look after Camberwell. London was her city and she had to do more to get her house in order.

CHAPTER TWELVE

Miles Bunyan opened the door. 'She's upstairs. Asleep.' He had purple rings under his eyes and when he turned around Lydia could see that his hair was in need of a wash and was sticking up in the back where he had missed with the comb.

'You want tea?'

'Thank you,' Lydia said. She always accepted drinks when offered. It was investigator training basics. People found it easier to talk when they were busy doing something and the normality of it helped to build intimacy, which increased the likelihood of trust and honesty and openness. At least, that was the theory.

Back in Miles' house and Lydia was reminded of her initial impressions of him. A good dad, for sure, but there was something she didn't trust. Or, more accurately, didn't like. He was talking about Lucy, describing her changeable mood, deteriorating behaviour, the way she had become more withdrawn. 'All since... Well. You know.'

Lydia did know. She accepted the mug of tea and sat with Miles at the kitchen table. 'You know that contract you told me about? With your father's old company? May I see it?'

'I burned it,' Miles said, surprised. 'You told me to.'

It was typical, of course, that the one time a client had decided to actually obey Lydia was the time she would have wished he hadn't. Ever since Miles had rung, she had been nursing a small hope that the contract would provide a clue or confirmation about the business structure of JRB. Or another contact name for her to follow up. Another crumb of information. Instead, it was another dead end. And, looking at the beaten and exhausted Miles, sipping tea while his disturbed daughter slept upstairs, another damaged family that Lydia had let down, she thought that maybe she should step down as the head of the Crows. Perhaps Maddie would do a better job.

Back in her office, Lydia planned to do some work or, at the least, think of some new ways to tackle the problem of the missing cup. She couldn't settle and her mind kept jumping from problem to problem. Outside on the terrace, she stood in the London drizzle and listened to the sounds of the city, traffic, sirens, a distant voice shouting obscenities. The urban symphony usually calmed her mind and helped her to think, but all she could see was the shape of a man hanging from a tree, strung up to look like one of the crows that was currently strutting across the paving. She went back inside and paced the room instead. Movement had always helped her think, but today not even the well-worn track around her office was working. And she felt odd. The nausea was back and her hearing felt as if she was at the bottom of a swimming pool. Then the room tilted, and she felt herself fall.

Lydia came round on the floor of her office. She saw a slice of her desk, the patchy paintwork of the ceiling and Fleet's concerned face. The back of her head hurt. She must have cracked it when she had fallen and she was extremely glad there was carpet, however thin and functional. Her thoughts came back in bits, the pieces sliding together until she was fully conscious. She realised that Fleet was speaking, he repeated her name.

'I'm okay,' she managed. 'Just fainted.'

'Can you sit up?'

'Yeah,' Lydia said and then felt the room swoop and had to lie back down. 'No.' Her body was tingling and her mind was a tunnel, the black edges threatening to send her back under. 'Lift my legs.'

Fleet did so, and she felt the blood returning to her head and the faintness and nausea retreat.

'What made you pass out?' Fleet was frowning down from what seemed like a very great height.

Lydia closed her eyes and tried to remember what she had been doing. She had been struggling to focus, pacing the room to calm her mind.

'Have you eaten today?'

And there was the problem in a nutshell. She had eaten. She had been feeling fine. It had just happened.

'Were you working?'

'I was stretching my legs.' Lydia tried not to sound defensive, but she was embarrassed. And worried. She was already at a severe disadvantage facing Maddie. If she was going to start keeling over at random moments, too, her chances of survival were diminished further.

'You need to get checked out,' Fleet said. 'Could be anaemia.'

She sat up without passing out again. Progress. 'I'm fine.'

Fleet didn't say anything else, but she could see he wasn't happy.

'I'll call tomorrow,' Lydia said, to appease him. Although they won't be able to help, she added silently.

HAVING BEEN POKED AND PRODDED BY HER GP TO no avail, Lydia was sure that her first hunch was correct. Whatever was off and causing her system to misfire was related to being a Crow. Unable to see any other option, she called home and confirmed that her dad was at his usual afternoon haunt, The Elm Tree in Beckenham, just a few streets from her childhood home.

Henry was sitting alone with an open newspaper and a half-drunk pint.

'Hello, love,' he stood when he saw her approach and they hugged. 'This is a nice surprise.'

It still felt miraculous that her dad recognised her and that she could speak to him without confusion. Whatever else had happened, she would always be grateful to Mr Smith for reversing the cognitive degeneration which had taken Henry Crow prematurely from the world.

Henry was frowning lightly. 'Did your mother send you? Did I forget you were visiting?'

'No, no. I haven't been home. I just came to see you.'

'Right.' He was clearly relieved. The ghost of his previous confusion was still a powerful spectre. 'What would you like to drink? Are you hungry? They do a decent Ploughman's here. Or the steak pie is good.'

'I'm fine.' Lydia sat opposite her dad, keen to get to the point. Just because Mr Smith had cured her dad and that he was no longer denying his Crow nature in the same way, didn't mean that she didn't act like a battery on him, still. By amplifying his Crow power, she was giving him more to siphon off. And they were working on the theory that this would keep him from getting ill again. It was by no means a certainty. For the first time, Lydia could see the point in Mr Smith's department doing actual scientific research on the Families and their abilities. It would be nice to have some hard data. Guide-lines to follow to keep them all safe and healthy.

But for now, she didn't have a choice. She needed to know more and there wasn't anybody else to ask. She didn't know if she had truly expected her ancestors to answer her questions after she had visited the cemetery, but she hadn't had so much as a vivid dream. 'I need to know more.' She glanced around to make sure that nobody was listening. She knew her father wouldn't appreciate her being indiscreet. 'About our Family. My Crow power.'

'Why?'

'So that I can control it.' *So that I don't murder*

anybody else by accident. Or pass out when I'm fighting for my life.

'I'm out, you know that,' Henry said, his voice gentle but with an undercurrent of steel.

'But you can tell me what you know, whatever Grandpa Crow told you?'

A shadow passed across Henry's face. 'I have no wish to pass on my father's lessons.'

'There's something else,' Lydia said, gripping her coin for strength. 'I've been feeling unwell.'

Henry stiffened. 'How so?'

'A bit off, I guess. Faint at times.'

'Have you told your mother?'

'No,' Lydia said. 'But I've been to the doc and been checked over. Physically, I'm fine. But we know that our power can have adverse effects.'

'That was different,' Henry said, clearly hating every second of the conversation. 'You're using yours. It's not... building up or whatever was happening with me.'

It was time. She couldn't tell her father that she had killed a man. Accident or not, he would see her differently and she couldn't stand it. Instead, she went with the other pressing reason she needed help. 'Maddie is really strong,' Lydia said.

'Maddie?' Henry frowned. 'Your cousin Maddie? Didn't she leave London? John said something-'

'The very same. Well, she can control a person's body, move them against their will.'

Henry narrowed his eyes. 'You know this how?'

'I know this,' Lydia said, putting emphasis on the words. She didn't want to worry her dad but, right now, she needed him to be Henry Crow, not her father. 'Now I need to know how to beat her.'

Henry shook his head. 'No you don't. Feathers, Lydia, you don't know what you're asking.'

'Tell me, then. Explain. Because if I can't match Maddie...' She left the sentence unfinished, unable to say the words out loud. She didn't want to make it real.

Henry took a sip of his pint, thinking.

Lydia had just decided he wasn't going to answer when he began speaking. 'Back in the day, I was next in line and doing my duty, toeing the line for your grandfather because, well, because there wasn't a lot of choice. My heart wasn't really in it, though, even before I met your mum.' Henry smiled a little sadly. 'I fell for her, Lydia, one look and I was a goner, but it's also true to say that she looked like a lifeline to me. A way out. She was this whole other...' He waved his hand, at a temporary loss. 'She represented something different. A whole way of being, of living, and I wanted it almost as much as I wanted her.'

Lydia kept quiet, not wanting to interrupt the flow of reminiscences.

'But Charlie. He was always hungry. He wanted it all. And when it came to it, it seemed like the perfect solution. We would both get what we wanted. Your grandpa wasn't too happy, of course, but I stood up to him.' Henry paused, looking uncertainly at Lydia. 'Are you sure you want to hear this?'

'I really do.'

'Right,' he looked down at the table before continuing. 'I've told you before that I wanted out, but I don't think I told you why. Not really.'

Lydia had assumed it was the whole slightly dodgy business thing. Wanting a less criminal life for his wife and daughter.

'Charlie was stepping up to me. It wasn't anything personal, but he was ambitious and I was... Well, I was in his way. He was doing anything and everything to get an edge. He would scheme, he would work all the hours, he would take any job from our father and never ask questions, but most of all, he would train. Hours and hours he spent working on his speed, his strength, his fighting skills. And he tried to work his Crow angle, too. He always wanted me to show him anything I could do, to see if he could learn it. Any bit of power from anyone, Crow or Silver or whoever, he was drawn to them. It wasn't healthy. He had a hunger for it.'

Lydia found it hard to imagine Charlie as a young man, everything laid bare for her father to see. The man she knew was closed and controlled and moved through the world like he was cutting it to pieces.

'Your grandpa encouraged it. He liked us at each other's throats. Called it healthy competition. Luckily, Charlie hated the old man as much as I did, and we didn't let him break our bond. We were close. We liked each other.'

'What happened?'

'Our father told Charlie that the only way to increase his power was to take it.' Henry paused. 'From me.'

'Is that even possible?'

Henry looked down for a moment. He seemed to be deciding whether to continue or not, but Lydia hadn't come to Beckenham to be sent away with an intriguing silence. She needed her family to start being straight with her. Feathers. She was the head of the Family. She was, she realised with a rush of embarrassment, her father's superior. 'Tell me,' she said.

Something moved behind Henry's eyes and he straightened in his chair. 'I don't know if it was true, but dear old dad told Charlie that he could take a person's power by killing them. And since I would need to be out of the way if he was to become the head of the family, anyway, it was a done deal.'

Lydia stared at her father. 'You're not serious. He can't have been serious. He can't have meant...'

'Yeah. He did.'

'That makes no sense,' Lydia said. 'Putting emotion and morality aside, why would he want to lose a member of the Family? A trusted part of the business? What had you done?' She winced with how cold that sounded, but still. The point stood. Why would Grandpa Crow deliberately reduce the ranks of main bloodline Crows?

'He thought I would kill Charlie.' Henry said flatly. 'In his mind, it was a neat solution to the problem.'

'What problem?'

'The Charlie problem. Grandpa Crow was a complete bastard, don't know if you've gathered that by now,' Henry smiled wryly, 'but he was a good leader. And he wasn't crazy. He saw something in Charlie which concerned him.'

'If you're concerned about your son, you get them

counselling. You don't set him against your other son in the hope that the favourite kills the younger one. You don't do that.' Lydia had always known her Family was half myth, but that was ridiculous. 'There had to be another reason. Or you both misunderstood his meaning.'

Henry smiled sadly. 'This was why I kept you away. This is why I'm out. There is poison in this Family.'

'No,' Lydia said. 'I don't believe that. There are people. And some of them are awful, but that doesn't make the Crows cursed. It's not poison. Or predestination. That's the easy way out.' Lydia was aware that her voice had got faster and was in danger of cracking. She would not be cursed. She was her own woman. She made her own choices.

'You have to be careful,' Henry said, tapping the back of her hand. 'Promise me. Don't kill in anger.'

Lydia noticed he didn't say 'don't kill' full stop. Not for the first time, it struck her that her life was weird. Pushing down the sudden urge to laugh, she nodded her agreement. 'Fine,' she said. 'Now will you promise to tell me how to get better control? Maddie's nearly killed me two times already. I need to prepare for the third.'

To his credit, her father didn't even blink. 'You have to practise.'

'Fine. What else?'

Her dad looked uncomfortable. 'You have to really practise. You need to practise killing.'

'How?'

'Animals. Birds.'

'No.' Lydia said flatly.

Henry shrugged. 'That's what I was told. I wasn't any good at it either, but Charlie was. And, let's be honest, Maddie is, too. If you want to win, you have to be able to play the game.'

'No,' Lydia said again. 'What else can I do?'

'I don't know.' Henry looked as miserable as Lydia felt. 'Maybe put yourself under pressure? See if you can maintain focus even while other things are going on. Or when you're in danger. It's not very easy to artificially create those kinds of situations. Not safely, anyway.'

'And if they're safe, they're not really putting me in danger.'

'Yeah,' her dad said. 'That's the issue. Sorry.'

'It's not your fault.' Lydia touched his hand.

'Be careful, won't you?'

'Of course,' Lydia said and ignored the taste of feathers on her tongue.

CHAPTER THIRTEEN

I t was almost midnight and Lydia was still wide awake. She knew she wasn't even close to sleep, so she got out of bed as quietly as possible. There was a shaft of orange light coming through a gap in the curtains and Lydia thought she would be able to get her clothes without putting on a light.

'What's wrong?' Fleet's voice drifted from the humped-up duvet.

'Nothing. Go back to sleep.'

The sound of the covers shifting and then Fleet was propped up on one elbow. 'Can't sleep?'

'No,' she said. 'I'm just going to sit up for a bit. Watch Netflix.'

'I don't think so,' Fleet said. 'You're going out.'

'Maybe,' Lydia conceded. 'If the TV doesn't work.'

'I'll come with,' Fleet was already reaching for his clothes.

'You don't have to,' she said. 'Go back to sleep.'

His eyes gleamed in the darkness. 'Can't. Got a bad feeling.'

Lydia paused, the door handle smooth under her palm. Fleet had always had a particular signature, a special something that wasn't Crow or Silver, Pearl or Fox, but was definitely not nothing. Most non-Family people were just that. Nothing. They smelled of after-shave or perfume or sweat, they might seem dodgy or give out a good, kind vibe, but that was it. With Fleet – and Mr Smith – Lydia got the same hit of impressions that she got with the Families, only she didn't have a convenient label for it. Fleet's was just Fleet. When she had met him, she would have laid money that there had been some-thing a bit magical way back in his family. Now, after so much time in close proximity to Lydia, that power had intensified and sharpened. Its edges more defined. The impressions quick and clear. And now, when Fleet said he had a 'bad feeling' it was perfectly possible that he was getting a premonition. 'You saw something.'

She saw his head nod.

'And you want me to come back to bed?'

Another nod.

'It's bad?'

'Yeah.'

'Right.' Lydia's mind flashed with images of Maddie out there in the dark. Black against black, stepping out of the shadows with a length of wire or a sharp blade. She stepped away from the door, dropping her clothes on the floor. She got back into the warmth of the bed and Fleet's arms encircled her, pulling her close.

'Thank you,' he breathed into her hair.

LYDIA WOKE UP STILL FEELING ANTSY. SHE contacted Paul for a meeting and agreed to meet him halfway between their territories. 'Potters Field will be busy,' Paul said, and suggested a park a little further from the river. It was technically closer to Camberwell, which gave Lydia the advantage, so she agreed. Less than an hour later, she arrived at the meeting. She had decided to walk in the hopes it would calm her jangling nerves. No such luck.

Paul Fox was sitting on a bench in Leathermarket Gardens, his face tilted to the sun. He spoke without moving and she wondered whether he had excellent peripheral vision or similar senses to hers. Or whether he would have greeted anybody the same way, just for the chance of appearing superhuman. 'Hello, Little Bird.'

'I just wanted an update on the surveillance,' Lydia said after sitting next to him on the bench. She hoped that keeping it all business and her language professional, it would keep the Fox from getting any other ideas.

'I love the spring,' he said, eyes still closed.

Lydia waited to see if he was going to say anything else, studying his face without the disturbance of him looking at her. He didn't, just kept his eyes shut like he was too busy enjoying the warm spring sun to bother himself with anything else. Lydia didn't have time for

143

games so she spoke again. 'On Emma. Any sign of my cousin?'

'All quiet,' Paul said, finally opening his eyes and looking at her.

Lydia appreciated that he had dropped his habitual teasing tone.

'There's been no indication of Maddie approaching your friend,' Paul added and Lydia realised she must be frowning.

'Thank you,' she said.

'No sighting of her at all, in fact. And I've got everyone on the alert.'

Lydia wondered how large a number 'everyone' included. She had been around town, alerting the sources she had been cultivating, like the lads running the food booths along the embankment by Westminster Pier, but it felt like a drop in the ocean. Especially when looking for a professional ghost. 'It's scary,' Lydia said. 'She could walk past our people. Hell Hawk, she could probably walk past us, and we wouldn't have a clue.'

Paul looked surprised. 'Wouldn't you do your,' he waggled his fingers. 'You know, sensing thing?'

Lydia hesitated. Then she realised that he was helping her and looking out for Emma and that, after everything that had happened with Maddie and the Pearl King and the Silvers, the Foxes were probably the closest she was going to get to a real alliance. 'About that... There's nothing from her. I don't know how she's done it or what has happened, but she doesn't feel like a Crow anymore. It's disturbing.'

Paul was quiet for a moment. 'I've never heard of

anything like that. I mean, people will say "they're not acting like a Fox" or they're not a "real" one if they want to insult someone, put them in their place, but it's not literal.'

'I know.' She leaned back and closed her eyes. It felt like she was dealing with too many questions. Too much was at stake and she didn't know what she was doing about any of it.

'Is it possible that it's you?'

Her eyes snapped open. 'What do you mean?'

'Could your power be on the fritz? You look a bit knackered, could be that. Or was it the adrenaline?' He held up his hands. 'No shade intended. She's scary.'

'It's not me,' Lydia said. 'I'm firing on all cylinders. You, for example, are giving off an unbearable amount of Fox.'

'Unbearable, is it?' Paul said in a low voice.

Lydia felt her whole traitorous body respond. 'Stop it.'

He grinned. White teeth flashing. She could see red fur, feel a warm body moving against her in the dark, smell good earth and fresh rain.

'I'm serious,' Lydia said, producing her coin and squeezing it in her fist.

He raised his hands in mock surrender. 'Okay, okay.'

Lydia took a few deep breaths. She could feel the Crow power rising through her, the urge to spread her wings and take flight, the thousand tiny hearts beating an urgent tattoo. A warning call. A swell of support. Both. She could feel the urge to tear into flesh with her sharp beak. The world was tilting, and she caught herself before she fell.

Her head was between her knees and she was aware of a firm hand on the back of her neck. Paul's thumb was rubbing small circles on the skin at the top of her spine and that wasn't helping to clear her head. Or perhaps it was. She was definitely anchored into the seat and the ground and the reality of the closeness of the Fox. She was no longer soaring high on a warm thermal or pecking at a carcass.

When she straightened up, the first words which came out of her mouth were 'I need a drink.'

Paul removed a flask from his inside jacket pocket and passed it over. The fine smoky whisky moved over the tongue and throat and, seconds later, she felt a welcome calm. This was the problem, she realised, she had cut down on alcohol and it had put her out of balance. Maybe the whisky had been keeping the Crow power damped down to a manageable level. Of course, the problem with going back to that coping method, was that she wouldn't be getting stronger. She needed the strength, needed the full power in case she had to face Maddie, but she also needed to be able to control it. And to not faint.

Of course, Lydia thought, in a moment of optimism, there was every chance that Maddie had headed off of her own accord. Paul hadn't seen her in Beckenham and neither Uncle John nor Aiden had sounded the alarm. Maybe she was on the other side of the world, back in the MI6 fold and merrily killing for the government.

CHAPTER FOURTEEN

B ack at The Fork, Lydia was thinking about raiding Angel's fridge before heading upstairs and was preoccupied by thoughts of food. It took her a couple of seconds longer than it should have done for her to notice that the closed cafe wasn't empty.

There was something in the air. Vibrations, perhaps. Or her Crow senses setting off the alarm. She felt her shoulders raise and her coin was in her hand as she scanned the dim room. It wasn't dark outside but the overhead lights were off. A green light blinked on the coffee machine.

'Angel?'

A figure rose from behind the counter.

'Ta-da!' Maddie was wearing a wavy blonde wig today and her lips were the colour of fresh blood. 'Pleased to see me?'

'Not exactly,' Lydia said.

'Now, now. That's no way to greet your own flesh and blood.'

'I thought you didn't want me to look for you.'

Maddie pulled an expression of faux sympathy. 'Oh, Lyds, I'm sorry. I didn't mean to hurt your feelings. Just because I don't want you tracking my every move, sticking your beak into my business, doesn't mean I don't want us to be friends.'

Lydia scanned the room for her nearest escape route, while trying to pretend she was doing nothing of the sort. Her heart was hammering, and she felt the itch in her arms. She wanted to spread them wide, take off for the clear blue sky. Get far, far away from the woman leaning against the counter. 'You want to be friends?'

'I told you, I didn't know it was you on the roof. And I blew off the job. That's got to show affection.'

'I'm very grateful,' Lydia said, trying not to sound like a sarcastic witch.

Maddie's mouth twisted, so she wasn't sure she had succeeded. 'And that's not my first peace offering. I've been on your side for months.'

'You have?'

Maddie blew out a sigh. 'Who do you think took care of that Kendal problem? And what thanks have I received?'

'Kendal?' The name fell into place. Mark Kendal. 'The guy who ran the phone shop on Southampton Way?' It took Lydia another beat to realise what Maddie meant. 'You killed him?'

Maddie smiled. 'Of course.'

'Why?' She was mystified. Kendal wasn't exactly the preserve of high-level assassins and he had nothing to do with Mr Smith, as far as Lydia knew.

'To get your attention, silly.'

'But you didn't sign your work. How was that getting my attention?' As she spoke, Lydia remembered the ten-shilling note she had found in Kendal's wallet. She had assumed it had been Mr Smith, but perhaps it had been Maddie's idea of a calling card.

'I know you like a puzzle,' Maddie said. 'Besides, I have my standards. Ghosts never leave a trace.'

Lydia had the sudden, inappropriate urge to laugh. She could picture a line of cereal bowls and mugs of tea on her kitchen counter, Jason making yet another hot chocolate. She made herself nod thoughtfully instead.

Maddie had moved from behind the counter and Lydia didn't like it one little bit. She tried to think of a way to distract her. If she could just get outside or upstairs and behind the locked door of her flat. Somewhere she could phone for help.

'You said you were helping me. I don't understand...'

'Hell Hawk, Lyds. Where is your head?' Maddie twisted a strand of blonde hair with a finger, her head tilted as she contemplated Lydia. 'Kendall was moving product on a massive scale. Quite impressive ambition, really. But it looked bad for you. Made you look weak. People were whispering that you had no idea, that you were asleep at the wheel. Seems they were right.'

'He came to me for help,' Lydia said, hating the confusion evident in her voice. 'Wanted me to stop the hairdresser over the road from selling phone cases.'

'No,' Maddie shook her head. 'He wanted you to pay them a little visit. And if you didn't take lethal action, he could arrange a cleansing fire and solve his problem with you in the frame as the arsonist. Everyone would know that the big bad Crow had paid them a warning visit.'

'Why did he want them dead? If he was moving drugs, why would he care about phone cases?'

'Oh, Lyds,' Maddie said. 'You really are lost in the clouds, aren't you? Keep up, babes.'

Lydia was distracted from her fear by embarrassed fury. She had believed the little twerp. He had played her. Or tried to play her. She would kill him. Lydia remembered a second later that he was already dead.

'The woman who runs the salon. She offers extras in the back room, cash payments only, but that's beside the point. She didn't like Kendall or the police attention he was risking with his activities. Perhaps if Charlie was still in charge, she would have been worried about Crow attention, too.'

Lydia ignored the barb. 'And?'

With exaggerated patience, Maddie explained. 'She made the mistake of confronting our man Kendal, asking him to keep things quiet. He decided to make sure she was going to keep quiet, instead. You know how important the flow of information is, how you've got to mark out your territory and make sure that everybody in it knows that you're in charge?' Maddie let the insult dangle before continuing. 'Well that applies all the way along the chain. Even the rats in the gutter have an order to maintain. But I wasn't going to have Kendal disrespect you like that. It really didn't look good. So I dealt with it.'

Lydia tried to come up with a response but her mind was unhelpfully blank.

'You're welcome,' Maddie said, a note of irritation creeping in. 'No charge. This time.'

By this point, Lydia had recovered enough to reply: 'There's always a charge.'

Maddie nodded approvingly. 'Quite right.'

'I'll pay it,' Lydia said, 'of course. But no more unsolicited help. I'm handling things.'

'Is that what you truly believe?' Maddie asked, looking genuinely interested.

'Why? Do you want the job?'

Maddie's laugh made all the hairs on the back of Lydia's neck stand up. 'I hadn't thought of that.'

Well, that had the ring of a lie.

'But it's not my style. I'm more a moves-in-the-shadows type. I could be the power behind the throne, though. Your trusted advisor. Right-hand woman.'

It was the old offer and Lydia had been half-expecting it since discovering that Maddie was back in town. 'Isn't it time to get a new tune?'

Lydia didn't see her intention or her movement but there was Maddie toe to toe, holding an extremely sharp knife to her throat. She felt the sting as it nicked her skin. 'Don't be rude, Lyds,' Maddie said and her eyes were dead.

Lydia didn't answer, just returned Maddie's gaze as best she could.

After a moment, a spark returned to Maddie's eyes and they widened ever so slightly. She moved away, the knife stowed as quickly as it had appeared. 'I'll leave you to think on it.' She made a show of checking the time on her phone. 'Oh my days, is it two already? Got to motor, babes. hope you don't mind. You know how it is? Places to be, throats to slit.'

Lydia stiffened as Maddie swooped forward, but she just kissed Lydia on each cheek. 'Ciao, bella.'

AFTER MADDIE HAD SAUNTERED OUT THROUGH THE front door, Lydia's first urge was to be sick. Instead, she locked the door and pulled the deadbolt. Upstairs in the flat, she found Jason pouring the last of the cereal into a bowl. More accurately, he was pouring the last of the cereal onto the counter next to the bowl and Lydia guessed he was deep in thought. She hated to be the bearer of bad news, but if Maddie was going to start showing up at The Fork, she had to tell Jason. He was almost certainly safe from her, but she could still give him a fright.

Jason didn't go pale in the way that a living person did, but his outline shimmered and he became more translucent. Sometimes he disappeared altogether. Right now, Lydia would say he was about seventy per cent solid. 'What does she want?'

Before her cousin had found her professional calling, Maddie had tried to throttle her and had then offered a partnership. To say she was dangerously unpredictable would be quite the understatement. Now she was a loose cannon and seemed to want to taunt Lydia. Or help her. It was very hard to tell. 'Your guess is as good as mine,' Lydia said.

'She might be playing with you. Like a cat with a

mouse,' Jason said, pushing at the folded cuffs of his baggy eighties suit jacket. 'Sorry.'

'I think that's likely.' It wasn't as if it hadn't crossed her own mind. She smiled robustly, still trying to reassure Jason. 'Lucky I've got you.' The first time Maddie had attempted to kill Lydia, Jason had saved her life.

'I'm not with you all the time,' Jason said.

Lydia pressed down a flare of annoyance. He was just being concerned, and she knew her anger wasn't with Jason. It was with Maddie for making her frightened. 'I'm a lot stronger, now. And it won't exactly be unexpected. I'll be ready.'

'I'm not sure that's true,' Jason said. 'She's nuts.'

'We don't say that anymore,' Lydia said, trying to lighten the mood and ease Jason's anxiety. 'It's mental health issues.'

'She's a fucking psycho. Is that better?'

'Maybe,' Lydia smiled at him. 'It's a specific diagnosis, at least.' And accurate.

'I'm being serious,' Jason said, still looking dangerously transparent.

'I know,' Lydia said and touched his arm.

AFTER CALMING JASON DOWN, LYDIA CALLED FLEET and asked him to meet her at Charlie's for some training. She couldn't face updating him on the phone and she needed to expel some of the terror-induced energy with some exercise.

At the training room in Charlie's house, Lydia kicked the join between the crash mats she had bought and lugged up to the room so that they lay together neatly. Then she went through her stretches and some strength training, ignoring the distracting sight of Fleet doing the same. Feathers, the man looked good.

When she was ready, she got into the middle of the mat. 'I want you to come at me.'

Fleet hadn't been fully on board with Lydia's new training plan when she had first described it and the intervening days didn't seem to have improved matters. He made a half-hearted feint and went to grab her, circling his arms around her waist in an easy-to-duck manoeuvre.

'Not like that,' Lydia said. 'Come. At. Me.' Practising spinning coins was all very well when she was on her own in the studio, but she wanted to see if she could maintain focus while under stress.

'I don't want to hurt you,' Fleet said. He held up his hands. 'I know you're perfectly capable of defending yourself, but-'

'Then you've nothing to worry about.'

Fleet rolled his shoulders. 'Fine.' His attack came quickly and without warning. Lydia was on her back on the mat, her whole spine vibrating with the impact. When she could draw air into her lungs again and her mind was unscrambled enough to form words, she said 'good' and got herself upright. 'Again.'

AFTER AN HOUR OF BEING FLUNG TO THE MAT BY Fleet, Lydia was sweaty and exhausted. She followed

Fleet down to Charlie's kitchen to make a post-workout coffee using Charlie's excellent machine.

She tried not think about Maddie standing in the same room and how much she didn't want to tell Fleet that she had visited her again. Once they were leaning against the cabinets, sipping coffee, Fleet ran through the rest of his week. He checked on which nights they were going to stay at his flat and which ones they would be at The Fork. After a while she realised that he was no longer speaking. 'Sorry? I zoned out there for a moment. I need another coffee.'

'That is never true of you,' Fleet said. 'You are ninety-eight per cent caffeine at this point.'

'That takes work,' Lydia said, switching on the machine.

'I was saying that I have some work to catch up on and I need a shower, but I could come over later. Are you around for dinner?'

'Maybe. Can I let you know?'

'Sure.'

She could see that Fleet wanted to say something else. 'What is it?'

'What was that about? Just now.'

'I have to get stronger,' Lydia said. 'I told you.'

'You're already strong.'

'More focused, then. I can't lose control. People will get hurt.'

Fleet watched her for another moment. 'It wasn't your fault. It was self-defence.'

There was a sudden lump in her throat and she swallowed hard. This was the moment when she should tell Fleet about Maddie's continuing interest. She knew that, but she couldn't. He would want to fix it. He would urge her to tell the police. However much he had embraced her weird life and her magical Family, he still believed in the system.

'It wasn't your fault,' Fleet said again and wrapped his arms around her. She could smell the clean sweat from the workout and the indefinable odour that was 'Fleet'. With her head on his chest, she could hear waves rolling on a distant shore and feel fine white sand between her bare toes.

CHAPTER FIFTEEN

When Lydia woke up, Fleet's arm was heavy across her body, as if he had been anchoring her in place even while unconscious. She turned over to wrap herself around him.

'What's on the agenda today?' Fleet asked a little while later, stretching his arms above his head in a distracting manner. Lydia was out of bed and pulling on her clothes but she paused to reconsider. She could be ten minutes late.

'Meeting mum for lunch,' she said, dropping her jeans and climbing back into bed.

Fleet kissed her before asking about the time. 'You have to get up, then,' he said, sitting up. 'Come on. I'm not going to make you late for Susan Crow.'

'You could come with,' Lydia said impulsively. 'If you want.'

Fleet's smile was like sunshine. 'Thank you.'

. . .

157

THE RESTAURANT WAS AN AUTHENTIC AND, considering its central location, refreshingly unpretentious Italian. Susan Crow had always been excellent at finding good places to eat and Lydia made a mental note to suggest that she and Fleet come back as soon as possible.

She ploughed through a plate of fried courgette flowers and a perfect tomato, basil and mozzarella salad, while Fleet held the conversational fort. She had never realised how charming Fleet could be. It wasn't like they had lots of mutual friends or spent lots of time in purely social situations. She was used to seeing him in copper mode, which she found alarmingly attractive, or in his private mode, which was just for her, but this was entirely different. He made her mum laugh, encouraged her to have a second glass of Sauvignon Blanc, and discussed, with all evidence of genuine interest, the merits of planting geraniums next to green beans as a natural pest deterrent.

When he had gone to the bathroom and, Lydia had a hunch, to settle the bill before anybody could argue with him, she fully expected her mum to compliment Lydia on her excellent choice of man.

Instead, Susan Crow leaned forward and took hold of Lydia's hand. 'Please don't ask your father about that stuff again.'

The warm glow snuffed out. She didn't need to clarify what 'stuff' her mum was talking about. 'Who else am I supposed to ask?'

'I know it's not fair. I'm sorry.'

'It's not fairness I'm concerned about,' Lydia said,

hating that she sounded petulant. She wanted to explain to her mum that she had to find out more about her Crow power and the legacy of being the head of the Family, that she was likely to be fighting for her life, quite literally, and that she needed to be ready. What was a bit of upset compared to that?

'He can't do it,' her mother said. 'He just can't. Please trust me. It will kill him.'

Lydia let the words sink in. Susan Crow wasn't given to hyperbole. And she loved Lydia. That was one thing Lydia had never questioned, not even for a single second, not even when she was at her teenage worst. If the woman opposite her was saying she couldn't do something, then she couldn't do it. If she said it would kill her father, then it probably would. Still. Lydia couldn't help the way her stomach plunged to the floor. She had wanted some firm ground to stand on. She had hoped Henry would be able to reach out a hand and lead her where she needed to go.

Her mother looked like she wanted to say something else, but Fleet arrived back at the table, and Lydia watched her expression alter. She favoured Fleet with a warm smile. 'That was delicious. We should do this more often.'

On the way home, Lydia was quiet and, after a while, Fleet ran out of conversational openers. Once they were parked, he said. 'I thought that went well.'

She put a hand on his leg. 'It went extremely well. I think she likes you more than she likes me.' The words came out more seriously than she intended and she felt stupid tears in her traitorous eyes and had to swipe at them unobtrusively. Unfortunately for her, Fleet was a sharp copper and he didn't miss a trick. Instantly, his arms were around her. 'What's wrong?'

Lydia started with the fact that her mother had warned her off asking her father for help with her power and ended with Maddie's most recent visit. He didn't take it well. 'We need to meet with Sinclair. And you need to make a deal. I'm serious, Lyds. You are in real danger.'

'No deal,' Lydia said. She couldn't explain it to Fleet, but the business with Mr Smith had made her feel like she was losing pieces of her soul. She would not do it again.

'She's showing signs of obsession. With you. This is really bad and you can't handle it alone.'

'I'm not alone,' Lydia said. 'I've got you.'

'You do, but I'm not with you all the time.'

It was an echo of Jason's concern. And it just made her feel worse. Like something fragile to be protected. She was the head of the Crow Family, not a damsel in distress. 'I'll figure it out. We don't need Sinclair. I promise.'

'It's escalating, her behaviour, I don't know why you can't see that.'

'Please, can you just drop it? Let's go upstairs. Work off lunch.'

Fleet looked through the windscreen, his hands tensing on the steering wheel. He was clearly struggling to hold his temper and Lydia wanted to tell him not to bother, to just let it out. To stop being so bloody careful around her. 'I've got a load of paperwork to catch up on,' he said eventually. 'I should go home.'

'I'll come with you,' Lydia said. 'I don't want to fight.'

'We're not fighting,' Fleet said tightly. 'I'm just worried.'

'I know. I'm sorry.'

He blew out a sigh. 'Don't be sorry.'

Fleet insisted on escorting Lydia to the flat, as if he thought Maddie might be waiting to jump out at her. Once he had checked the place through, examined her door and window locks and generally acted like she was a victim, which made her want to kick him in his soft parts, he accepted a coffee.

Before leaving, Fleet made a call, pacing the roof terrace while he spoke. 'I've posted a couple of officers to keep an eye tonight. Don't give them a hard time.'

'I won't. Thank you.' Lydia refrained from pointing out that if Maddie wanted to kill Lydia, then a couple of coppers sitting in an unmarked car along the street weren't going to stop her. She could see that Fleet needed the illusion of control. And, in the privacy of her own mind, she could admit that it was comforting to have them there.

WITHOUT FLEET'S CALMING PRESENCE AND THE knowledge that Maddie was most definitely in London and seemed keen to progress some kind of relationship with Lydia, sleep did not come easily.

When she had finally dropped off, it seemed like no

time at all had passed before her phone woke her. The ringing was muffled by the duvet on Fleet's side of the bed and she realised that she had fallen asleep with it under her pillow, just in case he had rung.

'No news,' Lydia said, expecting Maria's assistant.

'That's disappointing,' Maria's voice was cold. 'It is difficult not to take your lack of progress as a sign of your disinterest.'

'That's not...'

'And disinterest in my case is disrespectful. Disrespectful to me. And to the Silver Family as a whole.'

'I'm not disinterested,' Lydia said, gritting her teeth. A thought which had been lapping at the edges of Lydia's mind for some time burst into technicolour. Of all the people who would be likely to know about the whereabouts of the silver cup, Maria would have been top of her list. Surely Alejandro would have left it for his daughter? Or at the very least told her about the replica. Perhaps she was sending Lydia on a wild goose chase? An impossible mission that she was destined to fail, either keeping her busy and distracted from something that Maria was planning and didn't want attention drawn to, or forcing her to let Maria down and provide an excuse to break their shaky alliance.

'Let me prove it,' Lydia said. 'I'll come in and see you today. You are right, I do have something to share.'

Maria sounded thrown, which added to Lydia's paranoia that Maria was playing her. She recovered to say, 'I can fit you in at eleven. For ten minutes, anyway.'

· · ·

162

It was a relief to have a clear mission and, after dressing in her usual uniform of jeans, black T-shirt and leather jacket, Lydia forced herself to eat some toast before spending time on her roof terrace. She tilted her face to the sky and tried to calm her thoughts. She didn't have high hopes for a zen state of mind, but she was willing to try anything to get better control of her power. Even meditation.

The Silver offices on Chancery Lane were bustling with suited people with shiny hair and serious brief-cases. It was a very nice building, but it was filled with the sound of telephones, eye-scorching lighting and an undeniable atmosphere of stress. It gladdened Lydia's heart and reminded her that, in some ways at least, she was living life right.

Maria's assistant greeted her politely and offered a choice of beverages. 'I'm fine, thanks,' Lydia said. 'I'll go right in.'

Not waiting for an answer, Lydia strolled into Maria's office. The bright taste of Silver intensifying as soon as she stepped into the room.

Maria was standing in front of the floor-to-ceiling windows with her back to Lydia, speaking on the phone.

Lydia sat in an uncomfortable chair facing Maria's giant desk and waited while Maria took her time in wrapping up her conversation. The room looked the same as the last time she had seen it, when Alejandro had been in situ, down to the treadmill and the modern wood panelling.

Maria looked as groomed and terrifying as always. She was dressed entirely in black, in the kind of tailoring that brooked no argument from the mortal flesh beneath. Her waist was drawn in so tightly that she resembled a wasp and the red soles of her high heels flashed as she crossed the room and sat in the large leather chair opposite Lydia. 'Sorry about that,' she said with absolutely zero sincerity. 'I believe you have news for me?'

'What can you tell me about the cup?'

Maria's brow didn't crease but her eyes flashed with displeasure. 'Is this a joke?'

'No joke,' Lydia said. 'The more I know about it, the better. Maybe a detail will help me find it.'

'I don't see how. This is clearly a waste of time. I had hoped that you had grown out of this sort of game-playing, but clearly not.' Maria stood, motioning for Lydia to leave.

She stayed put and flipped open her notebook. 'You commissioned me to do a job. This is how I work. What did Alejandro tell you about it?'

Maria sighed and sat back down. 'Not much. It's the Family cup. It's solid silver and very old.'

'Made in the early sixteen hundreds as part of the agreement for the use of Temple Church.'

Maria's eyes narrowed. 'You've done your homework.'

'It's my job,' Lydia said evenly. 'And I like to be thorough. You sent Yas Bishop to purchase a silver statue to use as a bribe for Robert Sharp.'

Maria didn't flinch. 'Did I?'

Lydia didn't bother to elaborate. Both Robert Sharp and Yas Bishop had suffered a personality change and Lydia had suspected that the statue had been enchanted in some way that caused psychosis. 'The shop you sent Yas to was in the silver vaults on Chancery Lane. I wish to speak to the proprietor of the shop, Guillame Chartes.'

'Well go and see him,' Maria waved a hand. 'Sounds like part of your job.'

'The shop is no longer there.' It had disappeared without a trace, the people either side of the unit claiming to have never heard of the man or the shop.

'If it was easy to find the thing, I wouldn't have bothered commissioning you,' Maria said. 'What do you want from me?'

'I think you know how to contact him,' Lydia said. 'And the fact that you are avoiding telling me is curious.'

Maria's eyes slid left.

'Okay. Let's leave that. Now that we're in alliance, all cosy like, I need some information on one of your clients.'

'That's not possible,' Maria said smoothly. 'Client confidentiality, blah, blah.'

'JRB.'

Maria's expression didn't so much as flicker. 'What about JRB?'

'They are your clients. I am now pretty sure that Mr Smith, a government spook who arranged to have Fleet shot among many other transgressions, is JRB. That JRB is a shell corporation held by said spook and other spook or spooks as yet unknown.' Lydia did not like being honest with Maria. It went against all her instincts, but she hoped that being transparent would encourage the same in return.

Maria didn't seem impressed. Her lips remained a tight little line.

'I need every detail you have on them. Who was your contact? Apart from Yas Bishop.'

'No one,' Maria said. 'Yas Bishop was our sole contact.'

Which was convenient, since Maria had killed her in cold blood to cover tracks. Maria probably had her filed under 'cost of doing business' in some neat ledger tucked in the back of her mind.

Lydia balled her fists and then released them. She wasn't going to waste anger on Maria Silver. And she couldn't afford to lose control. She forced a political smile. 'Well, I appreciate your time. If you remember anything else which might be useful, you'll let me know?'

'Certainly,' Maria said. 'I thought you would be coming with news for me.'

'Not yet,' Lydia said, standing up. 'But I'm working on it.'

Leaving the office, Lydia turned and raised a hand in goodbye. Maria was sitting behind her gigantic shiny desk looking like exactly what she was, a deadly insect, but Lydia hadn't been waving to her. Just to her left, shimmering and translucent in the sunlight pouring through the copious glass, Jason raised his hand in return.

CHAPTER SIXTEEN

Getting back into the offices to collect Jason was always going to be the tricky part of the equation. Lydia had thought about leaving her jacket or a hat or something that she could collect, but she was concerned that it would put Maria on her guard. The woman wasn't a fool and Lydia wasn't in the habit of getting comfy in her office.

Then it occurred to her that all she needed to do was lie.

She called Maria at six that evening expecting her to still be in the office. She was not disappointed. 'Twice in one day, what a treat,' she said. 'This had better be good.'

'It is,' Lydia said. 'But I'd rather discuss it in person.'

'If you insist.'

MARIA WAS WORKING AT HER DESK. THERE WERE piles of documents and, although still immaculately made up and with lipstick that looked as fresh as it had in the morning, there was tiredness around Maria's eyes. Lawyers might have been backed by the devil, but they weren't enjoying a free ride.

'Have you heard from Alejandro?'

Maria held her gaze. 'What kind of question is that?'

'Just interested. And I'm showing sympathy. Asking after your old dad.'

'You are being obnoxious. Deliberately so. Why?'

Lydia shrugged. 'Old habits.'

'You said you had something important to share.'

Maria's irritation was palpable and Lydia calculated she had exactly zero seconds before she called some of her private security and ejected Lydia from the building. Painfully. 'There were three replicas made. You've got one in the crypt so that leaves another two floating around.'

Maria placed the top back onto the fountain pen she had been using and placed it neatly beside the pile of documents. 'I see.'

Lydia had glanced around the office casually when she had arrived and hadn't spotted Jason. Since then she hadn't been able to look away from Maria without it being obvious. She felt a coolness on the back of her neck and hoped, fervently, that it was Jason appearing behind her.

'It's not in your interests to tell me this. If I didn't know there were further replicas, you might be able to give me one and keep the real cup for yourself.'

'I've agreed to find the cup for you,' Lydia said, not clarifying that she never agreed to give the cup to Maria.

'If this alliance is going to work, we need to trust each other's word.'

'That's true,' Maria nodded. 'I don't, I must be honest, but perhaps in time.'

'It's a starting place.' Her neck was freezing, now, and the urge to look around was almost unbearable. 'I'll let you get on. Looks like you've got a lot of work. No rest for the wicked.'

Maria made a little shooing motion with her hand, dismissing Lydia in a practised manner.

Lydia stood and, as she turned, caught a glimpse of Jason, flimsy and almost entirely see-through in the bright office lighting. A second later and he was flowing into her body, lodging a block of ice in her stomach and seizing her lungs for a terrifying few moments. She couldn't speak to say 'goodbye' so left Maria's office in silence.

Back at The Fork, Lydia sat with Jason while he recovered his equilibrium. She was tense with antici-pation, but didn't want to rush him. There was no earthly reason for Jason to help her out, after all. Most ghosts would be enjoying a gentle retirement, maybe with a little light poltergeist action just for fun, not hacking into national databases and running around London playing spy.

'Okay,' he said, once his outline had stopped shaking and his body had solidified again with Lydia's touch.

He still didn't look quite right and Lydia could see that the excursion had cost him. 'Take your time.'

He rolled his shoulders, the movement jerky like he had forgotten how to move naturally. 'After you left, she made a call.'

Lydia waited, letting Jason marshal his thoughts. 'She thinks you have it.'

'The cup?'

'Yeah. There was a break-in at her father's house, just after he "died".' Jason made bunny ears on the last word. 'At the time she didn't think anything had gone missing, but when you told her the cup in the crypt was a fake, she realised that the real cup might have been the target of the robbery.'

'Why didn't she tell me this?' Lydia wondered if she had been right and that Maria was setting her a deliberately difficult task, withholding information so that she would fail.

'Because she thinks you took it. Or a Crow, at any rate. That's what she said to the person on the phone. She commissioned you to find it because she thinks you have it and it's an opportunity for you to return it without losing face.' He shrugged. 'Although she didn't put it quite like that.'

'Who was it? On the phone?'

'I don't know,' Jason said. 'She didn't say their name. And she stayed in the room after, working for ages. By the time she went to a meeting, I was too weak to press the buttons on the phone and I couldn't access the dialling record. Sorry.'

'No, no. Don't be. You did a brilliant job. This really helps.' Somebody had broken into Alejandro's home and, most likely, taken the cup. If it hadn't been the target, other items would have been taken. So whoever was responsible knew about the cup. 'Who knew about the cup? Mr Smith, I guess. Although I would have thought he would have pressured Alejandro to hand over the cup as part of his immunity deal and wouldn't have needed to nick it.'

'What if it was just a random burglary? A thief could have just seen an expensive looking antique and taken it?'

'I bet Alejandro had a lot of other expensive stuff lying around. Seems unlikely that it would be the only thing taken. I'm guessing the Silvers didn't file a police report? They wouldn't want any evidence of weakness getting out.'

Jason nodded. 'True. So, apart from us, the Silvers, and Smith, who else knows about the cup?'

'The person who made the replicas. We need to find Guillame Chartes.'

'There's another possibility,' Jason said.

'What's that?'

'The other Families. I mean, you all put items into the museum for the truce, right? That means the Pearls and the Foxes also know about the cup.'

LYDIA DIDN'T SEE THE PEARLS SNEAKING INTO Alejandro's house in order to steal a silver cup. Apart from anything else, they were trapped in their underground realm. It was a strange liminal space which didn't obey the normal rules of time and one they didn't seem able to leave. They had descendants all around

171

London, of course, people with varying amounts of Pearl blood and residual magic, but they hadn't shown any indication of having formed a meaningful hierarchy or purpose. The Pearl Court underground were the power-house, and they used children as their emissaries above ground, running errands, luring new playthings like Lucy Bunyan for the pleasure of the king, and, occasionally, following Lydia.

It was early evening and Lydia hadn't contacted Fleet during the day. She figured he needed a bit of time to process the latest news about Maddie. And to calm down from his annoyance that she hadn't told him about it straight away. She would go round, now, and update him immediately on her progress with the cup. She could even tell him about using Jason as a listening device.

Fleet buzzed her into the flat and then went back to what he was doing. Which was folding a shirt and putting it into a suitcase.

'You're leaving?' Lydia's body went cold. This was it. The other shoe. Dropping like a stone.

'Only for a little while.'

'How long?' Lydia had wanted him to stop treating her like a fragile thing that needed constant monitoring, but she hadn't meant for him to leave her altogether.

'Not sure,' Fleet was concentrating on packing the case, didn't look at her. 'A couple of days. Might be longer, but I hope not.'

Lydia pressed her lips together to stop herself from saying 'stay'. Or 'why now?'.

Fleet finally turned to look at her. 'It's important. I wouldn't go if it wasn't.'

'Is it work?'

'Sort of. It might help, but I don't want to get your hopes up.'

'I'd rather know,' Lydia said. 'Aren't you always telling me that communication is key?'

He smiled gently. 'That's definitely something we need to work on. But right now it's better if I don't tell you.'

'That makes no sense,' Lydia said.

'You know you can trust me. Remember that.'

At the door the panic was sudden and overwhelming. They were hugging, and she pulled away to look at his face. Afraid of what she might find there, but needing the truth. 'Is this because I didn't tell you about Maddie?' She wanted to ask if it was because she had told Paul Fox first, but couldn't make herself say the words. It would be like conjuring a curse.

'No,' Fleet said, but his eyes flicked away.

'Go then,' Lydia said, stepping back. If he didn't go, now, she was going to start crying, and that wasn't going to improve matters.

He looked anguished. 'You must understand-'

'I don't,' Lydia said. All she could feel was the abandonment. This was why you shouldn't trust other people, *rely* on them. They only let you down in the end. What had Jason said about 'everybody leaving?'. Turned out, some left earlier than others.

'This isn't about us,' Fleet tried again. 'I swear I'm not running out on you.'

173

'But you are leaving.' She refused to make it a question. She couldn't stand the hope.

'Yes. But it's just temporary.'

Lydia wanted to believe him. She reminded herself of all the ways in which Fleet had proved himself to her, proved to be a reliable, loving partner. He had always been on her side. She knew that. She forced a weak smile. 'Okay. Stay safe.'

He kissed her, again, and left.

Lydia closed the door and felt unshed tears hot behind her eyes. Fleet had always had her back. The man had taken a bullet for her. So why was he leaving now?

CHAPTER SEVENTEEN

Lydia went for a walk and called Paul Fox on the
way. The sky was a uniform grey and a one-eyed
pigeon followed her as if hoping for crumbs. She wanted
to tell it not to bother. That it ought to look after itself
because those it trusted would fly off on a secret mission
leaving it to peck for crumbs alone but she was aware she
might have been projecting. Just a bit.

Paul answered. 'Hello, Little Bird. Always a
pleasure.'

'Someone broke into Alejandro's house and stole the
Silver Cup. I think it was a Fox.'

Paul was quiet for a few beats. 'Just when I think
we're making progress, you make a baseless accusation
like that...'

'I'm not accusing you of anything,' Lydia side-
stepped an abandoned Styrofoam kebab container. 'I'm
trying to help.'

'You've lost me,' Paul said, his voice dangerously
even.

'I'm worried about whoever has the cup. Maria is looking for it. She's commissioned me, but I'm betting I'm not the only one she has put on the case. She had deep pockets and, as you know, she's utterly ruthless. If it's someone in your den, I thought you would want to know. So that you can protect them.'

'She hasn't got any leads,' Paul said. 'Unless you're running to her with your tall tales.'

'I am not,' Lydia said. 'I have no wish to be your enemy. I hope you know that by now.'

'There you go, then,' Paul said.

'It might have a psychological effect. On whoever is holding it. I've encountered enchanted objects before and they made a man go off the deep end. This is a friendly warning to be careful with it.'

'I told you, I don't run the family. We don't have an official hierarchy or anything like it. But I will ask around. See if some young cub decided to take a trophy.'

'Like I said, it's just a friendly warning.'

LYDIA DIDN'T HAVE HIGH HOPES THAT HER OFFERING to her ancestors in Camberwell Cemetery would have resulted in some kind of answer, but she headed to the family tomb anyway. The sky was bright blue and she didn't need her jacket on the walk through the graves. It was peaceful in the cemetery with wide paths and benches and not many people. A man was sitting on a bench with a box of sandwiches and a Thermos and a couple were standing in front of a fresh-looking plot, holding hands in silence, while their small girls ran around the nearby stones shrieking.

The English weren't great with death, Lydia thought. Everybody pretended it wasn't going to happen and, when it did, spoke in hushed tones and anodyne euphemisms. Like it was something unseemly. Or a curse that you could summon by naming it.

The air at the rise of the hill was thick with the scent of bluebells, which seemed even more rampant than her last visit. Lydia went to the yew tree and peered up through the branches, trying to locate the scrap of black silk she tied there. She couldn't see it and didn't feel inclined to climb the tree, again. Once had been enough. A crow landed on the stone surface of the tomb and tilted its head.

'I've come for my answer,' Lydia said, after bobbing her head in greeting. 'I need to know how to control my power. I wanted to be strong enough to beat Maddie, but now I seem to be misfiring. I keep fainting or being sick. I don't know if it's because I have too much power or that I'm not using it right...' Lydia sank down among the flowers and leaned her back against the trunk of the tree. 'And I'm so desperate I'm talking to myself.'

She closed her eyes, feeling her head swim. *Not now.* She produced her coin and spun it in the air. With her head tipped back against the tree, she watched her coin and let the branches and sky in the background of her vision blur. She focused on the flash of gold as the coin revolved. The image of the crow was in flight and then standing and then in flight, and then the wings seemed to be moving, flapping in time with her heartbeat.

A black wing was flapping in the tree. Or was it the black silk? Lydia blinked. It was a fledgling taking flight from a nest in the tree. It was no more than a couple of metres from the nest to the top of the tomb where it sat for a moment and then, with an encouraging caw from the waiting adult, fluffed its stubby feathers and made it back up to the tree.

'Is that my answer?' Lydia asked. 'Because I don't get it.'

That's when she became aware of something moving in the grass to her right. In the shade of the spreading branches, another fledgling was twitching its wings. It fixed Lydia with one bright and frightened eye and made a clumsy hopping movement. One wing wasn't opening the way it should, and Lydia realised that it was probably broken. It had fallen when it had tried its first flight. Or the parents had realised it was sick and had shoved it out of the nest to conserve resources for the successful offspring. If *this* was the answer, then she wished she hadn't bothered coming back.

Her heart tugged with sympathy as the young bird tried to spread its wings, the damaged one clinging uselessly at its side. The more she looked, the more clearly Lydia saw. The bird had a wet-looking head and its feathers were dull and patchy. It settled down low in the grass, its small chest heaving. Henry had told her that she should never touch a fledgling. Even when they were on the ground and seemed to be alone, their parents were probably nearby and she would do more harm than good by scooping it up. He had also told her that if one was injured or sick, it was kinder to finish them off with a rock. Not that she ever had.

The adult crow was still on the tomb and Lydia could swear it was waiting for her to make a move. 'I'm not going to do your dirty work for you,' Lydia said. 'I can't.'

The fledgling was close to death, she could feel it now. Its tiny heart was beating so loud that the sound was filling her ears. Henry had told her that the only way to get strong enough to beat Maddie was to practise. That she had to kill. She had rejected the idea that she had to take from another life in order to save her own, but her own father had told her that her Grandpa Crow had expected Henry to kill Charlie. To become the strongest version of himself. She hadn't wanted to believe that was the way, but the spirits of her ancestors seemed to be telling her the same thing. Unless she had completely lost her marbles and it was a perfectly ordinary crow waiting for her to leave so it could feed its fledgling.

Lydia got up to leave. Either way, she knew one thing was certain. She didn't have what it took, and she wasn't willing to kill to get it. Which, possible insanity aside, meant there was one essential truth – she was going to die.

CHAPTER EIGHTEEN

Guillame Chartes' shop in the silver vaults had disappeared, seemingly overnight. With a professional crew of movers and the ability to glamour – or pay – the surrounding businesses to say they had never heard of you, it was perfectly possible. But only with at least one of two things; money or power.

Lydia searched for him online and asked Jason to do the same. She also forced herself to practise producing coins and trying to move her mug around her desk without touching it while she searched, figuring that every second she wasn't training was a wasted second.

With the realisation that she couldn't beat Maddie came the knowledge that it was only a matter of time before Maddie killed her. And it turned out that knowing death was imminent was extremely motivating. She was determined to get as much done as possible. She was going to lose to Maddie, but she would do everything she could to protect those she was leaving. Which also meant doing her very best to take Maddie with her.

There was a Guillame Chartes listed by the London Assay Office, but no way to contact him. Lydia called the office number and pretended to be calling from the British Museum. No dice. The man she spoke to was either genuinely unable to give her an address for Guillame, or unwilling.

Jason, however, had no problem in nosing around in the Assay Office's database. 'It's not exactly high security,' he said. 'They're using a cheap cloud-based system and they've only got native encryption, not continuous.' He shook his head fondly. 'The muppets.'

'Did you find him?'

'Oh, yes. All entries for Guillame Chartes as a registered maker. Same name, different dates going back a couple of hundred years. Either there is one hell of a naming tradition in that family, or it's the same guy.'

'That's impossible,' Lydia said automatically.

'Said the magical PI to the ghost.'

THE ASSAY OFFICE DIDN'T HOLD HOME ADDRESS details, but they did have relevant places of business for the makers. These were mostly galleries, shops, and smithing studios. The database still showed Guillame's shop in the silver vaults, so it needed updating, but there was an additional piece of information in the 'biographical notes' section. Lydia read it three times to be sure, before calling to make an appointment.

Lydia couldn't help feeling, somewhat superstitiously, that the man would manage to remove his current location from existence before she managed to speak to him. Of course, that would be quite some conjuring trick, Lydia mused as she tramped through Kensington Gardens at the edge of Hyde Park and approached the palace. It was a modest palace, as these things go, but still pretty tricky to erase. People would notice for one thing.

Once she gave her name and confirmed that she was here to see the 'Surveyor of the Queen's Silverware', Lydia was waved through security. A woman who was definitely carrying a concealed weapon patted her down and led her deeper into the palace. She tried to make conversation, but the woman answered with two word 'yes, ma'am' or 'no, ma'am' responses until Lydia gave up and let silence prevail.

GUILLAME CHARTES LOOKED EXACTLY AS LYDIA remembered. Like a lizard in a suit only somehow less appealing. He was sitting behind a polished hexagonal table which was laid with a delicate china tea set and was holding a pair of silver tongs. 'Tea? Or I can call for coffee...'

'No,' Lydia said, the word coming out fast and instinctive. She added a 'thank you' and forced herself to approach.

'I won't pretend I'm pleased to see you again, Ms Crow,' Guillame said, dropping a cube of sugar into his tea and replacing the tongs. He picked up an ornate spoon and stirred, not looking at Lydia.

'That's good,' Lydia replied. 'I won't either.'

'In what way do you believe I can help you?'

After parsing the sentence, Lydia took the information she had printed from the London Assay Office. 'This is your mark, yes?'

Guillame didn't even glance at the paper. 'I'm but a humble conduit. I buy and sell silver. Very nice pieces, if I may be so bold, and I have a modicum of historical knowledge which is useful in the assessing of pieces, but still that is the extent of my skill.'

'Why are you lying?' Lydia raised the paper slightly. 'This is your maker's mark.'

He smiled and Lydia's skin prickled in horror. 'I believe you are mistaken.'

'Your mark is on the base of a cup that was made for the Silver Family. They wanted a suitable gift for the king. James I to be precise.'

Guillame had lifted the teacup to his lips and now he took a delicate sip before replacing it on the saucer with the faintest of sounds. 'I think you must realise that is an impossible accusation. James I was on the throne in the early seventeenth century.' He gave her a slimy smile. 'That's a long time ago, Ms Crow.'

'I'm in the business of the impossible,' Lydia said. She produced her coin and flipped it, slowing its spin and moving it through the air so that it danced between them, curving lazy arcs and dips.

His eyes widened a fraction and his tongue darted out, moistening his lips. It wasn't much of a tell, but it was something. She leaned forward a little, pressing. 'Could you do it again?'

Chartes seemed to relax. 'You want to commission me?'

'Yes.' An idea had been forming in the back of Lydia's mind. She didn't trust this man, naturally, but if she could imbue an object with Crow power, just as the cup was imbued with Silver magic, then maybe it would work to keep Jason powered up when she was gone. Like a battery. It wouldn't last forever, of course, but it would give Jason more time and maybe let him decide when he was ready to go rather than have consciousness ripped away. 'Can you work with gold?'

'Easily,' Chartes said. 'But you can't afford me.'

'Don't be so sure,' Lydia said.

He produced a card and fountain pen from inside his jacket and wrote down a number.

Lydia glanced at it, keeping her features immobile. 'What if I offered a favour? In return for a steep discount. As well as my discretion regarding your unnaturally long life. How do you do that, by the way? You're not the first I've met, but you don't smell like a Pearl.'

'Silver is an extremely healthy substance,' Guillame said.

'So, I've heard. Doesn't quite cut it as an explanation, though, does it?'

'I jog,' Guillame said, producing that slimy smile again. 'I eat a healthy diet. Don't get involved with dangerous people.'

'Now I know you're lying. You enchanted that cup for the Silvers, for starters. Was it a surprise or did you know you could do it? Did someone teach you?'

Guillame's tongue darted out, again, licking his lips. 'It would have to be a very large favour.'

Lydia spread her hands wide and fixed Guillame

185

with her shark smile. 'A favour from the head of the Crows. What could be bigger?'

He stared back at her, impassive, but considering.

In the end, the worst part had been shaking on the deal. Guillame's hand wasn't damp, but cold and dry with a subtle waxiness. Lyda had never handled a snake, but she imagined it would feel the same.

There were smithing studios for hire around the city, and several in the Hatton Garden area. 'You don't have your own workshop?'

Guillame had given her a pitying look at that. Of course he wasn't going to let her into his private domain. 'Safer to be in public, I believe.'

Too late, Lydia realised the truth. He was wary of her, too. Lydia had always been scrappy, but true strength was such a new thing, she kept forgetting she had it. The studio was on the middle floor of an old industrial building off Greville Street. There was a pub on the ground floor and an advertising agency above.

As directed, Lydia had hired a bench for a day. She wasn't entirely certain Guillame would show up, but there he was, on time and carrying a battered leather bag. Inside the studio, there were three other people, spaced out around the large room. Two were chatting, takeaway coffees in hand, while the third was sketching on paper, head down. All of them ignored Lydia and Guillame, which was a relief. Lydia's stomach was in knots and the idea of making small talk seemed even more impossible than usual.

Guillame opened his bag and began laying out tools on the bench. Lydia recognised the hammer and pliers, but couldn't name the others. They all looked extremely old and well-used, the wooden handles worn smooth and ashy. He pulled out a blackened canvas apron which reached right down to his ankles and a pair of leather safety goggles.

Lydia had settled on a simple curved bracelet made from a single band of gold. She wanted to spend as little time with Guillame as possible. Besides, it wasn't as if Jason would be too fussy. She wanted it to be a wearable item, in case it turned out that he needed constant contact for it to work.

Guillame had a lump of raw gold which he placed into a crucible. Fitting his safety goggles over his head, he told Lydia she should do the same. There were some hanging up on a rack with stringy rubber straps. She put a pair on, knotting the straps to make them stay in place. Guillame pulled on heat resistant gauntlets and used a blow torch to heat the block. Using long-handled tongs, he brought it to a hand-powered machine with iron wheels. It looked a bit like a mangle and, as it turned out, acted similarly, too. The heated gold went in one side and came out the other in a flattened lozenge.

'This is it,' Guillame said, clipping the edges with a cutting tool and picking up a small hammer.

Lydia produced her coin and focused her attention while Guillame tapped the surface of the band, creating dimples in the surface. He worked steadily and without hurry, looking to Lydia before each tap. Lydia imagined her Crow power flowing from her and into the hammer so that with the blow, the power would transfer to the gold. She wasn't sure if it was working, but she kept picturing it and pushing.

The warmed gold was dull in colour, but after a few taps it had darkened to an ochre. Just as Lydia was going to ask Guillame if they should start again, that it didn't feel as if anything was happening, he hit the metal and left a spot of shiny black. Black like a shadow. Black like a crow's wing. The kind of black that Lydia saw in her dreams, that made her want to spread her arms and take off into the sky. She almost lost her wits and stopped concentrating, and Guillame tutted. The next blow was the same and the area of shiny black extended. Lydia pushed more Crow to the hammer, focusing everything she had on that one point. The place where the metal head of the hammer was meeting the band of gold.

Once the tapping finished, Guillame picked up pliers and a thick wooden pin. He laid the band over the wooden cylinder and smoothed it down with his gloved hands, like he was moulding plasticine. Lydia didn't know if that was usual, but she was light-headed from concentrating and the fumes and the flow of power which had left her body, and couldn't spare much brain-power to question it. Once the band was shaped into a circle, Guillame flattened the ends with the hammer and slid it off the wooden cylinder. He removed his gloves and used a file on the hammered edge. The band tapered at each end and the filing made this more pronounced until two points emerged. They looked sharp, like they might cut into the wrist of the wearer if they weren't extremely careful.

'It's done,' Guillame said, dropping the piece onto the bench as if it was still hot. 'Anything else would be purely decorative.'

'Why did you file it like that?' Lydia said, reaching out and touching one of the points. It was as sharp as it looked.

'I don't know. It felt right.' He gave her a look. 'Things like this? They become the shape they're meant to be.'

The black colour which had begun halfway through the process, seemed to have set. Guillame had a cloth and was polishing the band's surface. Half was now a shining warm gold and then other half the strange black. A black that looked like no material Lydia had ever seen before. The bracelet was heavy in her hand. 'Do you have something to wrap it in?'

Guillame took a clean rag from his bag and passed it over. 'No extra charge.'

CHAPTER NINETEEN

Lydia parked around the corner from The Fork and scoped the cars lining the side streets as she walked home. She spotted the undercover officers with zero trouble, which meant that Maddie would be able to do the same. She hoped they were armed and experienced. She also restrained herself from tapping on the roof as she passed and saying 'boo'. Fleet would be proud. A thought that was instantly followed by the gut punch of missing him. Where the hell had he gone?

Angel had already left for the night and the cafe was dark. Lydia raided the kitchen for some lasagne and took the plate upstairs to nuke it in her microwave. Despite the surveillance reminding her that Maddie was a clear and present threat, and the absence of Fleet that made her chest ache, Lydia realised that she was humming as she waited for her dinner to ding. She also didn't feel queasy or faint. She took the bracelet out of the cloth bag and ran her fingers over the strange black surface. The crow power was there, vibrating beneath the surface of the metal like a tuning fork. She tucked it away and ate her lasagne sitting on the sofa. Perhaps making the bracelet had siphoned off some of her power and that was why she felt better? Had Guillame shown her a way to keep on top of her abilities without having to kill?

She was almost asleep when her phone rang. It was Paul and he didn't sound happy.

'Do you know what time it is?' Lydia rubbed her face, fighting the feeling that a good night's sleep had just been snatched away.

'I need your help.'

That woke her up. Paul Fox rarely spoke so plainly. 'What's happened? Are you all right?'

'I put the word out about that robbery. Turns out one of my lads did knock over Alejandro's. Said he nicked the cup and was going to bring it to me. Not that I believe the little shit.'

'Was going to?' Lydia latched onto the past tense.

'Yeah. He sold it on sharpish. Said it gave him a funny feeling.'

'Smart little shit.'

'Foxes ain't stupid,' Paul said. Then a pause. 'Not as a rule, anyway.'

'Did he tell you who he sold it to?'

'Eventually.' Paul's voice was grim and it sent a shiver down Lydia's spine. 'I'm going to buy it back and I want you to come with.'

Lydia was just about to ask why, when Paul answered her question.

'You said the one under the church was a fake. I want to know if this one is real before I pay for it.'

Lydia was privately surprised that Paul was planning to offer cash. She would have assumed he would take a more violent approach, but she also wanted to be invited along so she didn't say so out loud.

THE BUYER LIVED IN KNIGHTSBRIDGE WHICH seemed like the kind of place someone would be shopping in Harrods for solid gold spoons, not plundering the dark web for stolen silverware. 'Your boy sold it to this guy online, right?' Lydia asked Paul.

'Apparently. Kids today, eh?'

Paul looked as out of place as she did. Two black-clad chancers walking among the social climbers and upper middle class of London. Lydia had convinced Paul to go for an early morning visit the next day. He had been hell bent on going straight round after their chat in the middle of the night, but Lydia had pointed out that there was a high chance of things going pear-shaped with a midnight visit. People were just generally more wary of folk who showed up under cover of darkness and asked to do a deal. If he wanted this to be all nice and professional with a neat exchange of cash, it would be better not to act like crazy gangsters.

The street was tucked behind Cadogan Square and filled with smart brick terraces. Number eighteen had steps leading up to an arched entrance with stonework balustrades and ornate black iron railings. The door was freshly painted and there was a keypad entry lock with a row of buzzers. 'Flat four doesn't have a name,' Lydia said. 'Hope your info is solid.'

Paul shot her a look.

Lydia pressed the buzzer for flat three. When it crackled into life she said, 'parcel for flat four, can you buzz me in?'. She hadn't even finished speaking when the door unlocked.

The shared stairs were extremely clean, the white walls lined with tasteful framed photographs, and the air smelled of polish and expensive perfume. It was, in other words, a far cry from any rental place she had ever lived.

Lydia was hoping the buyer was home and this could remain a legal and friendly exchange. She had come prepared for plan B, though, with her pick set in her pocket, and Paul was carrying a duffel bag with some power tools, but they didn't need either. The flat door was already ajar and the place where the lock had been a splintered mess.

They exchanged a silent look and Lydia put her ear to the gap and listened. A muffled thump came from inside. Lydia stopped thinking and pushed through the door.

It opened into a short entrance hall with doors leading off. There was a shoe rack overflowing with trainers and an expensive looking bicycle leaning against the wall. The place might have looked fancy, but the buyer clearly still didn't want to risk leaving his bike in the communal area.

'Wait,' Paul whispered. He seemed as confident as he always did, but there was a wariness to his gaze as he looked around. There was another sound from the end of the hall. The door was half-open and Lydia moved toward it. She was aware, in her peripheral vision, of family and travel photographs lovingly framed and displayed on the walls, and of Paul walking behind her. She glanced at him, eyebrows raised and he nodded. She pushed the door open, muscles tensed, hoping and praying that the room was empty and that whoever had broken the front door was long gone.

The room was not empty.

'I told you to stop following me,' Maddie said, straightening up from a figure lying in the middle of the carpet. She was covered in blood up to her elbows. Bright, wet, red. Very recent.

'I wasn't,' Lydia said, her gaze skipping over the dead man on the floor. He looked young, but it was hard to tell at this point. His clothes looked young at any rate. 'I'm looking for that,' Lydia pointed to the cup, which was in the dead man's hand. He was still clutching it by one handle, which can't have been easy during the attack. 'For a job.'

'Finders keepers.' Maddie tilted her chin. 'Long time no see, Paul. How's tricks?'

Lydia was trying very hard not to stare at the blood. She glanced at the man on the floor. He really was a mess. Her stomach flipped over and bile rose. She swallowed it down. She couldn't see the weapon Maddie must have used. Her hands were empty but that didn't make her any less deadly.

'Not so bad,' Paul was replying to Maddie and his tone was impressively even. 'I can see you've been keeping busy.'

'I was very clear,' Maddie said, flicking her gaze back

to Lydia. 'You can't be showing up at my work. You want to see me, you call. Okay?'

'Maria Silver commissioned me to find that cup,' Lydia said, pleased with how steady her voice sounded. 'I swear. I didn't know you would be here.'

Something fluttered behind Maddie's flat eyes. 'You're helping the Silvers?'

'Not helping. Doing a job. A return favour.'

'Charlie was in Alejandro's pocket, but I never thought you would be the same...' Maddie looked disgusted. 'And what's our old squeeze doing here? Looking for a threesome?'

Lydia didn't look at Paul and she didn't give him time to respond, either. 'I'm not in Maria's pocket. Just trying to keep the peace. That's all I want.'

At once, Maddie was toe to toe with Lydia, her face unnervingly close. Lydia had blinked and missed her moving. Her speed was breath-taking. And terrifying. Her breath was warm on Lydia's skin and she could smell her perfume, fighting against the metallic tang of the blood. Still no Crow, though. Not even the tiniest taste of feather. What had her cousin done? 'Don't you get bored of peace?'

Lydia swallowed, feeling every part of the movement. 'No.'

Maddie's eyes were searching her own. Looking for what, Lydia hadn't the faintest idea.

'Liar,' she said, eventually, stepping back. She picked up the cup and Lydia winced.

'What?' Maddie had caught Lydia's reaction.

'I don't know how you can touch it so easily,' Lydia

said. She had no idea if being honest with Maddie was sensible, but with the waves of Silver coming from the cup and the man slumped in a pool of blood and the terror of being this close to Maddie, Lydia had no room for strategic thinking. 'It makes me feel ill. The Silver.'

'The silver?' Maddie frowned. 'I didn't know you were allergic to silver.'

'Not the metal,' Lydia said. 'It's full of Silver power. I can feel it. It's enchanted.'

Maddie laughed, disbelieving. Lydia understood how she felt. She had had the same reaction initially. 'An enchanted cup? This isn't a fairy story.'

'I am aware,' Lydia said drily. 'Nonetheless.'

'And you don't like it?'

'Not particularly. It's giving out a bright silver flavour. And a light. It makes my head hurt.'

'That's your thing?'

'That's her thing,' Paul chimed in. 'Lame, right?' He had put a hand on the small of Lydia's back and she felt his warning. *Don't be so interesting. Don't engage the crazy killing machine.*

'Yeah,' Lydia said. 'I sense Family power. It can be useful, but it's not very exciting.'

Maddie shifted. 'Oh, come now. Don't be so modest. I know what you're doing.'

'I'm not doing-'

'You think that if you play possum, I'll think you're dead already. It won't work,' Maddie nudged the dead man's leg with her foot. 'Just ask this guy.'

Sirens sounded, suddenly, approaching.

'That's my cue,' Maddie said, stepping away. She paused. 'You could come with.'

'No, thank you.' Lydia was still struggling to hold on to consciousness.

'Suit yourself,' Maddie said. 'I won't keep asking nicely, though.'

At least, Lydia thought she heard Maddie say those words, but the darkness had crowded in from the edges of her vision until it filled her mind completely. Her stomach lurched as she fell and then there was nothing.

WHEN SHE CAME ROUND, THE ROOM WAS FILLED with police and there was no sign of Paul. A woman Lydia knew was senior from her commanding tone, was issuing orders and a paramedic was crouched next to her, fiddling with the straps on a back board.

'I'm fine,' Lydia said, starting to sit up.

'Stay down,' the paramedic said, placing hands on her shoulders. 'Don't move. We're going to lift you onto the board. Okay? One, two, three.'

'I don't need-'

'It's all right, we've got you. You're fine.'

Lydia wanted to say 'I know I'm fine, that what I'm telling you' but she decided to save her breath. The woman was clearly on a mission and Lydia was already being lifted onto the board. She closed her eyes and concentrated on taking slow breaths through her nose. The swaying motion of being carried, along with the natural terror of being strapped down, was making her feel sick. 'Let me up,' she said, eyes open and pulse racing. Something was wrong. Someone was there. Danger, her brain was saying. Get up. Get out. Fly.

'Shit,' she heard a muffled stream of swearing as her body lurched down.

'It's okay,' a familiar voice. Fleet came into view above her. 'Are you hurt?'

'I'm fine,' Lydia managed, suffused with sudden relief. He was back. Fleet was back. 'They won't listen.'

'Let her up,' Fleet said.

The straps were undone and Lydia sat up, rubbing her arms, and then got herself upright. The world tilted and she had to swallow hard to stop herself throwing up. She squeezed her coin for strength and waved the paramedic away. 'Thank you. I'm okay.'

'This is against my official advice,' the woman said, giving Fleet an extra frown.

He nodded, calm and unflappable. 'Noted.' He ducked his head to look into Lydia's eyes. 'Are you all right? Did you hit your head?'

'You're back,' Lydia drank in the sight of Fleet. Tall, dark and beautiful. Here.

'I'm back. Now, answer the question. Did you hit your head? Black out?'

'I'm fine. She was here.'

'It could be a concussion. Let me take you to A&E to get you checked out.'

She scanned the room. The dead man was on the ground, three SOC officers were securing the scene and the silver cup had disappeared along with Maddie. 'Hell Hawk.'

'You want to tell me what happened?'

'Of course, Officer,' Lydia said, letting Fleet know that she was going to give him the official version.

He nodded very slightly, indicating his understanding, and Lydia proceeded to give him a sanitised version of events, light on the details and even lighter on the truth.

BACK AT THE FORK, AFTER MAKING LYDIA SIT ON the sofa and drink a cup of sweet tea even though she had asked for coffee, Fleet undid his tie and slumped next to her. He looked exhausted.

'It was Maddie.'

He took it pretty well. Just raising his eyes to the ceiling for a brief moment.

'She has the cup.'

Fleet nodded. 'At least that makes sense.'

'You're being very calm.'

'You spoke to Maddie?'

'Briefly, yeah.'

'And you're still breathing and in one piece. That's cause for celebration.' His lips quirked into a smile.

'She took the cup. I'm guessing that's the real reason she's in London.'

Frustration broke through Fleet's calm exterior. 'I don't care about the bloody cup.'

Lydia paused in acknowledgement of his outburst. She took one of his hands in hers and squeezed gently. 'It's important. If I don't bring it back to Maria, she might break our truce. It's pretty shaky.'

'Wasn't the deal that you find it? You found it.'

Lydia smiled. 'That's definitely my planned argument, but I don't think it will fly. Do you?'

He breathed in deeply through his nose and passed a hand over his face. 'No.'

'So that means I need to get it back.'

'How are you so calm?'

Because I know I'm going to die.

She couldn't say that, so she made up something else about having a plan. About not giving up. Luckily, Fleet was used to her pig-headed determination, and he didn't bat an eyelid.

THAT NIGHT THEY SLEPT WRAPPED AROUND EACH other and Lydia needed every centimetre of contact. His scent, his presence, and the Fleet signature of waves on a beach, salted air and a fire crackling in the dark. She needed all of it. Felt like she could finally breathe. The stubborn part of her had wanted to be angry over the last week, to rail at him for leaving her at this time of crisis, but it had been a token effort. She had just been worried. And missing him. And wanting him back, safe and whole and hers. If there was anything important, he would tell her. She knew it. And, although she fully expected to dream of Maddie drenched in blood and smiling like a kid with an ice cream, she fell into a peaceful blackness, feather soft and mercifully quiet.

CHAPTER TWENTY

Early the next morning, Lydia woke with the realisation that Fleet was already awake. He had his arms crossed behind his head and was staring at the ceiling, deep in thought. She propped up on one elbow to kiss him good morning. He still looked exhausted, grey shadows under his eyes.

'Couldn't you sleep?'

'I'm all right.'

That wasn't an answer, but Lydia didn't press him. She knew very well what it was like to have bad dreams and, sometimes, you just didn't want to talk about them. Didn't want to bring them into the day with you.

Once they were up and eating toast on the sofa, Lydia's legs over his, he rubbed a hand over his face and gave her a serious look. 'If I tell you something, you have to promise not to do anything stupid.'

'You know me,' Lydia said.

'I do,' Fleet said. 'So I need you to promise.'

'Define stupid,' Lydia said, aiming for a little levity.

Fleet raised his eyebrows in response.

'Fine,' Lydia said. 'I promise. Spill it.'

'I made a deal with Sinclair to get information.'

'I told you, no more deals...'

'I made the deal, not you,' Fleet said. 'You aren't a part of it, I promise. We needed information and this was the only way to get it. I did it for you.'

Lydia forced herself to shut up and listen.

'The project being run by your agent has been wound up. Nobody really believed that the Families were any kind of threat. Bedtime stories and some good PR. They didn't think it was a good use of the budget, and I can believe that. Everything in my work has to be justified with finance allocation docs, they would have had a hard time funding research into magic.'

'So it's definitely just Mr Smith?'

Fleet shrugged. 'I mean, he might have some acolytes, fellow believers, but from an official point of view, yes. Mr Smith was a one-man crusade within the service and the Families his pet project. With global terrorism and fears over Russian interference in politics taking the headlines, it's not such a surprise. Organised crime on our home turf is important, of course, but it's left to the NCA.'

The National Crime Agency definitely had a dossier on the Crows. Organised crime was their area and back in the bad old days, the Crows kept them sweet with well-placed bribes. At least, that was what Lydia assumed. It was all ancient history, as far as she was concerned. 'What about the NCA? I don't think we've been doing anything serious enough to pull their attention. Charlie wasn't squeaky clean but it was small time, really.' A thought hit her. 'Unless they were interested in the rumours. The power stuff. That might have drawn them to Mr Smith. Could they have been working with Mr Smith's department? His project?'

'Not as far as anyone knows,' Fleet said. 'According to Sinclair, your man Smith has a personal obsession. She showed me some of his departmental files and they were really something.'

'Don't tell me he had a Crow shrine with pictures of me with the eyes cut out.'

'Don't joke,' Fleet said. 'He's been collecting for years. The company, JRB, you know he took it over in 2001 when it went from being a family firm to the corporation we know and love. There was a copy of the contract in the file, the agreement with the Pearls? It seems it was the closest he could get to owning them. And he's been searching for the Silver cup. He's got Charlie, and he wanted you to add to the collection. Plus, he has a few other artifacts in storage. A coat that belonged to the Foxes back in the eighteen hundreds and some pearls that may or may not be connected with the Pearl Family. His notes recorded some uncertainty.'

'I bet he wanted me to take a look, see if they were the real deal.'

'Probably,' Fleet agreed. 'But the main thing is that his department at the service really does just boil down to him. It doesn't go further in any meaningful way, which means we just need to neutralise one man.'

'So he bought JRB in order to acquire the contract with the Pearls? And he's the sole director, now?'

Fleet passed his phone over and Lydia swiped through the images until she found the articles of incorporation for JRB. Lots of legal language and a name which rang a faint bell. Oliver Gale.

Fleet was looking over her shoulder. 'That's your man Smith's real name. Sinclair confirmed it.'

'If you trust Sinclair. What would stop her from lying or only showing you some of the file and not the whole picture? She could be working with Mr Smith. She could be part of his department.' Lydia knew she sounded paranoid, but she felt like it was more than warranted.

Fleet shook his head.

'You really trust her?'

Fleet held her gaze. 'I do.'

Lydia wanted to just believe him. Fleet was an excellent judge of character, a talented copper with a nose for bullshit and a gleam which had been giving him an edge of precognition his whole life. Still. It was too important. And Lydia couldn't take anything at face value, it just wasn't the way she was wired. 'Why are you so sure she isn't stringing you along? Why would she give you the goods?'

Fleet touched her arm. 'Because I traded.'

'I don't...'

'If the information doesn't pan out, she doesn't get my offering and, trust me, she really wants it.'

'What is it?'

Fleet grimaced very briefly. A quick expression which Lydia almost missed. Almost. She felt cold. 'What? What did you offer to give Sinclair?'

'Don't worry about it.'

Lydia waited a beat. 'You're not going to tell me?'

'Best not,' he said, looking away.

'Yeah, that's not going to work this time.'

Fleet closed his eyes. 'I went to see my father.'

Lydia kept her mouth shut, waiting.

'Well, I went to find my father. Wasn't sure I would manage... It's been a while.'

The silence stretched on and Lydia reached for his hand. 'Did you find him?'

He nodded slightly, eyes still closed.

'What did he give you that Sinclair wanted?'

Fleet opened his eyes and looked at Lydia with clear anguish. 'I can't talk about this. I'm sorry. I just can't.'

Lydia couldn't stand the pain in his eyes. She put her arms around him and rested her head on his shoulder. 'It's okay.' If there was one thing she understood, it was not wanting to verbalise something difficult.

'There's something else,' he pulled back to look into her eyes. 'Sinclair showed me Maddie's file, too. She's a stone-cold psycho.'

'Tell me something I don't know,' Lydia said.

'I'm serious,' Fleet said. 'You need to stay away from her. You have no idea what she is capable of.'

'I'm not exactly looking to braid her hair,' Lydia said. 'But she's on my patch.'

'I have a friend, a psychologist I know through work. Will you speak to her?'

'You want me to see a shrink?'

'No. I thought it would be useful to know more

about Maddie. Maybe it would help to predict her behaviour.'

Lydia messaged Emma and watched for the blue ticks which showed she had read it. A reply came back quickly that all was well. Next, Lydia rang Paul. 'All quiet,' he said. 'Nobody sniffing around.'

'Thank you,' Lydia said. 'But I wanted to check on you after yesterday. Did you get away all right?'

'Little Bird,' Paul said, his voice shooting unwanted feelings through her body. Damn Fox. 'Are we becoming best friends?'

'In your dreams,' Lydia said. 'But you are doing me a favour. And I don't wish Maddie on my worst enemy.'

His voice went serious. 'She's changed.'

'You felt it, too?'

'I could see it. Something is broken in that woman. And the way she was looking at you... You need to be careful.'

'I am,' Lydia said. 'I'm not an idiot.'

'I didn't leave until she had, wasn't sure what she would do once you were taking a nap.'

'Thank you,' Lydia said with genuine gratitude. 'But I know my cousin. I know how to handle her.'

'You were out cold, you didn't see her face. She looked hungry.'

Lydia felt a fission on pleasure. It was nice to be wanted.

'And she kissed you on her way out.'

'What?'

'On the forehead. She didn't even look at me.'

In usual circumstances Lydia would have said something arch like 'jealous?' but Paul had watched over her until the psycho had left the flat so she kept her lip buttoned.

'You need to stay away from her. She is way too interested, and it's only going to end one way.'

'I know,' Lydia said. She didn't want to talk about Maddie anymore. 'I've got something for you. You know that company, JRB? It turns out there's one main driver behind their activities. A spook with a hard-on for us all.'

'That sounds uncomfortable.'

Lydia had regretted her choice of words the moment they left her mouth. She felt the traitorous blush creep over her face and thanked feathers he couldn't see her. 'He's been gathering information for years and he tried to recruit me. You know him as the guy who orchestrated the trouble between us. And got the Crows killed in Wandsworth. I call him Mr Smith.'

'He wants a war? Messy.'

'He wants us at each other's throats. If we tear each other apart, we're not a threat. Plus, we're more likely to work for him, give up power or information.' Lydia didn't mention the Silver Cup. She owed Paul Fox, but she didn't trust him. Not completely. 'He's vulnerable, though. He's been working outside his remit at MI6. They are looking to clean up his projects and won't be too sad if he disappears.'

'And how do you know that?'

Lydia wasn't going to mention Fleet, it would only provoke some macho posturing. 'I've gone to some

lengths to make sure it's good information. I can't guarantee that someone else won't pick up his research in the
future, but for now they've got bigger fish to fry.'

'It's not going to be easy to get to him. JRB is just a
shell.'

'The Pearls.'

'What about them?' Paul's tone was dismissive.
'Bunch of grocers.'

'You've only met the descendants,' Lydia said. 'I've
met the original family and, trust me, they're not to be
fucked with. They're more powerful than you, me,
Henry Crow, Maria Silver and Maddie put together.'

'Is that a fact?' Paul still sounded unimpressed.

'But they've been trapped. Bit of tricky contract
work. Some agreement with the original incarnation of
JRB.'

'A written contract? If they're so powerful, how did
that work?'

'I have no idea,' Lydia said. 'Maybe back in the day,
all kinds of things got imbued with power?' She was
thinking of the power in the Silver Cup, power that had
been contained in ordinary metal. Maybe power had
been contained in the ink and paper of the contract, or in
the pen they used to sign. Maybe the Pearls just believed
in the power of language to such an extent that it worked
its own kind of magic on them. It didn't matter. 'What
matters is that I've got a bargaining chip. I'm going to
deliver Mr Smith to the Pearls. He's the sole owner of
JRB and I bet they can make him renegotiate. They want
to be free.' This last part was the bit which made Lydia
sweaty with nausea. If this worked and the Pearls broke

their contract, what would their freedom mean? Would they stay to their underground realm out of choice? Or would they rise up into the city? All she could do was hope they would be feeling magnanimous toward the Crows.

'And what will they do with Mr Smith? The embodiment of the contract which has kept them trapped all of these years?'

Lydia shrugged, even though Paul couldn't see her. 'Not my problem.'

LYDIA DIDN'T THINK THAT A CLINICAL psychologist was going to be any help in predicting Maddie's behaviour, but she couldn't get the image of Maddie leaning over her unconscious body and planting a kiss on her forehead. It was somehow more disturbing than the times she had threatened to kill her. Uncharted territory.

Fleet was pleased when Lydia agreed to the meeting, too, which was a bonus. She could see the tension radiating from him and wanted to ease his concern.

The psychologist worked part time for the prison service and part time in private practice, and she agreed to see Lydia at the end of the following day. 'I can fit you in at five.'

Fleet was still at work at that time. 'Sorry,' he said, sounding distracted. Somebody else was clearly still talking to him in the background and a phone was ringing. 'I was going to come with you.'

Lydia reassured him that it was fine and made her

way to the psychologist's office. It was north of Camberwell Green in a converted Victorian house and former bakery. The inside had been gutted and remodelled to house several rental offices and a reception area.

'DCI Fleet's friend,' the doctor greeted her. 'I'm Emi Hase. Come in. How can I help?'

Lydia wasn't sure what she had expected from the label 'forensic psychologist' but it wasn't this small smiley woman in a floral dress that looked like it had been bought in the children's department.

'I'm not here to talk about me.'

'You'd be surprised how many people think that.' The doctor had her hands neatly folded in her lap and was unnaturally still. She had shiny black hair in a neat bob, held back from her face with a red Alice band.

'No, really. I'm an investigator and I'm here in my professional capacity. I want to ask about my client. Well, not really my client.'

'We can talk about whatever you want.'

'It's my cousin. She is disturbed and I want your professional opinion on her behaviour, her perspective.'

'You think your cousin has a problem?'

Lydia flipped open her notebook. There was something unsettling about the office with its calming pictures on the walls and the box of tissues on the low table. Something in the vibrations of the air which made her feel on alert. Like the woman opposite her had x-ray vision and could see straight into her heart. 'I know my cousin is a psychopath. I want to know how best to handle her.'

'Psychopathology is rare.' A pause. 'And it's not what you see in the movies. They're not all serial killers.'

Lydia quashed the urge to smile. The head doctor didn't look as if she would appreciate that. She would probably interpret it as a sign of Lydia's mental illness. 'What if I am talking about a serial killer? But the professional sort.'

The doctor paused. 'Military?'

'Let's say "yes". How do I get her to do what I want?'

'I can't talk specifics without meeting the person. And I would also be extremely wary of diagnosing them as psychopathic without a formal evaluation. Plus,' the doctor gave the smallest of smiles, 'I'm not in the business of teaching manipulation techniques.'

'I'm not a patient or asking about a clinically vulnerable individual. I need to know how to handle a person who I believe to be psychopathic. Or, if that's too difficult, then just some general pointers on what it means to be psychopathic. For example, if I had made a deal with a psychopath, what are the odds of them sticking to it? Are they more or less unreliable than the general population?'

'A clinical diagnosis is not a predictor of behaviour.'

Lydia stamped on the urge to sigh loudly. 'I am aware. But what can you tell me? Are they likely to stick to a prearranged deal or plan?'

'Unlikely,' Emi said. 'Psychopaths are impulsive. They don't see consequences in the same way as neurotypical people.'

'But they can be very effective. What about a high functioning psychopath?'

Emi leaned back in her chair slightly, settling in as if to give a lecture. 'I didn't mean they couldn't see the consequences, that was poorly phrased, what I mean is that they may well comprehend all the possible conse-quences of their actions, but they just don't care.'

'Right...' Lydia was lining up her next question, but the doc hadn't finished.

'No. You don't understand. The most important thing for you to know is that your cousin won't have the range of emotions that you or I experience. She won't feel fear or excitement or love or sympathy or anything. Psychopaths describe everything as monotone. They can tell they are experiencing physical reactions to danger, such as increased heart rate, but that doesn't translate to fear.'

'That sounds quite handy.'

'It can be,' Emi said. 'But it can lead them to harm themselves. Because they just don't care. About pain, about hardship, about dying. None of it. That can lead to extremely risky behaviours. Like most people with a mental health condition, psychopaths are more of a danger to themselves than they are to others.'

Lydia thanked the doctor for her help and made to leave.

Emi hesitated before speaking. 'Do you really think your cousin is a psychopath?'

'Yes. Without a doubt.'

'And they are trained to kill?' Em had gone pale, but with a prurient interest lighting her eyes. 'You know that they have killed someone?'

'Many people. She's good at it and she likes doing

214

things she's good at. We all do, I suppose, but with her...
It's like she doesn't have anything else.' As soon as she
spoke the words out loud, Lydia realised that they
applied to her. Or they had done. When she had started
Crow Investigations it had been a revelation. She had
been completely obsessed, so happy to have found something that she was good at after years of flailing and failing. It suited her and it made her feel useful. And, yes,
powerful.

'May I be direct with you?' The doctor didn't wait
for an answer. 'I'm concerned this may be the result of
projection on your part. This is nothing to be ashamed
of, but it does indicate the need for ongoing professional
support. Is that something you would consider? If so, I
would suggest you don't delay. I can provide you with
the details of some highly recommended specialists in
this area...'

Lydia was already on her feet. This had been a waste
of time.

'However,' the doctor held up a finger. 'On the small
chance I am wrong in that assessment and your cousin
does exist in the manner you have described, I would
advise that you do not approach them or attempt to
engage with them. And to notify the police.'

'Your advice is noted,' Lydia said. How wonderful to
hand the responsibility for Maddie onto the authorities
or to another person. Anyone. But she couldn't. Maddie
was a Crow and she was Lydia's problem to sort.

CHAPTER TWENTY-ONE

Knowing that she couldn't win was curiously freeing. After leaving the psychologist's office, Lydia had walked to Camberwell Cemetery and sat among the bluebells next to her family's tomb and thought through all of her options. There wasn't a better one as far as she could see and, as long as she managed to take Maddie with her, she felt like it wouldn't be so bad to die. Of course, given the choice she would prefer to live, but she knew now that Maddie wasn't going to stop.

Back at The Fork, she ran over her idea with Jason. He was horrified. 'I don't care about Smith. He's bad news. But isn't there a chance that they will break the contract?'

'I expect they will.' This was a problem and not one Lydia had been able to solve.

'But won't that free them?'

'I can't fix everything,' Lydia said, frustrated that she was close to tears. 'If JRB is no more, then there's no Mr Smith trying to fuck with the Families, killing Crows to start a war. If the Pearls get free and decide to cause hell once they are, then everyone will have to deal with it. Hopefully they'll abide by the treaty. And feel some gratitude to us, at least, for passing on the contract.'

Jason opened his mouth to argue.

'Besides,' Lydia said, cutting him off. 'It's not like they're exactly harmless at the moment.' They both looked into the middle of the room, where Ash had been tied to a chair for his own protection, his arms bound to stop him from hurting himself. The Pearl King controlling his body as effortlessly as a child playing with a doll.

'What aren't you telling me?' Jason said after a moment.

'I've got you something,' Lydia said, trying to keep her voice steady. She produced the package from her bag and unwrapped the cloth. The bangle looked as peculiar as it had in the studio. It pulled at her. Touching the black surface with one tentative finger made her stomach swoop as if her whole body had just lifted into the air. She felt wings spreading wide, shoulder muscles tensing, and the sharp stab of beak against skin and bone.

'What is it?'

'It's for you to wear. If you want. It will power you up. The way that I do.'

Jason was frowning, his expression between hope and consternation. 'Will that work?'

'I believe so,' Lydia said. She hoped so.

He reached out and touched it, a smile breaking out. 'Bloody hell, I think it might work. I felt something then.' He looked at her with wonder. 'Where did you get it?'

'I made it,' Lydia said. 'With help.'

'That's amazing,' Jason said. Then his expression fell. 'Why?'

'We should sit down,' Lydia said.

'I don't need to sit down,' Jason said. 'What's going on?'

'I might have to go away for a bit,' Lydia said, chickening out of the truth. She couldn't say it. The finality of it.

'Where?'

Then it hit her, the ridiculousness of avoiding death talk with the ghost. He wasn't just a ghost, either, he was her friend. Her close friend. Hell Hawk. 'Maddie. She's not going to stop. I have to stop her.'

Jason caught on immediately. 'You're not a killer.'

'Technically I am,' Lydia said. 'And I've got to try. She has a twisted idea that we're meant to be something together. Either running the Family or running around the world killing people, I don't know which. But sooner or later she is going to snap. She's going to get tired of waiting or I'm going to do something she doesn't like. She'll want to hurt me and that will mean hurting those I love. I can't have that happen. I can't.'

'What are you doing to do?'

'I can't beat her,' Lydia said. 'I'm not strong enough. I'm not ruthless enough. She's a trained killer and a psychopath, I can't win. So, I'm going to give her what she wants.'

HAVING MADE THE DECISION TO GO DOWN

219

swinging, Lydia felt a sense of peace. It might not be a good plan, but at least she had one. And she had always preferred action to waiting for the sky to fall. Her phone rang with Paul's number and she answered it straight away.

'She's here.'

Her stomach sank. 'Where?'

'Beckenham. Couple of streets from your folks place.'

'That's close to Emma's, too.' Lydia hadn't intended to produce her coin, but it was there in her hand nonetheless. She squeezed it.

'I know,' Paul said. 'She's just sitting there. Plain sight.'

'Where?'

'Bumble Bee Cafe on Bromley Road. She's been at one of the outside tables for the last hour.'

'I'm on my way.'

The traffic was mercifully light and Lydia made it to Bromley Road in record time. She parked at the more residential end and speed-walked toward the parade of shops, cafes and pubs. Paul was waiting outside the dry cleaners. 'She's still there,' he said. 'I don't know what she's doing. Well, she's eaten a toastie and an ice-cream sundae, but I mean...'

'I know,' Lydia put a hand on his arm. 'Thank you for contacting me. And for watching Emma all this time. I won't forget it.'

Paul looked sideways at her. 'That plan you mentioned... What aren't you telling me?'

'Nothing,' Lydia said brightly. 'Can you go to

Emma's? I'm going to try to redirect her attention, but if I fail...'

Paul nodded, his face serious. 'I'm the back up. I won't let her near Emma.'

'I will pay you back,' Lydia said. She was looking down the street, trying to see if she could see evidence of the psycho up ahead.

'I know you will,' Paul said, which wasn't entirely reassuring. And then he loped away, taking a side street in the direction of Emma's house.

THE BUMBLE BEE CAFE WAS AS NAUSEATINGLY cutesie as Lydia remembered, with cartoon bees decorating the windows and tablecloths. Maddie was pouring tea from a hive-shaped teapot and the juxtaposition was enough to make Lydia's head spin.

'Let's take a walk,' Lydia said. 'You've had enough tea.'

Maddie tilted her head and gazed up at Lydia from behind enormous sunglasses. 'And how would you know a thing like that?'

'My boyfriend's a copper. It has its perks.' Lydia wasn't going to throw Paul under the bus. 'You are being watched.'

'Please,' Maddie said, standing up. 'Don't pretend the Met has the resources. They're not interested in little old me.'

'You'd be surprised,' Lydia said, moving away from the cafe. 'Aren't you going to pay?'

Maddie pushed her sunglasses onto the top of her

head. 'When are you going to stop pretending to be normal? You're the head of the Crows. You should act like it.'

Lydia didn't answer.

'And I don't know why you're pretending things are all cosy with your policeman. I know you haven't been seeing him much lately. Has he lost interest?'

'He had to go away for work,' Lydia said, trying not to panic that Maddie seemed to know so much about her day-to-day life.

'That's men for you,' Maddie said, watching Lydia with bright eyes. 'Unreliable.'

Lydia didn't take the bait.

They were walking down the street toward Lydia's car and away from the busy parade. It was safer for the general public but probably not Lydia's smartest move. Her mind was racing at Maddie's proximity to Emma and her family, not to mention her own parents. She knew she had to refocus Maddie, but the chat with the forensic psychologist hadn't exactly buoyed her confidence.

They reached Lydia's car within minutes.

Maddie nodded at a bus stop over the road. 'This has been fun, but I'm going in another direction. You should think about what I said. You can't rely on your policeman.'

'I hope you're wrong,' Lydia said, trying to keep her tone friendly and non-confrontational. 'I've moved my stuff into his flat. It's what he has wanted and I said "yes". This is the last of my stuff.' She patted the roof of the car. Inside there were boxes, a duffel bag, a rucksack and a couple of bin bags of clothes. She had filled the car after Paul had called, figuring that she would need to sell the story.

Maddie went still. 'I don't believe you.'

Lydia forced a shrug. 'I don't want to lose him. And things have to change or we're just stuck. He's right. It's the next move for us. Anyway, I can't live at The Fork forever.'

'That's what I've been telling you. You need to spread your wings.'

'You understand then.'

'No,' Maddie looked stricken. 'This is the opposite of what I meant. Spreading your wings does not mean moving into a pokey little flat with your tame copper.'

'It's actually a really nice flat...'

Maddie had already gone. She was crossing the road just in front of the approaching bus.

Lydia stood and watched Maddie board, wondering if she would raise her hand in a 'goodbye'. If she waved then maybe she hadn't just set her off on an anger-fuelled rampage. She lifted her own hand ready as Maddie took her seat by a window, but she didn't turn and look at Lydia as the bus pulled away. Lydia put her hand down and took a couple of deep breaths. Mission accomplished, she told herself. Maddie was definitely now more interested in Fleet which should keep her away from Beckenham. Lydia got into the car and called Fleet to warn him.

CHAPTER TWENTY-TWO

She had a plan. Jason thought it was a terrible idea, the psychologist thought she should stay far away from her cousin, and even Paul Fox was dubious about it. Still, it was a plan. And her disturbing dreams had stopped. It was as if her subconscious had given up on her. She woke up early from a dead sleep and realised that Fleet was the one having a bad dream. He was sweating and muttering in his sleep. She woke him as gently as she could and made soothing noises until his eyes focused on her.

'Sorry,' he said, embarrassed. 'Nightmare.'

'Want to talk about it?'

He leaned over and took a swig of water from the pint glass on his side of the bed. 'Not really. I don't know.'

Lydia wrapped herself around him and waited, stroking the hair at the base of his skull.

'I couldn't see who it was, but I thought it was you. I was at my flat and I was just sitting on the sofa, waiting.

Everything was normal and then it wasn't. There was a woman in a hoodie, but I couldn't see her face. I thought it was you but she had a knife and then I felt really scared. I couldn't move, you know, classic nightmare stuff. My body was completely paralysed, and I knew I was going to die.'

'That's horrible, I'm sorry,' Lydia put her forehead against his. 'It was just a dream, though, right?'

'I think so,' Fleet whispered. 'I mean I get lots of visions. Things that are going to happen, but then they don't. The only ones which have come true have happened immediately after the vision. If they are too far in the future, I think there are too many variables. Chaos theory. Or free will. Or that thing about how you change the future as soon as you look at it. Is that a physics thing? Atoms behave differently when observed? I can't remember.'

Lydia stayed quiet and let Fleet talk it out. She knew that feeling. Half-asleep terror being eased by action of talking. When he had gone quiet, she asked if he wanted to try to go back to sleep.

'I don't think so,' he said. 'You can if you want. Sorry I woke you.'

'It's fine. How about just lying down?'

Lydia had just fitted herself into the hollow of his body when he said something she didn't quite catch.

'There was a fire. The woman in the hoodie was laughing and I couldn't move and my flat was on fire. I could feel my body burning, taste the smoke. Smell it. It was so real.'

. . .

Once Lydia was up and dressed, she went onto the terrace for a little privacy. Ever since she had taken Charlie's place at the head of the family, the crows gathered on the roof and along the railing of the terrace. She took the time to greet them all and then set to work. Producing her own coin was as natural and easy as breathing and, now that she had practised, she could create a room full of duplicates and have them dance in any way she wanted.

She wasn't after anything showy this morning, though. Just control. Ever since making the bracelet with Guillame Chartes she had felt steadier. The nausea hadn't returned and, although she had passed out in the presence of Maddie and the Silver cup, she put that down to heightened circumstances. Circumstances she was planning to repeat, but still. She would be prepared this time.

There was a light drizzle falling but Lydia barely noticed her clothes slowly saturating as she stared into the middle distance and focused on the idea of her coin. She could feel her power humming in the background and hear the thousands of hearts beating, the crows that lived in the space that wasn't physical but that she somehow could access. She called to mind the feeling of her power running into the bracelet as Guillame had twisted the metal and, now that she knew the shape of that feeling, found she could repeat it. She felt her power focusing and channelling and when she stopped she saw a single coin, larger than hers and jet black, hanging in the air. She clapped her hands together and it disappeared, but the feeling of calm remained.

Fleet was inside, working on his tablet. He looked up when she came in. 'You're soaked.'

'I've got a plan.' Lydia licked her lips. 'But you're not going to like it.'

He closed the laptop. 'I will support you whatever, you know that. I'm on your side.'

'I'm going to turn over Mr Smith to the Pearl court and let them deal with him. They hate JRB with a cold passion and I think they will deal with him.'

'Okay.'

To his credit, Fleet was hearing her out. It was a plan involving kidnapping and cold-blooded murder, but all he was doing was waiting patiently for her to elaborate. Probably for the part where she explained that it was a bait and switch and she wasn't really going to deliver a man to his almost-certain death. 'And I'm going to use Maddie to help me do it.'

Fleet remained calm. 'What makes you think she will help you?'

'She hates him as much as I do. And I will tell her that I'm going to work with her. She wants a partnership so I think she'll do this to prove to me that she's serious about that. That I can trust her.'

'I don't think she cares about being a good partner,' Fleet said.

Lydia knew there was truth in that, but she was pretty sure she knew that there was something else. 'She's lonely. She's sick of being alone. She wants a companion.'

'What makes you think she wants you?'

'She thinks we're the same. She's too narcissistic to

want to be with anybody except her own reflection. She seems to think I'm close enough.'

'But you're not.'

Lydia shrugged. She wasn't sure whether she agreed with Fleet. They were both Crows, they were both killers. Maddie was insane, but she wasn't stupid. There were similarities. Instead of voicing this to Fleet, she said, 'I can act the part for long enough to get her on board.'

'Then what? Maddie is the problem, not Smith. She's not listening to his orders anymore. If your plan works and you get rid of Smith, you've still got Maddie to deal with.'

This was the tricky bit. She couldn't have Fleet guess her plan or he would try to stop her. 'I think there's a good chance it will give her closure. And then she'll leave and go back to her contract work. It's not like the service won't be happy to keep her on the books. She's certainly effective.'

He looked doubtful. 'She went rogue. She killed her handler and then, if this plan works, an MI6 agent.'

'Sinclair says Mr Smith is on his own and out of favour. They might be happy for a quick solution. And from what I have gathered, talented assassins don't grow on trees.' She winced as the image of Sergio Bastos swinging from one jumped into her mind. 'I mean, I think they would be willing to keep her in work. She's a valuable asset to the service.'

He nodded. 'That's true. It's a bit of a gamble, though.'

'You traded with them, what do you think they'll do?'

Fleet's brow furrowed as he considered the question. 'I think they'll close the files on your Family and roll Smith's department into an existing one.'

Lydia nodded. 'It's settled then.'

Auntie's flat was quiet when she knocked and Lydia hoped there wouldn't be visitors and dogs this time. She wanted to speak to Fleet's aunt in private.

Lydia was just about to press the bell for a second time, when the door swung inward. Auntie looked unsurprised but not especially happy to see her. 'I brought alcohol.' Lydia raised the carrier bag in her hand.

'I don't drink,' Auntie said, but she stepped back and motioned for Lydia to enter the flat.

'It's for me,' Lydia said, toeing off her trainers.

'You had better come through.'

If the last visit had been a formal affair with teacups and comfy seating, this time Auntie was all business. She led the way to the small kitchen and got two small glasses down from a cupboard. She put them on the cream Formica drop-leaf table and sat down on the matching chair. Lydia unscrewed the bottle and poured them both a generous measure before sitting in the other chair. The room was dominated by an old-fashioned dresser, overflowing with mismatched china, and the open shelving above the sink was lined with handmade-looking pottery and houseplants. If she reached out an arm she could almost touch the sink, and she wondered how Auntie managed to work in the room without knocking things over.

'Is this a goodbye?' Auntie said taking the offered glass of single malt.

Lydia felt her eyes prickle with sudden tears. There was a gleam about the woman, just like Fleet's, and she had to struggle to keep her emotions in check. She realised that she wanted to lean into this prickly and unwelcoming woman and have her hold her and stroke her hair, tell her everything was going to be all right. Although it wasn't. Not for her. She raised her glass. 'Yes.'

Auntie raised her glass in answer and drained it in one.

Lydia followed suit and then refilled both glasses. 'I thought you didn't drink.'

'That was before I saw your purpose,' Auntie said. 'Occasions like this, they demand it. And you brought the good stuff.'

She wondered how much of Fleet's gift Auntie shared and how much she knew. Or had guessed.

'You're doing the right thing, child.'

Lydia blinked several times to stop herself from crying and drained her glass. The whisky burned her throat and warmed her chest and, most importantly, reminded her that she wasn't the type to dissolve in a stranger's kitchen. No matter what the circumstances.

She squared her shoulders. 'I want you to pass a message to Fleet for me. Ignatius.'

Auntie nodded. 'You're not coming back.'

'No. I don't think so.' Lydia had tried to write a letter for Fleet, something to explain to him what she had done and why she had done it. She had tried to find the words, but it had been too hard. Now, sitting opposite Auntie she wondered why she had thought giving a verbal message would be easier.

'What do you want him to know?'

Lydia swallowed. 'That I didn't have a choice. This was the safest way. The way to make sure he was safe. And Emma. And my parents. I had to be sure.'

Auntie nodded. 'Anything else?'

'Just that I love him. And I'm sorry I couldn't think of a better way.'

CHAPTER TWENTY-THREE

Finding Maddie turned out to be the easiest part of the plan as she responded to Lydia's first overture. Lydia had sent a message to what she hoped was still her phone, promising something of 'mutual benefit'. A text message invited her to 'come and play' with an address. And a random Bill Murray gif.

Lydia made her way to the address in Belgravia which turned out to be a five-star hotel with a smoked glass frontage and an abundance of planters overflowing with lush greenery. Maddie messaged as she approached the front steps with the words 'garden terrace'. Lydia wondered if Maddie was watching from a balcony using her sniper scope. She felt her skin prickling. Here she was again walking toward Maddie when she ought to be flying away.

Maddie was sitting on a low sofa in the corner of the terrace, surrounded with flowers and lush trellises. The retractable roof was pulled back to reveal the blue sky and spring sunshine and the air was scented with jasmine. She was sipping from a pale pink cocktail, which had a matching partner on the table.

'Drink up.'

Lydia eyed the cocktail. It had probably cost more than she spent on food in a week, but might also have a nasty surprise. She tried to see if there were visible crystals in the bottom of the glass or powder on the rim.

'Oh, give me strength.' Maddie swiped the glass and took a long drink from it, wiping away the lipstick mark after. 'There. Now stop hovering. You're making the staff nervous.'

Lydia sat on a padded velvet chair opposite Maddie. It left her with her back to the entrance but she figured her biggest threat was on the other side of the table. 'Cheers,' Lydia said, toasting Maddie before taking a sip of the pink drink. It was sharp and delicious.

'I was glad you got in touch,' Maddie said. 'I was beginning to feel like I was doing all the running in this relationship.'

Lydia decided not to tackle the use of the 'r' word. She was pretty sure Maddie wouldn't kill her in broad daylight in a busy hotel restaurant, but not certain enough to push her luck. Lydia kept her face neutral. 'I wanted to talk. To find out what you want.'

Maddie fluttered her eyelashes. 'You care about me. I knew it.'

'I just want to know if there is anything I can do to speed up your London visit.'

'I might settle down. London is my home, after all. Maybe I'm tired of living such a reckless life. I look at you and your friend, what's her name, Emma? And that handsome boyfriend. You've built a nice steady life. Makes me wonder what that's like.'

Lydia felt sick. Just hearing Emma's name in Maddie's voice set every nerve jangling. She had to keep Maddie distracted and away from Emma and her family. She said the first thing which popped into her mind. A corpse swinging from a tree. 'It was pretty reckless, killing your handler.'

Maddie frowned. 'Sergio? Trust me, nobody is grieving that sack of shit.'

'Was it your idea? Or an off-the-books commission?'

'Everything I do is off the books,' Maddie leaned back and prodded the crushed ice of her cocktail with the stirrer. 'And I'm very happy with that. They love my work and they pay me well for it.'

She was lying, Lydia realised. She wanted something else. Recognition? 'You killed your handler, I would have thought even secret ops aren't keen on that kind of thing.'

Maddie shrugged. 'I've not heard any complaints.'

'That's because they haven't found you, yet. When they do...'

Maddie smiled. 'I'm not losing sleep over it. And I never liked him. He was rude.'

Lydia wanted to say that it didn't seem like enough to warrant being murdered and hung from a tree, but there was a fervent glow in Maddie's eyes.

'Fine. You want the truth?'

Lydia resisted the urge to say 'this will be good' and just nodded.

'I fancied a change.'

'Of handler?'

'No, I wanted out. I thought it was going to be so different, but it was just like being back here. Some old man telling me what to do. But it's not that easy to stop working for them, you know? You understand. You had to do the same thing with Charlie. You have to do something definitive, it's the only thing people like that understand. They weren't just going to rip up my contract and wish me a happy retirement. I had to make a statement.'

Lydia was pretty sure that the order to kill her had come from Mr Smith but she didn't know if Maddie knew that. If she had a handler before, filtering the information, she might not have known the difference between on-the-books orders from MI6 and Mr Smith's pet project. 'But then they sent you,' Lydia caught herself before she said 'orders'. 'Information direct? Didn't you think that was odd? After you'd made it clear you weren't working for them anymore?'

Maddie shrugged. 'I told you, already. I'm too valuable to them. I got a text. It was a job and I was in London already so I went to do it. I had made my point, but that didn't mean I wasn't open to renegotiating terms.'

'But it was me.' Lydia stopped herself before she did something truly stupid, like pointing out that by failing to kill her, Maddie was blotting her own copybook, again.

'But it was you,' Maddie raised her glass in salute, her expression suddenly grim.

Ice poured down her spine. 'Are you going to kill me?'

Maddie stared for a long moment, unsmiling. Then she took a sip of her cocktail. 'Not today.'

Lydia worked hard on keeping her breathing even, keeping hold of the fear that was lapping at the edges of her mind. She forced herself to take a sip of her own drink, to mirror Maddie's movements in the hopes it would build some kind of rapport. 'So, what's next for you?'

'I go freelance. No handler.'

'Don't you need contacts for that?'

'What makes you think I don't have contacts?'

'Nothing,' Lydia said quickly. Everything about Maddie was a performance, but the flash of anger was real. Maddie definitely wanted to be seen as smart and capable and in control. Then it hit Lydia... Maddie wanted her to be impressed. She tried to think about what Maddie wanted to hear. But that she wouldn't see through immediately. 'It's just I struggled with that... When I started my business. I didn't know anybody, and it was hard to build a client list.'

'Is that why you took the job from Uncle Charlie?'

'Partly,' Lydia said, truthfully enough. 'I did need the work.'

'I suppose I can forgive that,' Maddie said. 'Besides. It's in the past. I'm not hanging onto the old ways, I'm looking to the future. I've had my chakras aligned and I'm ready for the new me.'

Lydia didn't know how to respond to that.

Maddie's laugh made her skin prickle. 'Not really. The old me was perfect.'

'I KNOW A WAY FOR YOU TO RESIGN PERMANENTLY. To make it stick.'

'Do tell.' Maddie was smiling so widely her mouth was like a red slash across her face.

'I can get you access to Mr Smith.'

'I can get to him any time I like.'

'Fair enough,' Lydia said and made to leave.

'Just like that? Finish your drink at least.'

'Look, I want him gone,' Lydia said. 'He is running a personal mission and has the Families in his sights. It's unacceptable.'

'I don't disagree,' Maddie said. 'He's overstepped. I could teach you to shoot. Get him from a distance with a sniper rifle, it's the safest way. Especially for a beginner.'

'I don't need a gun,' Lydia said, trying to distract Maddie.

'What are you going to do?' Maddie didn't change position. 'Investigate him to death? Sooner or later you're going to have to toughen up. I didn't like Charlie, but he had that bit right at least.'

'You don't know what I'm capable of,' Lydia said. 'I don't need a gun, because he's already a dead man.'

That made Maddie cheer up. 'He looked pretty perky last time I saw him.'

'I was thinking we could work together. For a common purpose.' Lydia outlined her plan while Maddie finished her drink.

The waiter appeared and Maddie ordered champagne which Lydia hoped was a good sign.

Once the business with the ice bucket and the glasses and the popping of the cork had been dealt with, Maddie picked up the long-stemmed glass and raised it in a toast. 'To us.'

'To us,' Lydia echoed, hoping that she hadn't just made a huge mistake.

CHAPTER TWENTY-FOUR

Lydia pulled up in Emma's suburban street. She had chocolates for the kids and a bottle of wine and was feeling strangely calm. She had weighed up the possibilities and decided that Emma was the most vulnerable. Fleet was prepared and she had warned her parents. They had left London for an impromptu package holiday and hadn't told anybody, not even Lydia, where they had gone. And, as she reminded herself repeatedly, Henry Crow was no longer helpless.

The car door shut with a reassuring thunk and she could hear birds in the trees which lined the road. Children were playing in a nearby garden and their young voices tugged something painful inside Lydia. She wasn't going to worry Emma, she reminded herself. She would just sit and have dinner and make conversation and play with Archie and Maisie. Be a good friend.

In Emma's warm kitchen-diner, the evening sun pouring through the large windows, Lydia tried to breathe normally. She had thought she would feel better once she was here, but instead she felt like a bad omen. She had brought the darkness with her. She wondered what Fleet was doing and whether he had sensed anything when she had said goodbye. It was good that she was with Emma. If she spent her last night with him, she wouldn't trust herself to walk to her fate in the morning.

Emma had poured three large glasses of wine and Tom was stirring something on the stove. He had a tea towel draped over one shoulder and was telling Lydia about his recipe for... something. She realised that she had zoned out and took a large sip of wine to avoid answering his question about coriander. She couldn't summon an opinion.

Emma had clearly noticed her distraction. 'Shall we sit outside?' She put a hand on Tom's arm. 'Is that okay, babe?'

THEY SAT ON THE SMALL PATIO IN FOLDABLE DECK chairs which Emma had hauled out of the shed. The garden was filled with plastic ride-on toys, a small climbing frame and slide, and a couple of abandoned bikes, one of which didn't have any pedals. It looked like an entire football team had been playing, not just two small children.

Although they weren't quite as small as they had been. Dispensing hugs and chocolate when she arrived, Lydia had been hit with the changes. Maisie was taller and her vocabulary had doubled. Archie had lost a tooth and it gave him a rakish look. Like a tiny pirate.

'I can't believe how big Maisie has got,' Lydia said. It was the kind of thing she had heard other people saying, proper grown-up people. Finding the words leaving her own mouth was odd, but not unpleasant. It made her feel responsible and capable. Which made a nice change.

Maisie and Archie were upstairs having something which Emma called 'special time'. She pulled a face. 'We decided that they could have a slightly later bedtime on weekends, but we've dressed it up as special time. If they have earned all their stars during the week, they can have an extra twenty minutes playing in their rooms before bedtime.'

'Cunning,' Lydia said. The secret service had nothing on parents for making loaded deals.

'So,' Emma regarded Lydia over the rim of her wine glass. 'What's going on?'

'I'm visiting. For dinner.'

'And you're staying the night?'

'If that's still all right?' Lydia raised her glass. 'Then I can have a couple of these.'

'Bollocks.'

'I'd prefer wine.'

Emma ignored the pathetic attempt at humour. She gave Lydia a serious look. 'You know what I mean. Tell me what's going on.'

Lydia briefly thought about playing the 'can't a girl visit her best mate' card, but she could see that Emma wasn't in the mood. 'You know my MI6 guy?'

'The one who wanted information on your family?'

'Yeah. I told him to take a hike, that I wasn't going to work for him anymore.'

'Hadn't you made an agreement?'

Emma wasn't accusing Lydia of anything, but she felt it like a blow, anyway. Her word should be her bond. That was the kind of code she had been raised to hold. 'He forced one on me. And I considered it fulfilled.'

'But he had other ideas?'

'He wanted me to join his department. Doing what, I'm not exactly sure. Using my Crow abilities in some way.' Lydia looked away as she spoke, finding it hard to look squarely at Emma when she referred to magic. The ways in which she was so different. So *weird*. 'He took it poorly when I refused.'

Emma was sitting very still. She was no dummy and knew something bad was coming. Lydia was glad they were outside as it wasn't the sort of thing that belonged in Emma's safe and normal house. She said it quickly, like that would make it easier.

Emma didn't react for a moment. She had always been calmer than Lydia, more able to take a breath and process things before acting. When boys started pinging their bra straps in class, Lydia had turned around and smacked the perpetrator without hesitating. Which meant she had ended up in front of the headteacher for violence. Emma had taken a moment to think, then bawled the guy out, and then been to see the head of year to demand immediate action. In short, Emma was smart. And had been a proper grown-up ever since Lydia had known her.

'Isn't that illegal?' She said now, calm and collected,

like Lydia had just told her that Mr Smith had had her car towed, not sent an assassin to murder her.

'Very much so,' Lydia said. 'But I think the secret service get special dispensation from the police. Or they do it without getting caught. Honestly, I'm a bit hazy on how it all works.'

'I'm guessing the secret service don't advertise their methods. They probably don't produce handy pamphlets, either.'

Lydia slugged her wine, relaxing a notch. She was relieved that Emma was still able to make jokes, but more relieved still that she hadn't immediately sent her packing.

'You're worried about me, aren't you?'

'Maddie got me on the roof by threatening you,' Lydia said. 'And it worked. Which means you're perfectly safe.'

'How so?'

'Because the threat of hurting you worked to control me. No one would throw away that kind of weapon. You're too useful.'

'Well, that's good to know.' Emma drained half her glass in one long swallow. After a few moments of thought, she asked the question Lydia really didn't want to answer. 'So, why are you worried enough for a sleep-over tonight?'

Lydia had rehearsed this. She wasn't going to tell Emma the truth. Not all of it, anyway. It was too much to tell her friend that this was, most likely, her last night and that she wanted to spend it in her normal, happy house, with Maisie and Archie and all their life and promise and energy. That she wanted to laugh with her best friend and go to sleep hearing the faint murmur of her voice, the timbre of it so familiar and comforting. So she went with the other part of the reason. 'I'm teaming up with Maddie to take Mr Smith out. It turns out he is a rogue element in the service and if he disappears, my problems with MI6 should disappear.'

'Just like that?'

'Well, hopefully disappear. There's no guarantee, but he's definitely the one with the Crow obsession.'

'And Maddie wants him gone, too?'

'Our goals temporarily align, so we're going to work together.'

'What aren't you telling me?'

Lydia widened her eyes. 'Nothing. Just that I don't trust her and I wanted to be here tonight on the off-chance she decided to pay you a visit.'

Emma frowned. 'Why would she...? Oh.'

'I don't think she will,' Lydia said quickly. 'She's got no reason to threaten you, now, I'm doing what she wants.' She had stumbled over the words 'hurt you' when she had practised, so had changed it to 'threaten'.

'We've been in danger for weeks,' Emma said, cutting to the truth of the matter with her usual clear-eyed efficiency. 'Why are you here tonight?'

Lydia couldn't look her square in the face. 'I just wanted to see you.'

Thankfully, Emma let it drop. They had dinner and Tom made them laugh with his descriptions of his new line manager. The food was good and the conversation flowed. Emma played along that it was a normal evening and Lydia was grateful.

Lydia was rearranging the sofa cushions when Emma walked in with an armful of duvet and pillows. 'Are you still with Fleet?'

'We're all good.'

'Aren't you worried about him, too?'

Lydia didn't want to admit that she had deliberately played up her relationship with Fleet to further distract Maddie from Emma. It was the truth, but it sounded cold. 'Fleet's got police protection.' It wasn't entirely a lie. Fleet was police. And he was protecting himself. It felt rude to tell Emma that Fleet could look after himself, like she was accusing Emma of being weak for just being a normal human being, for not being trained for violence and threat.

Lydia didn't expect to sleep, but she had brought a book to read. She dozed a little in the early hours, but started drinking coffee at five. Maisie and Archie were up just after six and Emma sent them downstairs to play with 'Auntie Lydia'.

Lydia was engrossed in building a complicated vehicle from random Lego bricks when Emma told her to check her phone. 'Local news.'

In the Camberwell and Peckham section of the BBC news site, there was a report of a fire in a flat. The building had been evacuated and fire fighters were on the scene. The amateur photo illustrating the article showed Fleet's block. There was a red block headline which said 'breaking news' and a video alongside the article. Lydia clicked it.

A reporter was standing in the street along from Fleet's flat. The carpark for the building was, presumably, filled with fire engines and police, but his position still gave a clear view of the smoke-filled sky and the damaged building. Lydia didn't need time to work out that the source was on Fleet's floor and side of the building. She could see it instantly.

The reporter was speaking to camera, his face serious. 'London Ambulance Service treated three people on the scene and one has been taken to hospital for smoke inhalation. There is one confirmed fatality. The identity of this individual is not being revealed at this time, although their next of kin have been contacted. We have information that it is believed to be a Metropolitan police officer and there is an appeal for witnesses to what may not be a tragic accident, but a targeted attack.'

CHAPTER TWENTY-FIVE

'Oh my god,' Emma had been watching over Lydia's shoulder and she wrapped her arms around her. 'Lydia...'

'It's okay,' Lydia said, her voice muffled by Emma's arms. 'It's not Fleet.'

'What?'

Lydia extricated herself from Emma's embrace and turned to face her. 'It's okay. I promise, he's fine. He wasn't in his flat.' She showed Emma the text message on her burner phone that had just pinged through. 'See. He's all good.'

'What's wrong?' Archie's little face was crumpled with concern.

'Nothing's wrong,' Lydia said quickly. 'There was a fire but nobody was hurt.'

'Fire?' Maisie said. 'Get engine.' She disappeared below the edge of the coffee table and reappeared carrying a Lego fire engine.

'Why don't you two go and make sure Daddy's up.

You can tickle his feet if he isn't out of bed.' She waited until the small people had thundered out of the room and up the stairs, before turning back to Lydia.

'Sorry... I hope I didn't worry Archie.'

'Was that-?'

'Maddie. Yes. I told her I was moving into his flat. I thought it would keep her focused on Fleet and away from you.'

'Oh God,' Emma sat down. 'She's properly psychotic.'

Lydia wondered which part of 'contract killer' hadn't given her the tip off, but she restrained herself from saying so. Her world had always been hard to comprehend. Especially in the cosy and comforting living room with cushions and lovingly tended pot plants and toys in the corner. It was completely fair that Emma was leaning forward, head between her knees and dragging in lungfuls of air like she was trying not to hurl. Lydia patted her shoulder and murmured comforting words. After a while, Emma straightened up and managed a watery smile. 'Sorry. I think I just hadn't taken you seriously before. About her, I mean. Your cousin.'

'That's okay. Best way to function.'

'How do you do it?'

Emma looked sympathetic and Lydia couldn't stand it. 'Practise. And denial.'

'And alcohol?'

Lydia grabbed her for a quick hug and then Emma left to hustle the kids to get ready for school.

. . .

Lydia took the opportunity to wash her face and brush her teeth, then she called Fleet, needing the reassurance of his voice more than she cared to admit. As arranged, he had rung his gaffer and had a false report fed to the press. Male police officer found dead at the scene.

'Sinclair came through on that one,' Fleet said. 'The gaffer wasn't going to say no with her backing me.'

'I'm sorry about your flat.'

'Nobody was badly hurt, that's the main thing. And hopefully it will sell the deal to Maddie.'

'She'll believe me,' Lydia said, injecting certainty into her voice. Now that she knew Fleet was safe, she couldn't let herself speak to him for too long.

'Call me as soon as you can.'

She was grateful that he didn't question her further. She felt like glass, as if the slightest thing could make her resolve falter. And if that happened, she would fall and shatter on the floor.

Lydia went to the safe house in Vauxhall, the place where she had met with Mr Smith when he had blackmailed her into sharing information. She waved at the cameras she knew were hidden in the reception area and held up a piece of paper with some handwriting in block capitals, then sat on the pavement outside to wait. She could have used the phone number that she still had for him, but she wanted to speak to him in person and she was pretty sure he wouldn't be able to resist.

The black car pulled up, tinted windows obscuring

the interior. The back door nearest Lydia swung open and Mr Smith, sharp suit and patrician smile in place, inclined his head.

She hesitated. This was probably a very bad idea. The man wanted her dead.

'In or out?'

She got in.

THE CAR PULLED AWAY AND SOON THEY WERE passing the hulking geometric mess of MI6 and crossing Vauxhall Bridge. 'Fleet knows I'm here,' Lydia said. 'As does your boss.'

'Which boss would that be?'

'Sinclair,' Lydia said, watching his face carefully.

He didn't so much as twitch. 'You're getting more cautious. That's undoubtedly wise.'

Swallowing down the urge to tell Mr Smith she didn't need his advice or his approval, she looked at the man in the front passenger seat. He was large and wearing a suit. The man driving looked identical except his haircut was, if anything, even shorter and neater.

She had been prepared for Mr Smith's signature but, having not seen him for a while, it still made her feel nauseous. She could hear planks of wood creaking, hear the slap of sails in the wind, and taste gold on her tongue. Salt air and brine and sunlight catching the surface of the waves, shattering the water into a thousand painful white diamonds. She had been practising on accessing her well of Crow power without having to move physically and she used it, now. Imagining turning down the volume on his signature until it was barely detectable.

Mr Smith was watching her carefully. 'I take it you want to trade?'

'I wanted to warn you,' Lydia said, pausing before she used his real name, 'Gale.'

His lips stretched into a thin smile. 'Sinclair?'

She nodded. 'I still think of you as Mr Smith, though. For old times' sake.'

'Warn me?'

'Maddie is very unhappy.'

'I am aware.'

'Yes, poor Sergio Bastos.'

This time she thought she did detect the tiniest flicker around his eyes. It felt like winning. 'And you know she is still in London.'

He inclined his head.

'You also know that she is no longer taking your calls. Does that make you nervous?'

'Not particularly.'

Lydia gave him a long look. 'It should.'

The car was moving smoothly through traffic along the embankment. This being London, they still weren't moving particularly fast and Lydia could see the large plane trees, benches, and statues which lined the route. She watched the scenery and waited. Back when she was playing this game with Mr Smith before, she had no idea how far he was playing her. Now, she still wasn't entirely certain, but she felt more prepared. And, ultimately, compared to the raw terror of Maddie, he no longer felt like a threat. The goons in the front were no doubt highly trained killers and carrying firearms, but Lydia felt her Crow power around her like a cloak. Next to Mr Smith, she felt invincible. She wondered if this was how Maddie felt all the time.

'Why don't you tell me what you want?'

'What did you do to Maddie? I know she went through training, but I think there was more.'

'She is very talented. It was more a case of honing what was already there.'

'There is something wrong with her, now. Something is missing.'

'I didn't do anything,' Mr Smith said, his voice dripping with faux concern. 'I think there was always something missing. That kind of asset, they're all the same. Damaged. It makes them mouldable. You take the broken pieces and you put them together however you want.'

Lydia felt a flare of anger. It was a strange, almost protective, feeling. Not that Maddie needed her defence. She squeezed her coin.

He smiled at her, clearly aware that he had hit a nerve. 'Don't be offended. She's a good one. Most of the assets aren't too bright. Doesn't matter what the films would have you believe most hired killers don't need that much spark. Up here.' He tapped his temple. 'They just need to be able to pull a trigger.'

'Plenty of military types can do that. And you must know hundreds in your line of work.'

'Killing from a distance. Or in self-defence. Or in service of an ideal. Protection of a country or leader. Something. It's actually harder than you think to find someone who will stab a stranger for money. More than once, anyway.'

'I would say I'm sorry for your inconvenience.'

'But that would be a lie.'

Lydia didn't reply. Then, after the thoughts kept swirling, she did. What did it matter, now? Mr Smith wasn't getting out of his alive. And she wasn't, either. 'Maddie wasn't entirely all right, I can accept that, but she wasn't broken. She used to be a Crow.'

'She's still got that dubious honour.'

'I'm not so sure,' Lydia said. 'I can tell what Family people are from, and whether they are packing any power. She has lost that signature. If I wasn't looking right at her, I wouldn't know she was a Crow.'

'They say that you lose a part of your soul every time you take a life.'

'That's it? That's your answer?'

He shrugged. 'She's taken a lot of lives.'

LYDIA DIRECTED THEM TO HIGHGATE. IT WAS THE only entrance to the Pearls' domain that she knew of, although no doubt there were many more.

Once the car was parked in the road between Highgate and Queenswood, Mr Smith turned slightly in his seat. 'Tell me why I would go with you?'

'I'm unarmed,' Lydia said. 'And your large friends can come with us. You'll be perfectly safe.'

'I'm not concerned for my safety,' Mr Smith said. 'But I'm a busy man. You made it abundantly clear that you are not interested in working with me so, I ask again, why would I go anywhere with you?'

'I'm meeting Maddie. Thought you might want to tag along. You two can catch up.'

He went still. Well, more still. It was subtle but the tension in the car increased sharply. 'You are hoping I will kill her?'

'Before she kills me. Yes.'

'And if I fail, she'll probably kill me.'

Lydia nodded cheerfully. 'That's about the size of it. It seemed like a neat solution.'

'Why are you telling me?' Mr Smith sounded genuinely curious, and it was nice to have surprised him.

'I'm not a killer. If you come with me, I want you to know what you're getting into. It's your choice.'

'Well, then,' Mr Smith settled back in the soft leather. 'I choose not.'

'Fair enough,' Lydia said, and grabbed the door handle. She had barely made it out of the car when doors opened behind her and she found herself being forcibly detained by one of the large men, while the other gave her a professional and thorough pat-down.

'She's clean,' the man that Lydia privately named 'Handsy' called to Smith.

He emerged from the car, shooting his cuffs.

The other man, the one who had grabbed her, and who was still gripping her shoulders with meaty hands, suddenly let her go. Lydia stumbled forward but regained her balance before she did anything too embarrassing.

'Uhhh,' Meat Hands was saying. It wasn't coherent,

but it got the gist across. Something unexpected and unpleasant had just happened.

'Let's go for a little walk,' Maddie's voice. Bright and chirpy like a talk-show host, emanated from behind Meat Hands.

'We...' Meat Hands began, in a triumph of hope over experience, before finishing with another involuntary noise as Maddie punched him in the kidneys. 'Uhung.'

'No talking, please, children,' Maddie said.

'What makes you think I'm going to come with you?' Mr Smith asked, not unreasonably. The plan had been for Lydia to lead Mr Smith into the woods to meet Maddie and for her to ambush them under cover of the trees.

'You still want them, don't you?' Maddie said and winked at him.

'Wait,' Lydia said. 'What?'

Maddie cocked her head. 'I made a little deal with our mutual friend Gale, here. Amnesty from the service and maybe a few contacts. Just a little retirement package that will help me set up on my own.'

'And in return?'

'The Silver cup,' Maddie said, still hidden behind the massive bulk of Meat Hands.

'And me,' Lydia said, the truth dropping like a stone.

'And you. Sorry, cuz.'

Maddie did not sound sorry. Lydia wasn't exactly surprised that Maddie was double-crossing her, but she was weirdly disappointed. She had known it was a possibility, but Maddie's attention had felt like affection in some way and that had clouded her view. And it had all seemed different, then. She had been running terrifying scenarios in her mind as a theoretical exercise. Now one of those terrifying scenarios was actually happening, Lydia wanted to go back in time and deliver a swift kick to her past self. 'So, why would I come with you, now?'

'Because I'm asking nicely.' Mr Smith had produced a gun while they had been speaking. The sight of it made Lydia's insides go liquid. She wasn't experienced with firearms and wasn't used to seeing them anywhere except the TV screen. 'We'll all go in a happy little party. Once I've got the cup, I'll transfer the money and the contacts and we'll be done.'

'That's the deal,' Maddie said.

The liquid fear was tinged with anger. Lydia focused on the anger, using it to keep herself together. 'You duplicitous little...'

'Careful, now,' Maddie peered around Meat Hands to wink at Lydia. 'Don't say anything you'll regret.'

WALKING THROUGH HIGHGATE WOODS HAD NEVER been Lydia's favourite activity and doing so with a gun held against the base of her spine did nothing to improve the experience. She concentrated on watching her feet and making sure she didn't trip over a stray root. It wouldn't do to get shot by Mr Smith just for falling over.

As they moved further from the main path and the trees got closer together, Lydia could taste the Pearl magic. It was dark green leaves, buds bursting on the branch and youth and beauty reflected in a thousand shining surfaces. Not exactly a chatty party to begin with, the group had gone utterly silent. Something pale slipped through the trees to their right, keeping pace. It was a small figure and Lydia assumed it would be the girl the Pearls used as one of their emissaries in the above-ground world.

'Why did you stash it out here?' Mr Smith said, his voice slightly strained.

Maddie was walking behind them, covering Meat Hands and Handsy with her own gun. 'I needed some-where you weren't going to wander past. Coincidences do happen, but I knew you avoided this place.'

'What makes you say that?'

'Don't be coy,' Maddie said. 'It really doesn't suit you.'

Mr Smith shook his head. 'I don't know what you mean.'

'So, you're not shaking like a tiny little leaf?' Maddie's tone was teasing.

'Shut up.'

That surprised Lydia. Mr Smith had never been anything other than coldly superior with her, except when he had been laying on the false concern. Hearing him snap made her like him a great deal more than she had and guilt stabbed her in the stomach. He prodded the gun a little harder into her back and she stopped feeling bad.

'What's that?' Meat Hands stopped walking. He was looking around at the trees which had been groaning for a while.

'Nearly there,' Maddie said. 'Keep moving.'

'Do as she says,' Mr Smith said.

Lydia couldn't remember the route through the woods very well, but she knew they were almost at the entrance. She could taste it. And the trees were leaning down, branches twisting and writhing. The inky sky was no longer visible, replaced with an impossibly thick canopy of green leaves. It was how the forest must have looked to Londoners hundreds of years ago, back before the roads and pollution and city sprawl had got in on the act. The Pearls probably considered the change a travesty. If Lydia had her way, the whole lot would have been bulldozed to make way for a nice cheerful shopping centre. Maybe a Nando's.

The small girl with the long dirty blonde hair stepped out from the undergrowth. 'Shiny?'

'Not today, kiddo,' Lydia said. 'Sorry.'

'I brought you something pretty,' Maddie said, showing her teeth in what she probably thought was a friendly smile. 'It's over there.'

The girl was no idiot, and she hesitated.

'It's really pretty,' Maddie said.

The girl tilted her head, considering. 'Is there glitter? I like glitter.'

'So much glitter,' Maddie said. She was visibly confused at the child's total lack of fear.

'They aren't expecting you.' The girl pulled at a thick strand of her tangled hair and began winding it around her fingers.

'That's all right,' Maddie said. 'Help yourself to your gift, anyway.'

The girl stepped over to a hillock of moss and stones. A red leather purse on a braided cord had joined the variety of rainbow plastic beads hanging around her neck and it swung forward as she leaned down to peer under the leaves and stones.

'Where is it?' Mr Smith said. He sounded agitated and Lydia hoped he didn't slip and shoot her accidentally. How much field time did Smith have? She was used to seeing him on the other side of a table or leaning back against the leather seats of his car.

'Don't worry, it's here,' Lydia said, as the Silver tang hit her nostrils and the back of her throat. It was bright and clean and cold and it cut through the choking taste of foliage.

'Bring it to me-' Mr Smith was saying, his voice urgent with need, when he was interrupted.

The sound of the gun was so loud and sudden that Lydia let out an involuntary noise. One she wasn't proud of making. On the plus side, she managed not to wet herself. Small mercies.

Meat Hands toppled like a tree.

Handsy had spun around at the sound, his own weapon rising to fire, but Maddie was too quick. Faster than a blink, she was behind the man and drawing a knife across his throat. He fell to his knees, blood flowing. His expression was so surprised it was almost comical. Almost.

'There was no need for that,' Mr Smith said and wrapped an arm around Lydia, pulling her up against his front. He was surprisingly strong and Lydia found she was up on tiptoe. She tried to move and couldn't.

With his signature mixing with the Pearl magic and the Silver rolling off the hidden cup, Lydia was finding it difficult to stay conscious. She was glad she had spent so much time training and she used that focus, now, finding the quiet space in the centre of it all and drawing her wings around her like a shield.

'Time to go.' Lydia could dimly hear Maddie's voice but it seemed to be coming from a great distance. 'You give me Lydia and the contact list and my new friend here will bring you the cup.'

'That's not what we agreed. I get Lydia and the cup.'

'Deals change. Just ask your friends.' She waved at the bodies on the ground. 'The cup is fair payment for the contact list. And Lydia will be more trouble than she's worth.'

'Maybe you're right. Maybe I'll just kill your cousin here, leave her body for the birds.'

Don't try to bluff the psychopath, Lydia thought, wondering how he could possibly still be underestimating Maddie.

'You want the cup and I want the contact list.' Maddie's gun was steady in her hand and she looked relaxed. She could have been discussing the purchase of a loaf of bread. 'All we have to do is swap. Don't make this more complicated than it has to be.'

Lydia felt Mr Smith's body relax slightly, even though his grip on her remained firm.

She was still concentrating on staying conscious, but it was much easier. She could feel strong wings wrapped tightly and taste soft feathers. Whether it was the training under stress or the siphoning of her power into the bracelet or a combination of the two, Lydia definitely felt more in control. She could still sense the bright Silver from the cup but it was no longer blinding.

She blinked and focused on the scene. Maddie was holding the little girl who was holding the silver cup and looking pissed off. The trees seemed even closer than before. The small clearing they had been standing in was now a tangled mass of roots and trunks and foliage. A branch the thickness of a body builder's thigh was snaking down behind Maddie's head. It had a cruel intent, like it was sentient, and it made Lydia's stomach flip over.

'Watch out!' Lydia shouted.

Maddie ducked, narrowly missing the sudden swipe. The branch plunged into the ground with a sickening crack and leaves rained down. The other trees had awoken, too, and there were more branches moving in unnatural ways. There was one to Lydia's left that she would have sworn was staring at her.

'We need to go if we're still going,' Lydia said, speaking to Maddie, and trying to stay calm.

'You're not going anywhere,' Mr Smith said and then he was maybe going to say something else but Lydia would never know because the next sound out of his mouth was a kind of 'mnumph' and he let her go.

Lydia knew that Maddie was back on plan and was now controlling Mr Smith. She glanced back at him, stock still and with his eyes bulging. His jaw was working but his lips were clamped shut. Even though it was something she had signed off on, it was still a freaky sight. She turned away and climbed over the tree roots to get closer to the girl. She crouched down as best she could and looked into her pale blue eyes. 'We humbly request an audience with the King. We bring a gift of great value.'

The girl sucked on the end of a piece of hair and regarded Lydia balefully.

'You can keep the shiny cup, kid,' Maddie said.

The girl brightened and hugged it closer.

And then the ground opened up.

CHAPTER TWENTY-SEVEN

The last time Lydia had entered the Pearl court, there had been a black door covered in a mosaic of mother-of-pearl hidden in the basement of a ten-million-pound house. This time, it was an archway of twisted tree roots lifted to reveal steps roughly cut from black earth.

The girl twisted away from Maddie and skipped down, her blonde hair a beacon in the dark.

'You first,' Maddie said, pushing Lydia in the shoulder. 'Then you,' she added to Mr Smith.

Lydia was concentrating on the steps and heard the sounds of Mr Smith stumbling over the uneven ground. He was making a low moaning sound which made the hairs on her neck stand up. She knew what it was like to have your body controlled by Maddie and she could empathise with the sound effects.

The air was dank and cold and the earth seemed to press in from both sides. Stray roots poked through the packed soil walls. They were a stark reminder that this wasn't a carefully engineered structure and Lydia could feel her heartrate kicking up. She wasn't a fan of going underground at the best of times and at this moment it was extremely hard not to picture the metres of heavy earth and rock above her head.

Finally the steps ended and a short passage led to a door. Lydia recognised it as the same kind she had seen in the mansion. Shiny black lacquer which seemed to be catching the light, even though there wasn't any. No candles. No lightbulbs. No torches. Trying not to think too hard about how little sense it made, Lydia put her hand to the door. The blonde girl had no doubt already gone through and she had left the door ajar.

The court was as Lydia remembered. The magic was thick in the air as a group of beautiful young things danced to a pounding bass rhythm. Music which clearly should have been audible in the passageway they had just walked along. Lydia swallowed down the urge to be sick. That was the problem when things didn't obey the laws of physics, the human brain rebelled and that made a person mighty queasy. No wonder most people just decided they weren't seeing what they were seeing or hearing what they were hearing. It was easier on the gut.

Lydia's stomach turned over again, and she summoned her coin. Squeezing it hard in her right fist helped a little, and seeing that Maddie had gone a greenish shade helped a lot.

Poor Mr Smith had clearly lost the battle with the urge to vomit and he kept lurching over and his face was pale and sweaty. His throat was moving convulsively as he, presumably, swallowed back the bile. Maddie seemed oblivious and Lydia decided not to request that she unseal his lips. She told herself that it was because she wasn't sure Maddie wouldn't see it as a challenge to do something worse but the truth of the matter was that his comfort was not high up her priority list.

The girl had disappeared and the Silver cup with her. Lydia didn't have time to worry about that, though, as the crowd had parted to reveal the Pearl King sitting on their throne and it was as if the whole cavernous space went instantly silent. Maybe it did, Lydia could no longer tell what was real, what was imagery cast by the Pearls and what was the white noise of her fear. The King was just as beautiful as Lydia remembered, but easily twice as angry. Their face remained immobile and fixed, but when they spoke the tone was truly terrible. 'You are not invited.'

The figures nearest the throne shrank back and Lydia thought, when the monsters are afraid it's time to run. Instead, she stepped forward. 'We come to pay our respects to the Pearl King and to offer a valuable gift, a token of our esteem in the hope of a new peace between our Families.'

The King inclined their head. 'The King will grant you audience.'

She had warned Maddie of the archaic way the King spoke and the need to lay on the courtly obsequiousness, but Lydia could see she still wanted to dive over and punch them in the face. Quickly, she tugged on the bound figure, pulling Mr Smith into the King's view. A murmuring chatter began among the crowd of Pearls.

The King's face flickered. For a split second their

habitually blank and bored expression became avid, and they leaned forward a fraction. It was the equivalent of most people falling over in surprise.

Clearly fed up of obeying the 'let me do the talking' portion of their plan, Maddie stepped directly in front of the King, dragging Mr Smith with her. 'After the truce between our Families you made another deal. Not an honest handshake one, like our truce, but a tricky one, written on paper.'

'We have not invited this one to speak.' The King looked at Maddie like she was something foul on the bottom of their shoe.

'You discovered after the document was signed that you had made a deal with a company, not an individual and that it didn't just die with that person. It held strong as long as the company existed, no matter how many times the directors changed or the company was sold.' Maddie wagged a red-nailed finger. 'That was very silly.'

The crowd surged as if ready to crush Maddie, but the King held up a hand. Their voice was flat and utterly devoid of emotion, which made their words more chilling. 'You will die screaming.'

Maddie stiffened and Lydia knew the King was probably taking control of her body. Or trying to, at least.

'Your Majesty,' Lydia said. 'My cousin means no offence. Just to underline the immensity of our gift. We have found the sole owner of the corporation trading as JRB. He holds the ability to release you from your bond. He can dissolve the contract between your family and JRB.'

The King's gaze moved back to Lydia. 'You should

not lie.'

It wasn't a question, but she answered it, anyway. 'This man owns JRB.'

Mr Smith was sweating profusely. Lydia felt bad for him, but she also knew she didn't have a choice. He had come for her, he had used Emma as leverage, he had tried to have Fleet killed. 'You did this to yourself,' she said, not meaning to speak the words out loud.

Smith's eyes rolled to look in her direction, the whites showing. She couldn't tell what he was trying to communicate, but it didn't matter. She couldn't trust a single word from his mouth.

'Is this true?' The King asked.

Mr Smith made a muffled sound but his lips didn't move.

'Why does he not answer the King?' A member of the court stepped forward.

'He can't,' Maddie said, clearly struggling to speak. 'I have... Him. Locked.'

The King waved a hand and Mr Smith's mouth popped open, a stream of vomit-tinged saliva immediately flowing out and over his chin. The muffled moaning became, abruptly, a loud gurgling cry.

'Enough.'

The cry stopped and his shoulders heaved as he fought to get control of himself.

'Are you the owner?'

Mr Smith nodded.

'Do you have sole authority to break the contract signed on the twelfth day of the twelfth month in the aboveground year two thousand and one?'

He straightened his spine and nodded. 'I do.'

His voice was raspy and the front of his shirt was flecked with vomit, but Lydia had to hand it to Mr Smith. He had regained his composure remarkably quickly.

'So do it, already,' Maddie said. 'But in return I want my cup. Where's the girl gone?'

Her mouth snapped shut, her teeth making an audible sound as they clashed together.

'Lydia Crow,' the King beckoned. 'Do you make a demand in return for this gift?'

'No,' Lydia said. 'It's a gift.'

'Safe passage out,' Maddie said over her, somehow managing to fight the King's control and continue to have the use of her lips, tongue and vocal chords.

Lydia had thought about this and she figured that if the King decided to kill her, he would kill them all. Being struck down by the King wasn't a pleasant thought, of course, but the result was all that mattered. Her friends and family would be safe from Maddie and Mr Smith. She closed her eyes and hoped it would be quick.

'I can break the contract here and now,' Mr Smith said. 'But what do I get in return? Apart from safe passage?' He nodded at Maddie. 'You can do what you like with her.'

The King smiled thinly. 'How quickly you turn on your friends.'

'They are not my friends,' Mr Smith said, 'they are my subjects.' Lydia realised instantly what he was doing. He was shooting for comradeship with the King, trying to position himself on a similar level. There was probably a seminar on it at MI6. 'Making Friends With Despots for Fun and Finance.'

'There you are wrong. They are the closest thing you have in this place. But you have shown your lack of loyalty. It has been noted.'

'It's simple,' Mr Smith began. 'I break the contract between your Family and my company and we both walk away free men.'

'I am not a man,' the Pearl King said.

'It's a figure of speech, I meant no-'

Whatever Mr Smith meant was lost as his head rotated a hundred and eighty degrees with a sickening crunch and he fell to the ground. Lydia stared at his body lying on the packed earth, his dead eyes gazing from their unnatural angle.

'Why did you do that?' Maddie sounded mildly irritated.

Lydia managed a step backward. She didn't think she could make it to the exit before the King snapped her neck, too, but she could try.

'No living entity owns the company,' the King said, their voice quavering very slightly with the tiniest betrayal of emotion. 'We are free.'

And this was the part that had always been hazy for Lydia. In her plan, she would die, that was almost a hundred per cent certain, and she had hoped that Maddie would be executed alongside her, but the question of what the Pearl Court would do with their new freedom was the big unknown. Would they be free to roam above ground? And, if so, what did that mean for London?

She realised that the ground was shaking. Then a thick root burst through to her left, narrowly missing Mr Smith's lifeless body.

Maddie was advancing on the throne and Lydia had a spark of hope that the King and the courtiers would be distracted enough for her to make it out. She couldn't back out, keeping her eyes on the King and Maddie, not with roots bursting through the ground and the unpredictability of the courtiers. She turned and moved over the pulsating, shaking ground toward the exit, pulling her jumper up and over her mouth and nose to try to filter out the dusty earth which was now whipped up through the air.

'It's over,' she heard a courtier say in wonderment.

'Free,' another said. The word was running around the cavern like fire. Free. Free. Free.

The place had already been thick with Pearl magic, but when Lydia was hit in the back with a solid blow and knocked to the hard ground, she had no doubt what it was. Pearl magic unleashed. All that potential, all that rage, all that power. The cork had been popped. Feeling too vulnerable on her front, tiny shoots and roots pushing up through the packed earth on either side of her face, Lydia flipped over as quickly as she could. She was just in time to see the Pearl King rise from their throne, face shining with terrible power and purpose.

They were unleashed. They were uncontained. They were...

Lydia blinked soil from her eyes. The Pearl nearest

to her, a girl with beautiful high cheekbones dusted with shining glitter, was screaming. Lydia had heard it as a whoop of joy, but looking at her face she could now see it was a cry of panic and pain. Her face was twisted, her large eyes suddenly grotesque, and she wasn't the only one. Around the cavern, through the swirling earth and plant debris, faces were twisting, lithe bodies convulsing.

Maddie had moved away from the King and Lydia could no longer see her. The King was staring wide-eyed, their beautiful features utterly impassive. Something was moving under their skin and it took Lydia a horrified second to realise what was happening. Their flesh was rippling and changing, becoming wrinkled and shrivelled. The King's shoulders rounded and slumped as their spine curved, their eyes clouded and lips thinned to the point of vanishing.

Lydia had glimpsed the true age of the Pearl Court once. A single split-second image which showed the wizened figures of humans long past their natural life-span. Now those images were developing all around, as if emerging in a photographer's dark room. The Pearls were withering and dying in a matter of seconds, like a gothic stop motion film or one of those speeded-up nature documentaries. The strong and the beautiful crumbled to desiccated figures which fell and began to decompose. The contract which had kept them contained in these liminal underground spaces and had prevented them from roaming London, had also kept them in a time capsule of sorts. Sealed from the world and sealed from the passage of time. It looked as if time was rushing back in and was eager to get to work.

As the Pearls died, their hold on the earth and rock crumbled. The whole space was shaking violently, the ground and walls and chunks of compacted earth and stray rocks were falling from the ceiling. There was going to be a cave-in any moment and Lydia turned and pushed her way toward the exit, praying it was still open. Her mind raced, trying to remember the advice for being caught in an avalanche. Her old boss at the investigation firm in Aberdeen had sent her on an outdoor skills weekend. Part of preparing her for some of the surveillance jobs which might take her into the Scottish countryside. She had, quite rightly, sized Lydia up as a southern softie who had never knowingly been further than ten metres from a Starbucks. That experience was mostly an unpleasant blur of stinging rain pelting her face and hiking for endless hours, while a barking ex-Forces man encouraged the group through the means of sweary shouting and telling stories of the hardships he had encountered while serving and comparing the group, unfavourably, with his old unit. Which, while perfectly fair, got a little bit old. Things like, 'if we were in Libya right now, you'd already be dead.'

The air was filled with the thunderous sound of the ground shaking and breaking and Lydia could no longer see the dead Pearls nearest to her, let alone the opening which led to the steps out. Finally, she recalled the outdoor survival instructor. His voice spoke loud and angry inside her head. 'In an avalanche, oxygen is your priority. You can live with broken bones but you cannae fuckin' last without air.'

Helpful. Thanks, pal. Lydia knew she was panicking,

now. Speaking to a phantom of her memory and one she hadn't particularly liked, was surely the first sign of madness. She couldn't see and her eyes were burning. She wondered if a mains pipe had been ripped open and that there was poisonous gas filling the cave. That wasn't a calming thought.

She gripped her coin until she could get a hold of her racing thoughts. She told herself it was just the earth and grit making her eyes burn and that she was breathing good clean oxygen and that she was going to survive. She just needed to think. The pep talk didn't exactly help, but her autopilot must have kicked in as she had already pivoted around and begun working her way back into the middle of the cavern. She realised, seconds behind her deepest survival instinct, that she was looking for the throne. The King might have aged rapidly, their body decomposing somewhere on the floor ahead, but the throne was carved wood and inlaid precious metals and stones. It hadn't dissolved in a puff of smoke. It was the largest intact structure in the place. Her arms were out, but she kicked it before finding it with her hands.

The roof was coming down in chunks and a boulder landed to her right, narrowly missing spreading her brains across the dirt.

She felt for the back of the throne and tugged to pull it over. It didn't move. A moment of despair. There was no light, and the air was chokingly thick with earth and the sounds of moaning. She was going to be buried alive under Highgate Woods. She would have been better off being knocked out. She tugged again, leaning back with all her weight and trying to get the oversized chair to budge. And then it did. It rocked up onto the edges of its legs. With what felt like the last of her strength, she hauled hard and felt the throne go past the centre of gravity and fall. With the long back of the chair resting on the churning ground, it formed a slanted roof. She scrambled into the space created and put both arms in front of her face, trying to form an air pocket. Even though the air was choked and foul, she inflated her lungs as deeply as possible, knowing that every centilitre of air could mean another minute of survival, another minute for the rescue crew to find her and pull her out.

THE SHAKING EARTH AND ROARING SOUND OF ripping, crunching, falling, eventually slowed and then stopped. It became strangely peaceful. Lydia could no longer see anything at all. There was no Pearl magic creating light in an enchanted subterranean playground, just dirt and rock and tree roots, churned up and thrown back, ready to start the organic process of rebuilding itself. Worms and beetles would tunnel through, seeds would grow, ripped roots would mulch down and new ones would be sent out from the trees. The ground would heal and it would be as if nothing had ever happened here. Except, Lydia supposed, the ground would be extra rich from all the human remains. Her body and Mr Smith's and, she fervently hoped, Maddie's. That was the tiny splinter she held onto in the dark. She had lost sight of Maddie and there was a small chance she had slipped away, making it back up the steps before the cave-in. If that had happened, Lydia had to stay alive. She had never realised what it felt to truly hate a person, but now she knew. She hated Maddie with an intensity which burned from inside and made her skin feel on fire. That might have been referred pain from her tissue compressing and slowly dying of oxygen deprivation, but she preferred to think of it as hatred. Bright, clear, burning, energetic hatred. She would survive so that she could check that Maddie was dead. Lydia couldn't grip her coin, her fingers didn't seem to be working. The space she had created with her arms was impossibly small. Who knew how many minutes of air she had left? The panic surged and she forced herself to ignore it. If she panicked she would gasp in air, use up her precious oxygen and die more quickly. The fallen earth was pressing against her folded arms, but she could lift her head a small amount. There was a pocket of space between her head and the back of the throne. It was a couple of inches at most, but it meant more air. She had enough, she told herself. More than enough. And Fleet would be coming.

IT WAS GETTING COLDER IN THE DARK. LYDIA HAD no idea how long she had been crouched beneath the fallen throne, but the intense pain from her cramped muscles told her that she couldn't take much more. Give Lydia something to hit, something to puzzle out, something to run from. Those she could do. Curled up here in the freezing darkness, lungs choked and a terrible silence blanketing her ears, unable to move, and she thought she might rather die.

CHAPTER TWENTY-EIGHT

Lydia had been dozing. She had been dreaming, at least. She couldn't feel her coin in her hand anymore, but she could picture it there. And she had imagined other things, too. An arch of blue sky. Stretching her aching arms out wide. Straightening her back and breathing deeply, her lungs expanding with sweet clean air. The pain was almost gone. No. That wasn't true. At all. But it seemed further away somehow. Like it was happening outside The Fork on the street while she was sitting cosy in her favourite seat, a plate of buttered toast and a coffee on the table.

She wasn't an idiot. She knew this new comfort was not good news. It meant she was dying. Friendly brain chemicals and, maybe her Crow ancestors, were easing her passage to the great beyond. She would be the wind in the branches of the tree which shaded the Family tomb in Camberwell Cemetery. That didn't seem too bad.

There was a rumbling coming from above or maybe the side. Lydia had no sense of direction in the pitch black. Her eyes were tightly shut against the grit and she could no longer tell if she was still crouched underneath the tipped throne or whether she – or it – had been tumbled into a different position. Her arms were still folded in front of her face and she couldn't move.

The rumbling was sending vibrations through the earth and Lydia's first emotion was irritation. She was floating away in the dark and the vibrations were bringing her back to her body. A body which was flooded with pain and fear. Soaring in the wide blue sky, wind ruffling her feathers or crouched in the cramped dark, pain searing every nerve, every muscle. No contest. No thank you.

A thunderous ripping was accompanied by a draught of air. She sucked it in. Automatically and unthinkingly first and then, gradually, with new awareness. There was a strange sound, muffled and distant but getting closer. Voices. Calling her name. One voice in particular set her pulse racing and brought her thudding back to full consciousness. Fleet.

Blinding light against her closed eyelids. Instinctively, she kept them shut, even though she wanted to see what was happening. There was new air, that was clear, but there was a pattering of earth all around. Then a shout. 'I've got something.'

'That's it,' Fleet's voice. Unmistakable. 'Careful. She's underneath.'

More digging. More shouts and more air.

'Hang on, Lydia,' Fleet was saying from somewhere above.

And then there was a release of pressure from around her arms and torso. A voice she didn't recognise told her to keep her eyes shut, and that they were going to cover them to be sure. 'Too much light too quickly can damage your retinas.'

Her eyes were stinging, so Lydia could easily believe that. It was nothing, however, to the pain which was flooding through her body.

'Careful. Careful. Okay, Lydia, stay put, okay? We're going to dig around you some more before we move you. Just hang in there, you're doing great.'

The rest of the rescue was a little hazy. Now that Lydia was back in her body, feeling the pain of her cramped muscles and the burning in her chest and throat, it was taking all of her concentration to hold still and not cry.

After what seemed like hours, but was later explained to be mere minutes, she was hauled out from underneath the throne.

Her face was rinsed with water and soft material bound over her eyes to stop her from opening them too quickly. Fleet's signature grew stronger and then she felt his hand taking hers and squeezing gently. 'We're going to the hospital to get you checked over.'

'Do it here,' Lydia said, her voice nothing more than a cracked whisper. She coughed violently and tried again.

'No can do,' the voice of the paramedic was closer

than Lydia expected. Her blindness made her feel vulnerable.

'You need to be checked. And hydrated.'

Lydia wanted to argue but her throat hurt too much to speak. She shook her head, but could feel a deeper darkness encroaching.

WHEN LYDIA WOKE UP, SHE KNEW INSTANTLY THAT she had lost the battle. She was in hospital. The institutional smell was unmistakable, along with the squeaking sound of footsteps on rubber flooring, and rings rattling on a rail as a curtain was pulled somewhere in the room.

Her tongue felt swollen, stuck to the roof of her mouth. She tried to produce some saliva, but her mouth felt desiccated. And her throat was raw. She peeled her lips open. 'Water.'

There was a rustle of movement.

'I'm here,' Fleet's voice was reassuringly close. 'Watch out, straw incoming.'

The water was possibly the best thing she had ever tasted. It beat the finest malt hands down. Although, now she had thought of whisky, she really wanted a nip. That would take the edge off the discomfort.

Besides, she'd had one hell of a day. She deserved a drink.

There was still something over her eyes. She opened them and saw the darkness of the material blindfold. Pinpricks of light exploded, and she waited for them to calm down before pulling the material.

'They said you have to keep... Never mind.'

284

Her eyes hurt, were streaming in the light, but Lydia blinked lots and the stinging gradually eased. Her vision returned, and the blurry shapes resolved into a bed with NHS blanket. A pale green chair pulled up close holding a worried-looking DCI.

'Hey,' Fleet said. 'That's gotta hurt.'

'Worth it,' Lydia said, drinking in the sight. 'You're okay?'

'I'm fine.' Fleet's mouth turned up at the corners. 'And I think I'm the one who should be asking that.'

'I'm sorry about your flat.'

'It's just stuff,' Fleet said.

'I'm sorry I pointed Maddie at you. The fire's my fault. I just couldn't have her go anywhere near Emma. Her kids...'

Lydia's eyes were stinging and she blinked furiously.

'It was the right call,' Fleet said, taking her hand. 'I'm just glad it worked.'

'Thank Feathers you were staying at The Fork,' Lydia said, smiling a little. 'What were the chances?'

Fleet's tentative smile matched her own. 'Yeah. Lucky that. Precognition paranoia for the win.'

'And listening to your very wise girlfriend.'

'That, too.' He squeezed her hand.

THE DOCTOR EXPLAINED THAT LYDIA WAS extremely lucky. She didn't have crush syndrome or any of the other nasty-sounding hazards of being in a cave-in. She had been dehydrated, but they'd run fluid through an IV and her vitals were all looking good. 'Your blood oxygen is normal, which is excellent news, and there is no sign of organ or tissue damage.'

'Did they find the others?'

'Gale's body was recovered, but nobody else so far.' He squeezed her hand gently.

Lydia hoped the Pearl girl had made it out. She wasn't a member of the court and moved above ground so she assumed she wouldn't have crumbled like the old ones. She might have been a Pearl and an emissary of the court, but she was still just a kid.

'Maddie?'

Fleet shook his head. 'No sign. Yet.'

Lydia let her head fall back on the pillows. Hell Hawk. Of course she had escaped. It would be too much to ask that Maddie would have conveniently laid down and accepted death under the ground. She was too determined and too strong to let a little thing like being buried alive stop her.

A nurse wheeling a blood pressure monitor arrived to check on Lydia. 'Visiting hours finish at four,' he said to Fleet.

Fleet presented his warrant card, and the nurse rolled his eyes. 'Suit yourself. But don't blame me if one of the others yell at you. It's for infection control, you know.'

'It's fine,' Lydia said. 'You can go and check on your place. Maybe it's not as bad as we think. You might be able to salvage some of your stuff.'

'I'm not leaving.'

'Really, it's fine. I'm going to take a nap before dinner.' The blood pressure cuff was inflating automatically, and the nurse was washing his hands and pretending not to listen. She lowered her voice. 'If you wanted to come back in later with some takeaway, I wouldn't complain. I'm not excited at the prospect of hospital food.' She glanced at the nurse. 'No offence.'

'None taken, treasure.' He released her from the cuff and Lydia rubbed her arm to get the feeling back. 'Especially if you want to bring in a little extra for me.' He winked at Fleet and moved to the next bed. There were four in the room, but only one other was currently occupied. Lydia assumed that wouldn't last and, if she had any intention of staying put, she would be worried about being able to sleep surrounded by strangers.

As soon as Fleet had left, Lydia got up and sussed out her exit route. Luckily, the staff were swamped with duties and the corridor outside the ward was deserted. There was a door open at the end which revealed a small office. She was in her rights to sign herself out, but it would be quicker and easier just to leave. She was still plugged into an IV, but after a couple of deep breaths, she pulled that out and held the puncture site until it stopped bleeding.

Clothes next. The locker next to the bed contained the bag that Fleet had brought and, thank feathers, it revealed clean jeans, underwear and a loose T-shirt. The curtains were closed around the other occupied bed so nobody had to witness the humiliating sight of Lydia getting winded after putting on her jeans and having to sit on the bed for a few moments until the room stopped spinning.

It occurred to her that it was a sign she should be

resting in bed, but she couldn't stay still. Maddie's body hadn't been found. That meant she was out there somewhere. Maybe she was hurt and lying low to recover. Maybe she was still trapped underground. Or maybe she had got out before Lydia, discovered that Fleet hadn't really been in his flat when the fire took hold and was, at this very moment, following him with a gun.

No. Maddie wasn't superhuman. Lydia did up the laces on her Docs while she calmed herself down. If Maddie had escaped from the cave-in, she wouldn't have been completely unscathed. She would check hospitals. Just because the crew hadn't pulled her out didn't mean she hadn't been hurt. If she needed help, she would have given a false name, or maybe she collapsed on her way out of Highgate and was picked up. She could be lying in a bed in this very building, about to wake up any moment. What would she do then?

Docs on, T-shirt over head and jeans done up, Lydia was ready to move. The drawn curtains seemed to grow larger in her vision. They were hiding the bed. What were the chances? Suddenly, she was seized by a sense of dread. What if Maddie was lying in the bed next to her, hidden by those anonymous blank curtains? Her mind flashed through the images. Maddie found unconscious or delirious with concussion, rushed into the emergency department, treated and then shunted up here to this room. Maddie lying awake and fully alert, listening to Lydia speaking to Fleet. Fury that her plan to get rid of him had failed. Was that a shadow behind the curtain? A figure standing just the other side of the pale material, gathering strength to attack?

She had no weapon. There was a plastic jug and a cup on the table and nothing else. Not even a pen or pencil. She didn't know if she would be able to stab Maddie with a pen, but it would be nice to feel she had the option.

She produced her coin and squeezed it. Whether it was the adrenaline spike or her Crow magic, strength seemed to flow through her body. She stood, every sense on alert. She could hear Maddie breathing, but there were no other sounds from behind the curtain. Maddie was standing very still. Waiting.

Lydia knew she had to act fast. If she failed, Maddie would kill her. And if they attracted attention, she might hurt the staff or other patients, too. She launched herself across the gap between her bed and the curtains, aiming for the middle of the shadow, hoping to wind Maddie with her first blow.

Lydia stumbled forward, almost falling. She had empty fabric gathered in her fists and forward momentum carried her onward, her feet hitting the edge of the bed. She released the curtains and fell through, palms out to catch herself.

A woman with grey curled hair and a pale pink nightdress was standing on the other side of the bed, a cup of orange squash in her hand. She looked at Lydia with undisguised disgust. 'What the fuck are you playing at?'

Lydia apologised. 'Tripped.'

'Aye, right,' the woman said, calming a little. 'Mebbe stick to your side, eh?'

Lydia apologised again. Her heart was hammering, and she wiped her palms on her jeans.

It was official. She was going mad.

She had just poured a glass of room temperature water from the plastic jug and was chugging it down, when her phone buzzed with a text. It was Maddie.

Roof. Now.

CHAPTER TWENTY-NINE

There was no choice. If Lydia didn't obey Maddie and meet her on the roof of the hospital, she would come looking for her. At this moment, there was a chance that Maddie believed Fleet to be dead. If she came to the ward, she might be there when Fleet came back with dinner.

Besides. This had to end.

At least she had seen Fleet one last time, Lydia thought as she got into the lift. At the top floor, she had to leave the lift and take the last flight of stairs to the roof. Her muscles seemed to be obeying her and she could breathe steadily, which was a relief. Still, getting trapped underground for a few hours wasn't the best preparation for tackling a trained killer in combat. She squeezed her coin and imagined strength and power flowing from it. She wasn't sure whether she could feel anything, but the shape and weight of the coin in her palm was comforting.

The sky was black and there was a little rain falling

when Lydia pushed through the door to the roof. The drops struck her face, stinging her raw skin. She hadn't looked in a mirror since waking up in hospital and it crossed her mind that she might be horribly disfigured. Another great reason to end it all today.

Maddie was standing near to the low metal fence which edged the roof. She turned as Lydia approached and smiled like she had won the lottery. It reminded Lydia of her recurrent nightmare. Maddie on the roof looking like it was her birthday, wedding and Christmas all rolled together. At least Fleet wasn't here. That was the small comfort. She had kept him safe. He would be angry that she had faced Maddie alone and the message she had left with Auntie wouldn't help much, but he would be alive to be angry with her. That was what mattered.

'You made it,' Maddie said.

'I didn't have much choice,' Lydia said, stopping a couple of feet from Maddie. 'Are you going to threaten to kill me, again, because that's getting old.'

Maddie's smile dimmed. 'You should show me more respect.'

'I'm here, aren't I?' Lydia had walked slowly and with a slight limp. Now, she shifted as if in pain, and made sure to keep her posture slightly bowed. Beaten. In pain. Weak. 'Speaking of which, how did you get out unscathed?'

In truth, Maddie wasn't looking too clever. Her face and arms were smudged with dirt and blood, and her hair was matted, sticking out wildly on one side. When she had turned, Lydia had seen her holding her side, as if injured, although she had dropped her hands, now. They hung, open and ready for action. 'That was wild,' Maddie said. 'You weren't lying about the Pearls.'

'So, what's next for you?'

'That depends.'

'You've got the cup. You've killed your handler. And now your handler's handler is dead, too. What is keeping you here?'

'I think you know the answer to that.'

'I don't.'

'I'm proud of you,' Maddie said, and it sounded strangely sincere. 'You killed him. I knew you could do it.'

'That was the king. I didn't...'

'You walked Gale into that place knowing he wouldn't come out. Same thing as pulling the trigger.'

Lydia shook her head, ignoring the throb of pain in her temples. 'It really isn't.'

'It's okay,' Maddie took a step closer. 'We're not like other people, you and me, we're special.'

Lydia wanted to say that she wasn't anything like Maddie, but her mouth was full of feathers, choking back the lie.

'I know you see it, now. We should be together. That's why I sent a warning to your pet policeman.' She pulled a mock-sorrowful face, bottom lip out. 'I hope you're not too cross about that. I gave him a fighting chance, at least.'

'You arranged the fire.'

'Like I said, he had a chance to get out. But he didn't, did he? I saw the news.'

'You murdered him.' Lydia didn't think she was a wonderful actress, but found she didn't need to dig very deeply to sound outraged and devastated.

'I set you free,' Maddie said. 'He was always going to hold you back.'

'You want me to come with you?'

Maddie laughed and shook her head. 'I think I should stay here. We could run the Family together. I can take it from you, but I would rather we teamed up. I'm tired of being alone.'

'It's hard to get enthusiastic after seeing your last business partner. I don't fancy ending up hanging from a tree.'

Maddie waved a hand, dismissing Sergio Bastos. 'He wasn't my partner. It would be completely different for us.'

'For a while,' Lydia said. 'Until you get bored. Or I piss you off.'

'You already piss me off,' Maddie snapped. 'I've never known anybody to be as annoyingly stubborn as you. Except me.' She smiled again, showing the impeccable orthodontic work that had no doubt set back Uncle John a fair whack. 'That's the point. We're made for each other.'

'Is that why you wanted Fleet out of my life?'

'Of course. I need space in your heart. I'm very needy. You know that.'

Lydia could feel Maddie's power plucking at her. She forced herself to relax, to let it happen. She had to let Maddie feel safe and in control. 'I can't do it. You killed Fleet. You killed Sergio. You're basically a monster.'

Anger and disappointment flashed across Maddie's face before her features smoothed. 'I guess I was wrong about you. You don't understand, after all. Oh well.'

Lydia felt her legs pulled by Maddie's power. In her mind, she welded her feet to the ground. In reality, she stumbled toward the edge of the roof, powerless to stop her legs from moving. She didn't have to pretend to show sudden terror. 'So, this is it? Bit unimaginative. Thought you might mix it up.'

Maddie laughed, and the sound cut through Lydia. She was so far gone, she barely seemed human. Whatever was left of the girl Lydia remembered from her childhood, it was surely burned away by her actions. That was something her mother had said when Lydia was very young. People weren't good or bad, they did good or bad things. It didn't matter what you thought, it mattered what you did.

'I will find everyone you have ever cared for, you know.'

The wind was blowing straight into Lydia's face, making her eyes water. She blinked to clear her vision and felt the salt water cold on her cheeks.

'Fleet was just the start.'

'They haven't done anything to you,' Lydia said, hating the wobble in her voice even though she knew it was a good thing. The weaker and more defeated Maddie thought she was, the more chance Lydia had of catching her off guard.

'You know that's not true,' Maddie said.

Hating herself as she did so, Lydia made a last attempt to protect Emma and her parents. If this plan didn't work and Maddie survived, she had to put her off the scent. Of course, that meant putting somebody else in danger, but Lydia had never claimed to be a good person. 'It's Paul. He's the reason I can't leave.'

'Fox?'

'You remember we had a thing? Back in the day? Well, it started again. I love him.'

'Nice try,' Maddie was smiling, but there was the smallest hint of uncertainty.

Lydia clutched that uncertainty to her heart, squeezed it close and prayed it would be enough to stop Maddie from hurting Emma. If this didn't work. But it had to work.

She was at the edge, now. If Maddie just nudged her over, using her mind, then Lydia would die for nothing. She had to get Maddie closer.

'Wait!'

'Last words? I don't think so.'

'You can't kill me.'

She felt her body lurch and for a sickening moment her feet lost purchase on the ground and she was hanging over the edge, all centre of balance off and only Maddie's will stopping her from freewheeling into the air. 'Wait! You don't want to do this!'

'I do,' Maddie said, eerily calm. 'I really do.'

'I left insurance.'

And her feet were making full contact on the concrete, her body tilted back and away from the edge of the roof. She felt the control release a little and she stumbled back.

Maddie had taken a step closer. Still not in arm's reach, but closer. 'I'm listening.'

Lydia was gasping for breath, tears still streaming down her face, so it wasn't much of a stretch to struggle to speak. She exaggerated a little, playing for time, and Maddie folded her arms, waiting.

Lydia had played this moment over and over in her mind. The confident part of her wanted to take Maddie on, to straighten up and throw her Crow power and see if she could beat her one-on-one.

But, as always, her mind ran through the possibilities. If she failed, Maddie would kill her instantly. And then she would hurt Emma. And Fleet. And, now, possibly Paul Fox. And maybe her parents, and anybody who had ever meant anything to her. It was too big a risk. Lydia had to make sure.

Maddie's hold over her was like bands of steel wrapping around her body, but also like having Jason on board, the sense of something inside stretching its limbs within hers and inhabiting her every organ and blood vessel and nerve. She wanted to test it, to see if she could break the bond, but didn't want to alert Maddie to her power. She hoped she was strong enough to overcome Maddie's control for a few seconds and, if she managed to catch her by surprise, that would be all she needed. If she tested it and failed, though, Maddie would be on alert and that could be all the edge she would need to keep Lydia's body under control. She was itching with the desire to flex and push back and it was taking every ounce of self-control she had to hold herself in check. All the while acting desperate and terrified and as if she was struggling. She hung her head down, doubled over as far as she could with Maddie holding her in place, and forced her words out in a strangled whisper.

'What?' Maddie took another step closer.

'Charlie,' Lydia said, using the only name she knew had ever frightened Maddie.

'What about Charlie?'

Another garbled whisper. She could feel the cold annoyance radiating from Maddie. Either her frustration would snap and she would shove Lydia over the edge of the building or, perhaps, pull out a knife and stab her to get it over with. Or, and this was crucial, she might take another step and bring herself close enough for Lydia to make her move.

She took another step.

Like a bird taking flight, Lydia unfurled her wings and threw everything she had outwards. Maddie's control over her body snapped in an instant and she was propelled forward. Before she could react, Lydia had wrapped her arms around Maddie and was pulling her over to the edge of the roof.

Maddie's split second of surprise had passed and she was fighting back with everything she had, both physically and with her controlling power. Lydia could feel the attack, trying to stop her muscles from behaving, trying to pull her away from the edge.

She was grateful for the hours she had spent being flipped and grappled on the mat, otherwise she wouldn't have lasted a single second with Maddie. She was throwing her Crow whammy at Maddie, too, blocking her and attacking with the same motion, feeling the thousands of tiny hearts, beating in time, wings sweeping the air and feathers filling her mouth.

Another step and she half-fell, half-jumped, dragging Maddie along with her.

CHAPTER THIRTY

The wind rushed past Lydia as she fell. She couldn't see as her eyes had filled with tears from the cold air and the world was a blurry mess in shades of grey and brown. She couldn't blink to clear her vision, couldn't think past the sharp terror, which was like a single high note screaming in her ears. She had been falling for a second and also forever.

The air finally whipped away the water from her eyes, enough that she could see the ground below. Her arms were spread wide, desperately trying to slow her descent and a tiny part of her brain, the oldest part, told her to flap her arms to give herself a little uplift to catch a thermal. But she wasn't a bird, she was a human. She knew she couldn't fly.

Another second and the ground was very close. There wasn't time. Lydia knew she was falling to her death and that there wasn't time to be thinking this much. It simply wasn't possible. Which meant she was probably already dead. Lying on the concrete with her wings smashed, and these were the last random firings of her neurons before the lights went out for good.

Her heartbeat was in her ears, pounding in panic, but the sound was like an orchestra. A thousand small hearts beating with hers, but much faster, filling in the gaps in her pulse so that it was a constant noise. Not overwhelming, but uplifting. The taste of feathers in the back of her throat and the sharp scrape of talons on stone. At once, she felt it. A draught of air from beneath, lifting her up and slowing her fall. She saw the block-work of the building, a window, and then another. Separate and distinct impressions which were like slow motion after the blur of before. There was something underneath her, cradling her body. She felt her shoulders straighten and her arms lengthen, her wings spreading wide.

Then she hit the pavement.

Her arms were slightly outstretched and took the force of the fall along with her knees. She felt her forearm snap, and the pain whooshed like fire up to her shoulder. She lay on the concrete as if at the bottom of a pool. The noise of the city was muffled and her ears were still pounding with the drumming heartbeats. Slowly they faded and Lydia began to make sense of what she was seeing.

Maddie was lying a few feet away, on her back. Her head was turned toward Lydia and her eyes were open and fixed. Quite dead.

The pain in Lydia's arm was vying for attention with a very bad feeling in her face. Her nose was broken for sure, and possibly some other small bones too. She didn't want to move her legs to test her knees for fear of what fresh pain she would unleash. Instead she rested her cheek on the cold ground and dragged lungfuls of air in through her chapped lips.

She shifted and felt her arm complain, but in that moment she knew she would heal. Maddie had hit the ground first which meant that whatever Lydia had felt had not been a hallucination brought on by mortal danger. She had slowed her descent enough to survive. A pool of blood was spreading out from beneath Maddie's head. A demonstration of what ought to have happened to Lydia, too.

She dragged another breath as the sound of sirens in the distance brought her more fully into the present. She couldn't smell the exhaust and blocked drains and dropped takeaway containers which made up the London bouquet, but she knew they were there. She had fallen and her city had caught her.

LYING IN HER DOUBLE BED WITH FRESHLY CHANGED sheets, a cup of coffee laced with a secret splash of whisky that Emma had provided, and Fleet in the kitchen making a late breakfast of scrambled eggs and crispy bacon, Lydia though that plunging several floors off a building had its advantages. She shifted and felt a bolt of pain from her broken left arm and sprained shoulder and thought that maybe it wasn't something that she ought to do on a regular basis.

She picked up her phone and checked her messages. Her mum had replied that they were having a lovely holiday and Maria had sent a terse email demanding an update on the whereabouts of the silver cup. She dialled her number, feeling magnanimous in her lovely aliveness. 'This isn't the service I'm used to,' Maria said. 'I hope you have good news for me.'

'I found the cup,' Lydia said. 'But I don't have it. Best guess, it's buried in Highgate Woods.'

'Is that a joke?'

'Nope,' Lydia said, wincing as she shifted. 'I know you think I stole it, but I didn't. And neither did any Crow. When I say your best chance of finding it is to excavate the recent cave-in in Highgate Woods, I'm telling you the truth. And that's the end of my favour. We're even.'

'I don't think so,' Maria began, 'this is hardly-'

'I am the head of the Crow Family and I located a highly important Silver relic as a personal favour. My advice is that you take better care of your things in future.'

Hanging up on Maria was always enjoyable and Lydia leaned back, closed her eyes, and savoured the moment. There would be fall out, of course, but that was for another day.

When she opened her eyes, she found Jason hovering at the end of her bed. He was staying out of the kitchen because Fleet was using it, but she knew it was taking an enormous amount of self-control. 'He won't be much longer,' she said.

'It's not that,' Jason said, pushing the sleeves of his suit jacket up even further. 'There's something I wanted to ask you.'

'Fire away,' Lydia said. Her stomach dipped at the nervousness in Jason's voice.

'You know the bracelet. It's not that I'm not grateful...'

His form was shimmering and Lydia patted the bed in an invitation for him to come closer. 'What is it?'

'I don't think I want to stay. After you... Go.'

'After I die?'

'Yeah. Or if you move to Fleet's place. Or somewhere else. I don't want you to feel responsible for me. And I don't think I want to be like this forever. I mean, it's good, now. I'm kind of happy. I like living with you and I like helping out but, you know, everything ends.'

'You don't have to feel guilty,' Lydia began. 'I like living with you, too. You're not a responsibility, you're my friend.'

His face brightened. 'I know. And I feel the same. I mean, you're my friend.'

Lydia felt a sudden lump in her throat. 'Well, I'm glad that's settled.'

They looked awkwardly at each other for a beat longer. Lydia tried to lighten the moment. 'I should jump off a building more often.'

Jason smiled sadly. 'Everything ends,' he said again. 'Or it should.'

Fleet pushed the door open and Jason slipped past him before Lydia could say anything else. 'Your grill pan is a disgrace.' Fleet had found a tray from somewhere, possibly one he had brought from his flat as Lydia was pretty damn certain she didn't own such a thing, and he placed it on her lap. 'Were you talking to yourself just now?'

'Jason,' Lydia said and watched Fleet straighten and look around the room.

'He's not here. You can relax.'

Fleet sat next to her on the bed, stealing a piece of bacon.

'What do you think John is going to do?'

'Can you just relax, woman? You did it. You don't have to worry about Smith or Maddie. It's over.'

Lydia dug into the eggs and bacon, trying to relax.

'No bad feelings,' Fleet tapped his temple. 'No premonitions, bad dreams. nothing.'

After she had finished her breakfast Lydia relaxed back against the pillows. Her eyes wanted to drift shut and, after a few minutes of battling, she let them. Fleet was right. She had won. Maddie was dead. Smith was dead. She was free. Fleet was safe. Emma was safe. She still had to deal with John and Daisy. And no doubt Aiden was hovering somewhere outside the building, kept at bay by Fleet for the time being, but waiting to march into her office with a line of complaints and concerns and new jobs. Being head of the Crow Family as well as running Crow Investigations was a crazy idea. Two full-time jobs squished into one life, but it was her life. Her choice. She was drifting off, now, could feel sleep tugging at her sleeve. Her stomach swooped as her centre of gravity altered. She was rising up into the air, wings stretched wide. The sky wasn't blue, it was a multitude of tones from pale grey to purple to a bright cerulean. The air currents were shifting within it, whirlpools and vortexes forming and disappearing, and a warm draught lifting her higher. She wasn't alone, there were crows flying with her. Hundreds of black shapes matching her every move. Lydia knew she was asleep, now, so she wasn't frightened when one of the crows came very close and its beak opened to greet her. Maybe it was her grandfather. Or great-great grandmother. Or maybe it was Maddie, finally arrived home to the flock.

One thing Lydia knew for certain, dream or not, was that she couldn't really fly. Not in the real waking world. But she also knew she no longer had a fear of heights.

She was no longer afraid of falling.

THE END

THE END

THANK YOU FOR READING!

I hope you enjoyed reading about Lydia Crow and her family as much as I enjoyed writing about them!

I am busy working on the next book in the Crow Investigations series. If you would like to be notified when it's published (as well as take part in giveaways and receive exclusive free content), you can sign up for my FREE readers' club online:

geni.us/Thanks

If you could spare the time, I would really appreciate a review on the retailer of your choice.

Reviews make a huge difference to the visibility of the book, which make it more likely that I will reach more readers and be able to keep on writing. Thank you!

ACKNOWLEDGMENTS

I am deeply grateful to you, dear reader, for embracing the Crow Investigations series. I am having so much fun writing about Lydia, Fleet and the Families, and can't believe I get to call it my job!

Thank you to my friends and family for their love and support, and to my brilliant publishing team. Especially my wonderful early readers, editor and designer.

In particular, thanks to Beth Farrar, Karen Heenan, Jenni Gudgeon, Caroline Nicklin, Paula Searle, Judy Grivas, Deborah Forrester, and David Wood.

Thank you to my lovely writer friends, especially Clodagh Murphy, Hannah Ellis, Keris Stainton, Nadine Kirtzinger, and Sally Calder. Our group chats and Zoom sessions in lockdown have kept me halfway sane - thank you! And I can't wait to see you all in Real Life.

As always, special thanks to my patient, clever, loving husband. You are the best. And I'm not just saying that because you do all the accounts.

ABOUT THE AUTHOR

Before writing books, Sarah Painter worked as a free-lance magazine journalist, blogger and editor, combining this 'career' with amateur child-wrangling (AKA motherhood).

Sarah lives in rural Scotland with her children and husband. She drinks too much tea and is the proud owner of a writing shed.

Head to the website below to sign-up to the Sarah Painter readers' club. It's absolutely free and you'll get book release news, giveaways and exclusive FREE stuff!

www.sarah-painter.com